Relatively Reckless

ANNE MARSHALL

BALBOA.PRESS
A DIVISION OF HAY HOUSE

Copyright © 2022 Anne Marshall.

All rights reserved. No part of this book may be used or reproduced by any means, graphic, electronic, or mechanical, including photocopying, recording, taping or by any information storage retrieval system without the written permission of the author except in the case of brief quotations embodied in critical articles and reviews.

Balboa Press books may be ordered through booksellers or by contacting:

Balboa Press
A Division of Hay House
1663 Liberty Drive
Bloomington, IN 47403
www.balboapress.com
844-682-1282

Because of the dynamic nature of the Internet, any web addresses or links contained in this book may have changed since publication and may no longer be valid. The views expressed in this work are solely those of the author and do not necessarily reflect the views of the publisher, and the publisher hereby disclaims any responsibility for them.

The author of this book does not dispense medical advice or prescribe the use of any technique as a form of treatment for physical, emotional, or medical problems without the advice of a physician, either directly or indirectly. The intent of the author is only to offer information of a general nature to help you in your quest for emotional and spiritual well-being. In the event you use any of the information in this book for yourself, which is your constitutional right, the author and the publisher assume no responsibility for your actions.

Any people depicted in stock imagery provided by Getty Images are models, and such images are being used for illustrative purposes only.
Certain stock imagery © Getty Images.

Print information available on the last page.

ISBN: 979-8-7652-2847-0 (sc)
ISBN: 979-8-7652-2845-6 (hc)
ISBN: 979-8-7652-2846-3 (e)

Library of Congress Control Number: 2022908462

Balboa Press rev. date: 05/18/2022

CONTENTS

Previously You Met vii

Good to Meet You 1
The Reason 8
When Will I See You Again 19
You're My Home 22
When I See Your Smile 26
One More Night 31
Come Sail Away 38
The Letter 43
If Not For You 45
Just the Way You Are 52
The Way You Look Tonight 58
In Too Deep 65
La Dolce Vita 69
Come Fly With Me 71
Say You Won't Let Go 76
Stand By You 79
Where Have All the Flowers Gone 85
I Got You (I Feel Good) 90
Wicked Game 93
I Wanna Hold Your Hand 100
I Wonder What It's Like To Be Loved By You 102
One Is The Loneliest Number 109
You've Got A Friend 112
If the World Was Ending 115
One Fine Morning 122
Having the Time of My Life 129

Take Me to the River	136
Save your Tears	139
Trust in Me	143
My Sweet Refuge	148
The Tracks of My Tears	151
He's Still A Mystery To Me	154
Talk To Me	159
Living La Vida Loca	163
You Can Count On Me	165
Harvest Moon	169
Don't Stop Believing	172
Need You Now	175
Baby, It's Cold Outside	178
Please Forgive Me	187
Something	191
I'm Dreaming of a White Christmas	196
If You Go Away	201
Auld Lang Syne	206
Blue Tango	210
It's A Mad World	218
What Do You Want From Me	227
Have I Told you Lately	232
Dream Believer	234
Getting to Know You	248
Something in the Way She Moves	253
Don't Let the Sun Go Down On Me	257
You've Got A Friend	260
It's the Most Wonderful Time of the Year	267
When I See your Face	269
And I Will Try to Fix You	275
Total Eclipse of the Heart	279
For You Are Mine At Last	281
Freeze Frame	288
I'll Be There For You	290
If Not For You	295
Walking on Sunshine	297
About The Author	303

PREVIOUSLY YOU MET

Madison (Maddy) Davis-Walker - gregarious Canadian woman moves to London for a year, falls in love with Sebastian, changes his life

Sebastian Walker - reserved, widower falls in love with Maddy, design architect

Henry - orphaned boy assigned to Sebastian in a mentorship program, becomes close to Maddy

Christian Gerhart - Bank Manager for Deutsche Bank London, friend of Sebastian, sailing friend of Maddy

Lambert - loyal assistant to Sebastian at the Architectural firm, friend to Maddy

Sam Brown (The Professor) - musician, owns Decades Night Club, friend of Maddy

Grace and Davi Patel - Maddy introduced her best friend Grace from the CoffeeHouse to Davi, driver for Sebastian, their son Chance

Giselle and Philippe - Maddy meets Giselle in France, Philippe is Sebastian's best friend, owns winery in France. Giselle and Philippe marry and take on Villa Mirage.

Father Dom - the village priest at Villa Mirage, friend of Maddy

Oliver Wainright III - teenage crush of Maddy, now JAG lawyer for the Marines

Dermot Matthews - former US Ambassador in London, friend of Maddy

Deirdre Putnam-Fontaine - London socialite, friend of Sebastian

Sorento - Italian designer, rescued from a gambling debt by Maddy, designs Azul Line for Maddy

Michael Riley - scrupulous investment mogul befriends Maddy, disappears mysteriously, trusts Maddy with his life story before his death

A global virus is threatening to shut down commerce, flights, gatherings and life as we know it. The pandemic will force people to stay home, wear masks, quarantine if exposed, communicate on-line and stop hugging loved ones.

GOOD TO MEET YOU

"Let me get the drinks." Lambert moved away from the group as they walked into the theatre foyer. The usual opening night buzz was subdued this evening as patrons wondered if the virus would affect the run.

"Are you enjoying the play Maddy?" Christian asked as he scanned the crowd. He saw several clients from his bank in the foyer eyeing Maddy, not sure if they should approach. Six months ago Sebastian Walker had been gunned down as he walked out of the Registry Office with his bride, Maddy. A young boy had also been shot - a young life with so much potential lost - the boy, Henry, had been especially close to Maddy. Christian mourned both Sebastian and Henry but he understood the loss was unbearable for Maddy. This was the first night she had agreed to come out.

Opening night, as a patron of the arts, usually an exciting event for Maddy, was a welcome distraction from being alone in her London flat. It felt right to be here with Sebastian's loyal assistant Lambert and his friend Christian, who were committed to watching over her.

Maddy turned to Christian, about to share her thoughts on the first act, when she felt a hand on her elbow and a soft voice said "Excuse me." Christian had engaged in conversation with the couple beside him. She tucked a loose strand of hair behind her ear, took a deep breath and turned to see who had spoken.

The voice belonged to a tall, athletic man with the darkest eyes Maddy had ever seen. She blinked and took in his beautifully tailored suit, cufflinks on his crisp white shirt, an exquisite hand-painted silk tie…Maddy smiled, her head cocked to encourage him to continue.

"Permit me to introduce myself, Mrs Walker. I am Adam Khan, a friend of Oliver Wainright. I understand you are working on a water treatment project off the coast of Africa and I believe I may be of assistance. I have extensive experience with water in warm climates, notably the Saudi desert." He extended his hand.

He was holding her hand in his cool grip. "I have studied your reports and have several options to share." His self confidence was unsettling, his voice hypnotic, his diction precise.

"Please call me Maddy. How very kind of Oliver to mention my project. It seems I am at a disadvantage as you know about my project and I know nothing of you."

"Oliver assured me you would be more passionate about the needs of the island than he was. Perhaps we could discuss this more at dinner, this evening. I will answer your questions so we are on equal ground."

"Dinner this evening?" Maddy asked, interested in his response.

"The Shard is quite acceptable, however, if you prefer something more traditional, may I suggest *Gaucho* at Tower Bridge? Either provide an expansive view of London at night." He was still holding her hand. His eyes boring into her.

"Thank you, however we are invited to the cast party at Joe Allens, the restaurant across the street, after the play. I think everyone is expecting a lockdown so the cast want to get together." She hesitated and added, "Please join us. If you like."

Mr Khan bowed slightly, taking a step back. A barely discernible look of disappointment on his face. He was not a man who was turned down.

"Oh, Mr Khan, I should warn you…" Maddy waited until he made eye contact, "there may be dancing." She smiled at his serious look. She wasn't sure why she had invited him.

A look of deep concentration on his face, Adam Kahn, with his hands clasped behind his back, gave a quick nod and walked away. Maddy felt giddy as she watched him meld into the crowded foyer. What a strange duck, she thought.

Christian watched the exchange, surprised that Maddy had no idea who Adam Khan was; amused at how calmly the legendary Titan had reacted to her refusal to have dinner with him. He was known to get what he wanted, at any cost. Christian would wait to caution Maddy. She should be aware of his reputation.

Lambert arrived with their wine, flustered. "Did you see Kahn go by? I can't believe he would attend theatre without his usual entourage of goons. He always looks so intense. I guess he's allowed - he's very wealthy and powerful." He raised his glass. "Cheers."

"I don't think we've seen the last of him." Christian raised his glass in return. "Shall we get back to our seats?" He waited for Maddy to enter the theatre and then turned to see if Khan was still in the foyer. He wondered why he felt uncomfortable about the introduction. He was protective of Maddy and hoped Khan would lose interest.

Several hours later, after a loud and enthusiastic cast had taken their bows and sat down to a pre-arranged meal at the bistro, the music began. The band was well known to the actors and a raucous party was underway.

Maddy returned from the dance floor and watched Christian, leaning towards the pretty, young star, his arm around the back of her chair. She smiled at his persistence - the head of the Deutsche Bank in London, acting like a schoolboy. Lambert was already dancing with several of the troupe, clearly delighted to be letting loose with fellow thespians - his acting aspirations limited to local productions in small playhouses.

Maddy felt a hand on her shoulder and when she looked up Adam Khan was standing beside her. "Am I too late?" He asked as he scanned the crowd.

"Too late for dinner, I'm afraid, although I'm sure we can have something prepared for you." She rose, aware she was standing very close to him.

"I've dined, thank you. Would you like to dance?" His eyes were intense, his lashes long - his gaze much too sultry for a man of his age. She guessed he was mid-sixties.

Maddy smiled and nodded, welcoming the chance to dance, to let the music carry her away from her sadness, her loss, the emptiness in her heart. Khan followed her to the dance floor, absently moving to the music, watching Maddy dance. He was relieved to hear the change of pace to a slow number. He held his arms out for Maddy, who easily moved into the waltz, her hand barely touching his shoulder, her head near his chin, close enough for him to feel heady from her scent. He was disappointed when the song was over and the band announced they were taking a short break.

"Do you enjoy dancing?" Maddy asked as they made their way to the table, holding up the hair on her neck - the room was definitely warm.

"You may ask all your questions at dinner, tomorrow." He stood behind her and started to braid her hair. "May I?" He asked as he deftly started braiding. "I'm told I'm very good at this." Maddy realized she had stopped breathing. Was this stranger, a man she had just met, really braiding her hair, in a crowded restaurant?

"Well, well, well. Adam Khan, international man of mystery, where have you been? It's been ages." A heavily made-up woman in a tight dress approached, her words slurred, her high pitched voice intruding. "When did you take up hair styling? You never offered to style my hair. Come to think of it, you never offered anything. Introduce me to your escort, won't you?" The woman was teetering on her expensive stiletto heels.

Adam continued to work away at the braiding, looking around for something to secure his perfect braid. One of the actors handed him an elastic, giving him a thumbs up on a perfect job. When Adam was satisfied the braid would hold he looked over at the woman, took a deep breath and spoke in a low, menacing voice.

"Ms Hartnell, you should go home, you have had too much to drink. My business is none of yours and I'm offended you would call my friend an escort. Good night to you."

"I know who you are." Barbara Hartnell, the entertainment columnist from the Guardian stared at Maddy with contempt, pointing a finger. "You're the merry widow. The woman Sebastian Walker unceremoniously dumped me for…" Her eyes narrowed as she recalled the incident. She turned to Khan. "Consoling the grieving widow? How nice. Does she do you…"

Khan moved between Maddy and Hartnell. "Good night." He said menacingly.

He placed his hand on Maddy's elbow and guided her towards the bar. "I'm sorry. I don't go out much for that very reason." The bartender placed two flutes of champagne on the bar and walked away. "Dinner tomorrow? I will call for you at 7:00 pm. May I drive you home now?"

Maddy's eyes were filling with tears. Too many memories came flooding back - Sebastian had been so upset by the Hartnell encounter, she had just been called an escort; a strange man had braided her hair, as if it was a normal thing to do, yet it seemed like an intimate gesture. This man was a friend of Oliver's, he knew about the water project, he wanted to help - she suddenly felt overwhelmed with emotion. She had been wrong to think she was ready to go out in public. It was too early.

Maddy shook her head, trying to compose herself. "I'll make my way…"

"No. Absolutely not. You are not my escort, you are my dinner guest and I would never allow a woman to arrive alone. Especially when she has so many questions." His voice was firm but his dark eyes looked amused.

Maddy smiled, wiping a tear away. "I do have a lot of questions."

Khan watched her wipe the tear away, wondering if he should dry the track of the tear with his thumb. He realized Maddy was not wearing make-up; women didn't wipe their eyes for fear of smudging their make-up. He turned away quickly. He must focus on the water treatment business.

Christian and Lambert approached them at the bar. "Maddy, did you have a good time? Ready to go?" Lambert was moving his gaze between Maddy and Khan.

"I'm ready to go if you two have had enough for one night. Mr Khan has been most solicitous and he's a great dancer." She turned to Adam and formally introduced him to her friends. It was civil but awkward.

"I have offered to see Ms Walker home but I see she is in capable hands so I will say good night. It has been a pleasure." He reached over and touched his lips to Maddy's hand. One last look and he was gone.

"That guy is major intense. He has a reputation for being ruthless in business, I see that." Lambert watched him leave. "Did he scare you?"

"No, but he did braid my hair." Maddy shook her head. "This was great fun. You were right, I did need a night out. Thank you both. I'm ready to go whenever you are."

Christian nodded, he had lost interest in the young actress - it seemed to require more work seducing young women these days. He did not comment on Khan or the hair but he wondered where this was going. He would check on it tomorrow. Maddy was too vulnerable right now.

The three friends left the restaurant, arm in arm, laughing at something Lambert was relating with great passion. When Maddy laughed, her head thrown back, it was a warm laugh. The trio crossed the street, singing a tune, none of them particularly interested in the black town car parked across the street.

THE REASON

"You have a date?" Grace asked, not sure if she was happy for Maddy or concerned. Grace had been the first friend Maddy had made in London, when she arrived, hoping to spend a year finding herself in London. That year had brought heartbreak, adventure and love with Sebastian. Since then Maddy had been involved in every aspect of Grace's life - introducing her to Davi, Sebastian's driver; buying out the previous owner of the coffee shop so Grace could have ownership in the business; arranging for a move to the bookshop where the elderly Mr Simpson had allowed Grace and Davi to thrive in a new coffee shop location; as well as being a wonderful friend.

"Well, it's more of a business meeting, really. This is a friend of Oliver's and he is interested in my water project for the island. Remember we went to the island and there was a coup - they need fresh water. Grace, he braided my hair last night."

Maddy was still unsure about the gesture.

"That's weird. Are you sure you feel up to this? You haven't been out much. Not that I don't think it's time for you to get out of the house but…what do you know about this chap?"

"Not much, but I did Google him and he seems legit. His name is Adam Khan, he's from the UAE, lives in Dubai, he's an engineer and…."

"Maddy, Adam Khan…Oh. My. Goodness. Be careful. He's notorious. Is he as handsome in person as he is in the tabloids? Oh Maddy, I can't believe it. Davi will flip when I tell him." Grace was gushing.

"It's just dinner and I'll know pretty quick if he really is interested in the water treatment plan - if not, I'll go back to being a hermit. I haven't been to the beach house since the funeral so it's time, before they impose any restrictions on travel. I hope you, Davi and little Chance are staying safe. Must go. I'll let you know how it turns out. Ciao for now."

Maddy rang off the call, smiling at the reaction of her friend. It was nice to know everyone was looking out for her. Having dinner with a strange man, discussing the water treatment plant, just getting out of the flat, dressing up again…Maddy was looking forward to having an appointment. Grief was exhausting.

At precisely 7:00 pm the doorbell rang and Adam Khan presented Maddy with a lovely bouquet of Gerbera daisies in various colours. How did he know they were her favourite flowers? How did he know where she lived? He was impeccably dressed in a dark silk weave suit. His shirt looked so crisp Maddy wanted to reach out and touch him, just to be sure he was real. Maddy had chosen a simple black dress, a colourful pashmina, her hair was swept back in a loose chignon. Adam Khan nodded, realizing he approved of her outfit. She looked so young and free…

Walking into the restaurant several of the other diners approached Adam, anxious to shake his hand or remind him who they were. When they were seated Adam was preoccupied adjusting his shirt cuffs. "I'm sorry. I dine here whenever I'm in London."

"Does this happen every time?" Maddy asked with a smile, glancing out over the room.

"No, but for some reason everyone is interested in you this evening."

"I'm flattered but not convinced."

He looked across at Maddy, admiring her.

"Champagne cocktail to start? Or would you prefer wine?" He asked in a soft voice. The man was too charming.

"I'm fine with wine. When do I get to start asking my questions?" Maddy certainly had many questions for this enigmatic man.

Adam ordered a bottle of dry Riesling. He suggested they let the Chef choose their meal, then he pulled out a folded document.

"Here is everything I think you'll want to know about me. Everything that isn't on Google. I have included a letter of reference from Oliver. Also, there is a page on my current water system and treatment plant in Dubai. You may find that particularly interesting as I believe it mirrors your own project. Now, may we enjoy the evening?"

Maddy laughed out loud, despite herself. "My friends accused me of flirting with you last night."

"Were you?" He found her laugh enchanting.

"I don't know. I'm not sure I know how…but it is pleasant bantering with someone who I just met. How did you become so adroit at braiding?" She looked directly at him.

"My daughter has long hair, she constantly challenges me to do something to contain her unruly curls when I am home. And no, cutting her beautiful locks is not an option, she tells me. It's the only time we have together these days - her life is so full of entertainments. No sons, I'm afraid, just one daughter and she is enough for any man. My wife passed away at childbirth so Angela and I are very close. She will marry soon and terrorize some other man. I will miss her, but it's time." He sighed and noticed that Maddy was encouraging him to go on. She made him feel like he wanted to keep talking about himself, something he was not usually comfortable with.

"May I ask how the project came up in conversation?" Maddy lowered her glass and looked over the candle flame at Adam. Her diamond tennis bracelet reflecting the light.

Adam took a sip of wine and returned her gaze. "Oliver and I were at school together - how ironic that a boy from the desert would befriend a marine, a man made to be on the water. When he was in Cyprus he invited me to visit and mentioned he thought my work would benefit a very close friend of his. He has been key to designing my security systems and providing legal advice over the years, how could I refuse such a request?" He moved back in his chair and continued.

"I have studied your notes and flown over the island. I'm not sure you realize the scope of the project you are proposing. The island is not well positioned for fresh water or sustainable living. There is an island several miles away, with a lush forest and a fresh water source. The foundation is better for building and the beach on the eastern coast has not eroded or moved with currents." Adam averted his eyes as his long fingers moved up and down his wine stem.

"I suggest you encourage your friends to move - they are in danger of losing whatever has been built to date. You mention the runway was to be improved - that did not happen. Your islanders are not very productive left on their own. I understand the development was faulty and it is crumbling, mainly due to the substandard materials supplied. I'm sure that is not what you hoped to hear, but I assure you, I have done my homework. I wanted to meet you and be sure you understood the situation. Now that I have met you, I think I want to help you rectify the problem. Ah, it appears we are to start with mussels. I hope you enjoy them."

Adam watched Maddy lean over the mussels, inhaling the aroma and smiling her approval.

He sat back, admiring his dinner companion, hoping the shock of his words would not ruin a perfectly civilized evening. "I come to this restaurant whenever I am in London. My friend Michael insisted on eating here. Since he passed away I don't seem to visit as much. We met once or twice a month - he was reputed to be as ruthless as I - he was Irish, great fun and fiercely competitive in business, but sadly he was the victim of an untimely sailboat tragedy right here on the Thames. Now I only return when I must."

Maddy had thanked the waiter for topping up her wine glass and was trying to concentrate on the plate in front of her. It looked delightful but she had lost her appetite with the words delivered. She bit her lip and tried to hold back the tears she felt welling up in her eyes. She had to toughen up - she wasn't upset by the report but rather of the image of her lovely Irish friend in his sailboat…

"Maddy. Maddy, are you alright? Look at me." His voice was soft and pleading. Adam reached for her hand.

Maddy looked up and blinked, willing the tears away, her eyes bright.

"Blue Eyes." He whispered. "You are *Blue Eyes*." Adam leaned back in his chair. "How did I miss that? You were friends with…"

"Michael Riley." They said simultaneously.

"Maddy, I should not have mentioned Michael or given you such a concise report on the project right away…I don't know why I didn't see it before. I've upset you. I'm so sorry."

Maddy rubbed her neck and then waved her hand over her plate. "This is a lot to digest…um, I should probably go. I'm sorry." She pushed her chair back. Adam could see her rubbing her thighs, fighting for control.

"Thank you for being so diligent - I appreciate your alternate plan but I need time to think about what you saw and what you propose. Don't get up…" she stood, feeling unsteady on her feet."I'm sorry. I'm overreacting to hearing Michael's name again. I didn't realize he knew you. I miss him. I'm actually writing his story, as he told it to me."

Adam was beside her, his arm around her. He helped her sit down and squatted beside her chair. "Maddy, please forgive me. Michael spoke of his friendship with *Blue Eyes* often - how he loved being with you, but he wouldn't tell us your name. I shouldn't have mentioned it. In retrospect, I should have deferred your questions until after dinner. Please don't go. Indulge me and let me enjoy having dinner with a beautiful woman."

He slipped into his chair, wondering why he was so concerned about her reaction - his synopsis was truthful, perhaps blunt, but that's how he would speak to any client. Michael had been gone for two years, surely she had come to terms with his death…

"I should go, it's a shock to hear Michael's name again…I just want to walk on the beach. It was wrong of me to accept your invitation, however charming. It's too soon."

Adam looked at the woman sitting across from him - her eyes were sad, although she looked totally in control. He knew she had suffered a loss recently, he had opened yet another wound and given her news she was trying to process.

George, the maitre'd approached the table, inquiring if everything was to their liking.

"George, we have had some terrible news and must leave. We'll go out the back." Adam nodded to the kitchen door.

"Certainly Mr Khan, follow me. I will have your meals prepared to go in a moment."

Adam held Maddy close as they walked through the kitchen into his waiting car.

"Not the evening I had planned but at least we will get to finish our meal. It would be a shame to deprive ourselves of a fine dinner. George will just be a moment." Adam opened the door for Maddy and then climbed into the far side of the car.

"Trust me?" Maddy looked across at Adam. She had slipped her shoes off. Adam smiled at her, not sure what she meant.

Maddy stepped out of the car and leaned into the driver's window. "Hello, I'm Maddy. Who are you?" She held her hand out but the driver seemed frozen in place.

"Kaleed, Madame." The driver responded cautiously, looking nervously in the rearview mirror at Adam, his eyes darting. He was not trained to speak to the clients his boss entertained. His job was to drive Khan and ensure he was always in sight.

"Kaleed, nice to meet you. We won't be needing you this evening. Do you have a wife or girlfriend, or both, who is waiting for you?" Maddy opened the drivers door, signalling Kaleed to disembark. "I'll drive. I know where we're going. Thank you."

Kaleed, frantically searched the car for his boss. He could feel beads of sweat on his forehead. He had never taken orders from a woman and no woman had ever driven his car…he wasn't sure what to do.

Adam could not contain his laughter as he watched Maddy take control of the car and his driver. The restaurant service door opened and their meals were delivered to the vehicle.

"Don't worry Kaleed, I am not kidnapping Mr Khan. I am taking him to a secret place and will return him, with your car, after dinner." She raised her right hand. "I promise. I'll try not to hit anything."

Adam nodded and his bewildered driver stepped aside. He had never been asked to leave his boss - was this a trick? He nervously looked back at the security team in the black BMW. Should he warn them? He watched his boss walk over to the car and speak to the driver. He motioned for Kaleed to join him and after a few moments of intense conversation the security team departed, with Kaleed.

Maddy beckoned to Adam. "Come on, let's go. You'll love the beach. I'm a good driver. Sit back and chill. You get to choose the music."

Adam hesitated, amused but unsure of what he had just done. He watched the security team disappear.

"You can sit up front. Come on, get in." Maddy laughed. "Would you prefer to drive?"

"No." Adam responded.

"Is this an armoured car? What a blast. You must just love getting in and driving away."

"I do not."

"Are you kidding me? You don't sneak away and just drive into the countryside on a lark?" Maddy asked. "Check out a village pub? Go rogue?"

"I do not." Adam sat in the car tentatively.

"Oh. I see. Do you know how to work the radio?" She asked with a smile.

Adam looked at the dashboard, realizing he had never been in the front seat.

"I'm usually on the phone when I'm in the car. My security team handles the details."

"So you don't get any privacy? Oh dear." Maddy nodded, leaned forward and chose a soft jazz station. "Okay, let's go."

Adam had to admit Maddy was a good driver and the hour long ride to the beach house was definitely an adventure - he had never been abducted, albeit willingly, by a woman who insisted on singing with the radio. She asked so many questions and he found himself wanting to talk to her. He surprised himself when he realized he felt relaxed - not a familiar feeling, sadly.

They ate on the deck of Maddy's comfortable beach house, listening to the waves crashing below them. The wine seemed to taste better out here. They had soft blankets around their shoulders and he noticed Maddy sat with her legs folded under her, like his daughter sat when she was at home with him. He wasn't sure what time it was, the evening had flown by but he could see the light of day trying to burst forth.

Maddy stood and touched his shoulder, disturbing his reverie. "Dinner was lovely. I'm going for a walk on the beach. You can sleep if you like." She had changed into a loose sweatshirt and leggings, her feet bare. Her hair was swept up and held in place with a scarf. He wanted to touch her face and pull her close. Maddy covered him with another blanket and suddenly she was gone, gone before he could respond.

He closed his eyes and thought about their conversation - she had challenged him and he had spoken about things he had long kept private. She wanted to know what aircraft he had flown over the island, what business he disliked, what made him happy, why he had a security team following him, why he never remarried, where he had travelled, how he knew Michael Riley, why he didn't drive, what he liked to eat, why he had a Christian name…nothing seemed out of bounds to her. He felt as though he had just completed a high level interview for a seat on the rocket to heaven.

He stood up and looked down at the water - he saw Maddy walking along the beach, the sun trying to break through the fog. He kicked off his *Brunello Cucinelli* deerskin loafers, pulled his socks off and rolled his pants up, laughing at his impulsiveness. He ran down the steps to the beach, feeling free and exhilarated. When he caught up to Maddy he was out of breath, making a mental note to return to the fitness club.

They walked in silence for some time, stopping to toss a piece of driftwood or pick up litter. When they turned back towards the beach house the sun had won over the fog, spreading a golden hue. As they climbed the stairs Adam felt a wave of fatigue and wondered when he had last stayed up all night. Maddy looked back, realizing he might fall asleep as he stood on the step. She reached for his hand and pulled him up the last steps. He followed her into the house and fell onto the sofa. He was sleeping before she covered him and placed a pillow under his head.

Maddy made coffee and then fell back on the bed, sinking into the duvet. She had meant to lie there for a moment but when she stirred it was early afternoon and the sun was reflecting off the waves. She sat up and looked around the room - collecting her thoughts; gathering her bearings. She stretched and walked over to the sofa, wondering if Adam was still sleeping. He was gone, the blanket folded on the arm of the sofa. She walked out to the deck and let the sun warm her face. Why hadn't she come here months ago, right after the funeral? It was so peaceful and so soothing, listening to the waves, watching the sky. Her stomach growled and she realized she had not brought groceries. Dinner seemed a long time ago. She turned and was startled when she saw Adam standing before her, a grocery bag in his arms.

"Good morning, or should I say, afternoon. I thought you'd gone. Did you sleep at all?" She had to admit she was happy to see him, and his groceries.

"I slept like a baby. I had coffee but realized we might want something more so I found a shop, all on my own…it was quite an adventure, shopping. I haven't been in a food shop for years, maybe decades. I did get help with the essentials, the shop girls were most helpful. Now I need your help to turn them into something we can eat."

Maddy laughed and took the bag from him. "Well done. Welcome to the real world."

After creating a toasted western sandwich with the ingredients Adam had so proudly purchased, they sat on the deck, enjoying a glass of sparkling wine.

"This was a most enjoyable getaway for me. Thank you Maddy. Now, I must return to Dubai. My team will be here shortly. Unfortunately they are not programmed for such impulsive behaviour and they expected me this morning. You keep the car, return when you like." He reached out to touch her arm.

"You are a breath of fresh air and I hope our paths will cross again. I am serious about flying you over the island and helping you determine the best course of action, whatever you choose to do."

Maddy smiled. "Let me look at your data. I want to understand what you propose. When are you next in London?"

"I have no plans. Ah, here's my car. Be safe, *Blue Eyes*." He kissed her hand and walked out to the waiting car.

Maddy watched him drive off and sighed. She had enjoyed the time with Adam - he was a pleasant distraction - she also enjoyed time with her friends in London - it was the time alone she found difficult. The loss of Sebastian and Henry left a big gap in her life. She leaned against the closed door wondering if she would ever see Adam Khan again.

WHEN WILL I SEE YOU AGAIN

"Angela, grab my phone. I'm expecting a call from Oliver. I'll be right there." Adam called out from the pool terrace at his Dubai home.

"Hello Uncle Oliver. Father will be right here. I'm acting as his secretary, it seems. Listen, he met your friend in London. Kaleed told me she made him get out of the car and she drove away with Father. He won't tell me anything but Kaleed said her name was Maddy so I looked her up - is she the one dancing with you on that dreamy YouTube video?" Angela gushed on, anxious to hear more about Maddy but her father stood beside her, ready to take the phone.

"I'll get the details from you later. Here's Father. When are we going to see you? You'll come to my wedding, won't you? Bring your friend…I must meet her."

Adam shook his head at his daughter's enthusiasm for gossip. He had purposely not spoken about his visit to London, knowing she would fantasize about him meeting a woman. He had no time for women. Then why was he thinking about Maddy whenever he wasn't in a meeting? Why couldn't he forget the way she laughed? He must be getting old and soft.

"Oliver, when I received the estimates on the boat repairs I must say I was shocked - I think a change of venue is required. Although Angela is keen to have the reception on board. Can you imagine how difficult it will be to keep the air conditioning ahead of the crowd on that old tug?"

Angela tried to eavesdrop on the call but Adam had moved into his office and closed the door. She would call Oliver later - he was her favourite uncle and he rarely said no to her. She wanted to meet Maddy and her wedding presented the perfect opportunity.

In Martha's Vineyard, Colonel Oliver Wainright III, of the Marine JAG Corps, placed his phone on the desk and looked out at the boats, swaying in the wake of a large cruiser leaving the harbour. Adam had been vague about his meeting with Maddy. He himself had not yet called Maddy to see how she was faring - he hoped to visit her within the month, if the threatened lockdowns allowed. He was leaving his seaside paradise later today for a month of discovery hearings onboard a submarine - he wanted as much sunshine as possible before the ordeal.

He had hoped to retire from the Marines after his Cyprus tour of duty but as he settled into life in Washington he was recalled to provide legal counsel for a controversial case - after several months of depositions, preparing for trial and then the actual trial, he was tired. Weary of the very thing he enjoyed about the law…interpretation and justice. One more assignment and then he was determined to retire.

Oliver looked forward to the wedding in Dubai. He was proud of the woman Angela had become - her father had done a good job of separating business and time with his daughter. Angela knew her father was a successful businessman but she knew little of his methods and his ruthlessness. It had been difficult for Oliver over the years, as he was aware that not all of Adam's dealings were above board. He had not wanted to jeopardize their friendship but he did feel there were aspects of life in the Middle East he did not understand or care to know about. He stood and stretched. He dialled Maddy's number, anxious to hear her voice. He did not leave a message. Time to go.

Maddy stayed at the beach house for another week. She was careful to stay in touch with Lambert, Christian and Grace, assuring them she was enjoying the walks on the beach and being alone. She had not called Rod, a childhood friend of Sebastian's who lived near the beach house - she wasn't ready to share her grief or be reminded of her life with Sebastian. She would return to the flat in London soon enough - back to her computer and her work.

She knew she must return to Villa Mirage in Italy, Sebastian's inherited property, at some point, but Giselle and Philippe, managing the Villa, assured her the business was doing fine, the vineyard was healthy and Father Dom, their neighbour and good friend, was still drinking and playing cards. She missed them all - she longed to see them when she was in a less fragile state. She was missing her dog Anza, who by all accounts, was also missing her.

She read the report on the island and came to understand how much time and effort Adam Khan had put into suggesting an alternative for the island inhabitants. He had attached preliminary monetary figures to the move, a great deal of detail on substandard conditions. She wavered between amusement and respect for the thoughts he presented. He was certainly thorough.

YOU'RE MY HOME

♥ ♥ ♥

Back in London, Maddy was pleased with the chapter she had just finished writing, Maddy closed the laptop and rubbed her eyes. She sat back and was startled when the doorbell rang. She wasn't expecting anyone. No one was visiting during the latest pandemic. She hadn't realized how late it was in the day - it was dark in the flat.

As she opened the door she was distracted by a letter on the floor. Someone had dropped a letter in the mail slot. She bent to pick up the letter and heard a familiar voice. As she stood she was engulfed in a full body hug.

"Hello beautiful. JAG Officer Wainright reporting for furlough. I'm just off a submarine with forty men and I really needed to see you. Sorry I didn't call first. I have to quarantine for fourteen days…if that's not A.O.K. with you I'll head to a hotel but I wanted to see you first." Oliver had not let go.

Maddy laughed and invited him in. "Welcome. You can certainly stay here. I'd love the company." He was wearing a mask with the Marine logo printed on it. She looked around for hers - it was suggested that masks could contain the spread of the virus and it made sense to wear a mask in public. She buried her head in his lapels and just enjoyed human touch for another minute.

"I come bearing gifts….beer, wine, gin, champagne and steaks. Oh, and chocolate." He pointed to a large box beside his duffel bag. "I'm afraid I need a shower and a beer before I answer any questions."

"Let me show you to your quarters, sir. Right this way. Towels in the bathroom, everything you need right here. Very private but no entertaining allowed. Get settled and I'll feed you." She left him and wandered into the kitchen to prepare a snack tray. It could be a long night of catching up.

Oliver was a wonderful companion; for two weeks they played cards, chess, board games and managed to complete several puzzles - talking and reminiscing well into the evenings. They had met as teenagers studying Spanish in South America and Oliver had visited Maddy in Italy before his tour of duty in Cyprus - they were easy together. Each morning they tried to get through a yoga class without laughing; the afternoons were for reading and preparing extravagant meals. They did not speak about Sebastian or Henry. Oliver knew the loss was too raw. They agreed they could only talk about happy times.

When asked about the visit with Adam Khan, Maddy was noncommittal. She shrugged and said he seemed like a decent person and his report on the water project was detailed. She was trying to reach someone on the island to monitor the mood, the water situation and the health of the villagers. She realized things were difficult because the world had basically shut down since the medical reporting was so dire. She wasn't allowed to travel to Villa Mirage in Italy and that was heartbreaking.

Oliver told Maddy about the upcoming wedding in Dubai, now on hold, and the closeness between father and daughter. He had not spoken with Adam since the lockdowns but hoped they would soon be able to golf or sail in either of their country homes. Oliver had hoped he and Maddy would become closer, he adored her. He had suggested Adam contact Maddy regarding the water filtration plant and yet he felt that might have been a tactical error on his part. It was possible Adam was interested in Maddy and that would be awkward. Who wouldn't want to spend time with Maddy?

The last day with Maddy was busy with arranging passage, collecting briefs on the next trials and packing. Oliver had been trying to reach Adam with information on a boat repair but they had not connected. As he was enjoying a picnic with Maddy on the terrace his phone vibrated. There was no polite way to ignore the call.

"Hey, good to hear from you. I'm flying out tonight after a great two weeks of quarantine here with Maddy. Say hello. I'm switching to video."

Adam leaned forward, self-conscious about how he looked. He had thought about Maddy ever since he had left her at the beach house. He imagined her sitting beside Oliver, pushing her hair behind her ears, a gesture he found endearing.

"How are you Adam? Are you in lockdown as well?" Maddy asked, genuinely interested.

Adam took a deep breath, "Yes, we are being careful. Oliver's not badgering you, is he?" He wondered why it bothered him to know Oliver was with Maddy, they were friends, after all.

"No, it's been great fun having him here. He actually seems to enjoy my cooking. It gets pretty lonely but hopefully this craziness is over soon." Maddy was so animated, he wished he could reach out and touch her.

"What do you hear from your island villagers?" Adam hoped his voice wasn't too high.

"Oh Adam, it's so frustrating, no phone or internet, no way of communicating. I've been in touch with every agency on the north coast of Africa, hoping they will stop in at the island and report back…I've even called Greenpeace. Thanks for asking." She sighed. "I have a few questions about your suggestions - but until I hear back from the village I really can't move forward." Adam smiled as she shrugged her shoulders and moved a loose tendril of hair behind her ear. He knew he had to see her again. "Oh, I still have your car." She sounded mischievous.

Adam found himself laughing. When had he last laughed out loud?

"I hate to impose, but if it's not too inconvenient, I may ask you to collect me from the airport next week."

"Of course, anytime. Just call." She looked over at Oliver. "Here's Oliver, I'm butting in on your conversation. Be safe Adam." She blew him an air kiss and stood up, walking away to give them privacy. She wondered how Adam would be in London without his security team but shrugged it off.

Waving goodbye to Oliver was emotional for Maddy. She would miss having him in the house. The zoom calls with friends were fine but they weren't the same as having someone beside you, someone to laugh with.

Oliver promised to return after his next tour of duty - it seemed crime didn't take a break during a pandemic. He was reluctant to leave Maddy - she had been the best companion - he wished she was more, but it was still too soon to make a move. He couldn't risk losing her now…not after all this time. He had so wanted to kiss her goodbye, to hold her in his arms, to run his hands through her hair, to kiss her softly and then passionately. He wanted her to wrap her arms around him, kiss him and not let go. Patience. Patience was required to win the prize…and getting rid of the damn masks.

WHEN I SEE YOUR SMILE

♥ ♥ ♥

"Hello Maddy. Ah, yes, I hate these machines. If it's not too inconvenient, I am arriving at noon tomorrow. Heathrow Terminal 2. Hmm, it's Adam Khan. Um, if you can't make it, no worries, I will take a cab. Yes, that's it. Thank you." Adam hit 'end call' and wondered why he couldn't deliver a simple telephone message to the woman.

Prior to landing, Adam shaved, brushed his teeth and donned a crisp white shirt, the collar and cuffs starched stiff - he felt ready to take over a corporation. He lowered his head, realizing he was nervous. He hadn't felt this way for so long, he was trying to understand why beads of sweat were breaking out on his forehead, why he was jumpy…it was so easy to build; buy and sell; move through life with no emotion - no women.

He kept a steady pace through the terminal and when he saw blue sky he knew it was a flip of the coin - she would either be there waiting or he would stand in the cab line. He should have ordered a limo. No. He took a deep breath and walked through the automatic door. He could see people looking back, smiling and pointing to a mass of colour ahead. He saw Maddy standing in front of his car, gripping a dozen colourful balloons emblazoned with 'Welcome'. She was smiling and she waved, oblivious to the crowds staring. He laughed, feeling self-conscious and yet very special. As he approached the car Maddy opened the back door for him and offered the balloons to a family walking by, except for one, which she placed in the car.

"Hope you had a great flight, sir. Welcome to London." She smiled and he felt awkward - he wanted to embrace her, to move her hair behind her ears, to look at her, watch her smile. She was wearing a baby blue sweater set and jeans with denim runners. Simple but refreshing. He closed the back door, opened the passenger door and motioned for Maddy to sit. He walked to the drivers door, still smiling.

"Best welcome ever. Thank you." He looked over at her, smiling broadly.

"You can drive? Where's your security team?" Maddy looked around.

Adam laughed as he started the car. "Of course I am able to drive. I went rogue and gave my security team the slip, just as you suggested. It was a wonderful feeling. I have you to thank for this sense of freedom, although I fear it will be short-lived."

Maddy gave a throaty laugh and absently reached over to touch his collar, her fingers caressing the hair on his neck. "Good for you. I'm proud of you."

Adam closed his eyes and tightened his grip on the steering wheel. It was such a simple gesture, Maddy caressing his neck, yet it seemed to take his breath away. He tried to focus on driving. He was worried he would reach for her arm and pull her close if she didn't move her hand.

"Would you like some lunch? I have a picnic basket in the boot or I can recommend a great take-put pizza place or if you prefer something spicy we can stop for curry at Auntie's take-out. Everything is take-out now. Either way, I did bring wine." Maddy was hugging her knees, her shoes off.

If only Kaleed could see her now, bare feet on the leather…he chuckled to himself.

"Maddy, before the team arrive and find me I have business to attend to - it's been months since I've been back in London. Are you free to have dinner with me this evening? Please say yes."

"Of course, you need to take care of business, especially since you've gone rogue. I'm so sorry. I just assumed, wrongly, that you had free time. Silly of me. Of course you have business here. It's nice to see you again. You can let me out anywhere here - I'm happy to walk and let you get to work."

"Maddy," he placed his hand on her knee, "I want a long, leisurely dinner with you rather than a quick lunch. Is that alright?"

"You know where to find me. When you're ready…oh, red light, I'll hop out now. Cheers." And she was out of the car, running across the intersection, her shoes in her hand. He hit the steering wheel hard with both hands, feeling out of control, watching her disappear. The light changed and he drove ahead, but only after the horns of the cars behind him blared, bringing him back to reality.

After a long walk, a lovely bubblebath and a cup of tea, Maddy sat at her computer and started another chapter. She lost track of time and was startled by the doorbell. She stood up and stretched. It was dark out, who would be calling now?

She opened the door to find Adam holding flowers and a bottle of wine. Several cartons and take-out bags at his feet. He looked repentant. Maddy motioned him in - trying not to laugh at the collection on the doorstep.

"Well, I am hungry. Thank goodness you're here." She bent to collect the take-out bags and cartons. "Please come in. You seem to have covered all the food groups."

Dinner choices included pizza, fish and chips, seafood linguine, burgers, chicken biryani, curry and a selection of desserts. The table was laid out, containers open, wine poured and candles lit when they sat down. The fragrant bouquet looked lovely on the counter as there was no room on the table.

Several hours later, sitting out on the terrace, they laughed at how much they ate, how they had tasted everything and how they might not eat ever again. It was a relaxing evening, sprinkled with light conversation, heated debate and friendly silences.

"Isn't this about the time you feel like walking on the beach?" Adam asked, watching the clouds swirl around the moon. He yawned, knowing he should go but not wanting the evening to end.

"I'll head to the beach house tomorrow and spend a few days there - I'm sure the dust bunnies are taking over. The forecast is for sunshine so it should be glorious. You're welcome to come down if you want to escape the city."

No response. Maddy looked over and realized he was asleep in the lounger. She touched his shoulder and suggested he take the guest room.

Maddy was speaking with Grace and her young son Chance when Adam walked into the kitchen in the morning. She had cleared the take-out feast from the table and had breakfast set. Maddy motioned to the coffee pot so he walked over to fill a mug and leaned against the counter, watching her wave to a child on the screen and sign off, promising to stop by on her way to the beach. It was clear from the air kisses and the repeated goodbyes, they missed her.

"Good morning. I am surely the worst dinner guest ever. Sorry, it was such a relaxing evening." Adam sighed, knowing his security team would be here shortly. He seemed to have forgotten about his car. Maddy had shown him the side entrance, exclusive to her flat. She could park and enter without anyone from the street seeing her. The vehicle was safe.

Maddy smiled. "It was a lovely evening. Very inclusive, in terms of dishes. Anything you want to take for lunch?" She looked over at the cartons and bags of food.

He held his hand up. "No, thank you all the same. I may not eat for a few days." He glanced at his watch and searched for his jacket and shoes. "My driver is here. I'll leave the keys. The car is yours to use. I won't be driving again this trip."

"I'm heading to the beach house for a few days. You are welcome to stop by, if you should find yourself in the neighbourhood. Please don't bring any food." Maddy laughed and Adam wished he could record the sound, to hear it later.

They were standing by the door and Adam felt faint, having her so close. He softly touched her cheek and then moved a strand of hair behind her ear. Her eyes were drawing him in and before he could control the urge to hold her, he kissed her. Slow, soft, teasing her lips, afraid to breathe, afraid she would turn away from his kiss.

Maddy had not anticipated the move and was confused that she had returned the kiss. Her knees were shaking, her heart racing.

Adam opened the door and briskly walked to the waiting car. As the car drove away he willed himself to look straight ahead, touching his lips. What a pleasant way to start the day. He barely heard Kaheel ranting about safety and protocols.

Maddy smiled as she leaned against the door. How was it Adam Khan always had a perfect white shirt and clothes that never wrinkled. How was it that she was smiling from that kiss? Neither had worn a mask…it felt relatively reckless, but so good.

ONE MORE NIGHT
♥ ♥ ♥

Maddy was chasing after a kite on the beach, pulling at the string, when her phone rang. She struggled with the string and the phone, answering breathlessly. The wind caught her kite and she let out a scream of delight just as she heard her name being called.

"Maddy, are you alright? What's going on?"

"My kite has finally left the ground…it's wonderful. Sorry, I missed who's calling. I can't let go now."

"Maddy, it's Adam. I'd like to see you this evening, I have a favour to ask, well, actually several favours. I wondered if you would join me for dinner. Secondly, if you would mind if I stayed over and thirdly, would you collect me from the train station in an hour? If you say no, not possible, I will have to jump off the train."

Maddy laughed and pulled on the string. "Yes, yes, yes of course." I'll meet the train, but only if you come and fly this kite with me."

"Whatever it takes." He felt like a schoolboy. He sat back in his seat, inserted his earbuds and listened to a podcast about changes to international trade laws as they pertained to the oil and gas industry. Sadly, he would have to listen to the conversation again as he barely heard the discussion - his mind was preoccupied with visions of flying a kite as a child.

Maddy was standing by the kiosk at the station when he disembarked. She was wearing a white tee shirt, wildly patterned leggings, a soft suede jacket. Her scarf hung carelessly around her neck and her sunglasses were perched on her head, giving her the air of an aviator. Her hair was tied back in a high ponytail and her cheeks were flushed, from the wind and the sun. He stopped to watch her as she greeted locals coming out to the platform, others leaving. She was there to meet him, he wanted to shout this out, to let the others know, she was there to welcome him. He shook his head and walked towards her. She smiled the most disarming smile when she saw him. As they met he wished she would throw her arms around his neck so he could hold her and tell her how lovely she looked. At that moment an older couple stepped forward and expressed their sympathy for her loss, the loss of her dear husband, Sebastian.

Adam stepped back and waited for Maddy to finish her conversation. She watched the couple walk away before acknowledging him.

"How was your train trip? How did you ever get on a train without your security team? Did you bring casual clothes? Are you hungry?" She stopped talking and laughed. "Sorry, it's good to see you." She took his hand and led him out to her car. "Are you okay with the top down? It's so beautiful out. Your car is still at the flat."

He tossed his bag in the small back seat and looked over the car. "I should be fine. Now, I heard there was a kite to be flown…let's go."

After several failed attempts, the kite having survived dragging on the beach and hitting the rocks, Adam regained his moves and demonstrated his skill - long forgotten. He enjoyed hearing Maddy laugh and scream with joy as the kite soared above them. Carrying the kite, they walked along the beach as the sun threatened to settle on the horizon. They climbed the stairs to the beach house, exhausted. They sat on the deck, watching the sunset, wine in hand.

"That was brilliant. I haven't flown a kite for years, I don't know why I never got a kite for my daughter. Cheers." He raised his glass. "What shall we do about dinner?"

"I was craving spaghetti and meatballs. I don't feel much like going out. Do you mind?"

"I defer to the beautiful Chef. May I help you in the kitchen?" He would try to be useful, although his meals had always been prepared for him. What a different world he was experiencing for the first time.

"You can be the meat ball roller - I'll handle everything else." She pointed towards the small kitchen and walked away.

Dinner was delicious. He watched Maddy create a salad, heat a baguette, cook pasta and taste the sauce with a wooden spoon in the time it took him to roll perfect meatballs for the oven. His next job was grating the parmesan...he made quite a mess but Maddy just laughed. They consumed a bottle of wine in the making of dinner and another as they finished the pasta.

Maddy lit a fire and they sat on the floor on large pillows. Soft music played and soon Adam was standing, asking Maddy to dance. They danced and talked and asked each other more questions.

Adam wanted to know if hearing about Sebastian made her sad - she explained she had such a lovely life with him it would be selfish to be sad now - her memories of loving him were strong. She had experienced loss before, with her parents, her lover in Paris, friends and acquaintances... but the greatest loss was young Henry, a young life so full of promise. Following each loss it seemed life had provided others who needed her love and here she was...alone, but not unloved.

Maddy asked Adam about his privileged life, his friendship with Michael Riley and how it seemed strange that he and Oliver had been school mates, especially since Oliver had joined the Marines. Adam spoke about Michael and how they had become business associates and then friends, how Michael had referred to *Blue Eyes* all the time, but had not wanted them to meet. Michael said Adam was too ugly for his girl - she had enough with one bad guy in her life. He also confessed he and Oliver had met at a regatta, in a marine biology session - Oliver had given him legal advice which proved to be quite lucrative and they had remained friends. Oliver had also been cagey about his relationship with Maddy.

"I came all this way, by train, no less, to ask you to be my 'Plus One' at the Tate Modern fundraiser - I've never taken anyone but suddenly I want to sit beside you and hear your thoughts on the auction items up for bid. Is it too soon? I hadn't thought about that. I would be honoured if you said yes. Social distancing and masks required."

"That's Friday night, isn't it?" Maddy recalled.

"Yes. If you need something to wear I am happy to shop with you. I have lots of practice, my daughter insists I adore and approve of every gown she buys."

"Although that is a lovely offer, I think shopping is limited right now and I'm all set. Shall I meet you there?"

"No, I will call for you." He stopped dancing and looked at her, "Thank you."

When they sat back down on the pillows Adam watched Maddy curl up and pull an Afghan over her hips. She closed her eyes and waved her hand towards the bed. "You can have the bed this time. It's better than the sofa. Good night Adam."

He watched her for some time, waiting for sleep to overtake him. He leaned over and kissed her cheek, moving her hair back from her face. He added a log to the fire and lay beside her, on the floor. "Good night Maddy." He whispered.

The birdsong blared in stereo, heralding morning. As Adam opened his eyes he felt he was shrouded in cloud. The sun was attempting to burn through the mist, it was too early to rise. Maddy moved beside him and he quickly covered her with the Afghan. His watch vibrated - of course his security team would be checking in. He responded quickly - no need to wake Maddy, she was sleeping soundly and he wanted this scene to last longer. She had agreed to accompany him to the auction…he smiled and drifted back to sleep.

They walked on the beach, speaking sometime, enjoying the sound of the waves without words, sometimes they held hands, they ran after waves and then settled on the deck for coffee. Adam had walked around the beach house and suggested an alarm system. Maddy teased Adam mercilessly about technology and working remotely. He teased her about the shoes he tripped on as he walked around the beach house - she preferred to be barefoot.

Adam stayed at the beach house for another night before driving back with Maddy - just in time for the auction. They both looked tanned and wind burned, relaxed and happy in each other's company. The security team was anxious to have Adam back in London, under their vigilant watch. Maddy didn't understand the need for security but then, Adam didn't understand why she didn't lock doors.

Heads turned when Adam arrived at the foyer with Madison Walker on his arm. Maddy wore a one piece jumpsuit in black with a white stripe on either side of her body. The gauzy white scarf wrapped around her neck flowed behind her as she walked. It was stunning, best described as a showstopper. Her hair was down in loose curls, and when she moved the curls bounced. She wore her diamond tennis bracelet, the first gift Sebastian had given her, and diamond earrings. Adam was aware of the stares and the nods of approval, and for a moment he wished he was in the crowd watching her walk towards him. Maddy had walked into the room with the air of someone who did not realize her presence was powerful. In his mind, that made her even more beautiful.

Guests were making their way to Maddy, to welcome her, to offer condolences, to ask how she was faring…she was quick to smile and assure everyone she was fine. She came away from each conversation with a full report on how everyone else had managed through the pandemic. Adam knew or was interested in, very few of the patrons. He was enjoying being Maddy's escort. When they finally sat at their table he squeezed her hand, hoping to relay support. Maddy whispered in his ear when she had comments on the art - she either knew the artist, thought it was outrageously high or suggested it would be better owned by someone else. He did manage to purchase one beautiful canvas, which he hoped Maddy would accept for the beach house.

Too soon the evening was over and Adam hated to leave Maddy at her door. She was gracious in her thanks for a lovely evening but didn't invite him in. "It's been a wonderful week Adam, thank you for spending time with me. You'll be anxious to get home, I'm sure."

Adam had earlier mentioned he was leaving the next day. He leaned forward and took Maddy's face in his hands. His lips barely touched hers, he was dizzy with anticipation. Would she kiss him back, like she had before. He had been so careful not to push her. His lips felt dry and his tongue darted out. He felt lost in the kiss. It was a kiss that made men want a release, to hold a woman closer. He moved his hand to the door frame to steady himself. Maddy was leaning against the door, her eyes closed, her breathing fast. He was unsure of what to do next. His blood was coursing through his veins - he wanted to make love to this woman.

Maddy pulled his jacket lapels towards her and kissed him, softly, slowly - filling him with desire. He wanted her, he had to have her. He stepped back, hoping she would invite him in, willing her to cry out that she wanted him to stay. But his sudden movement back had broken the spell and Maddy look startled. She whispered she hoped he had a safe trip home and then she was gone. The door was closed and the moment was over.

He stood there, looking at the door, not wanting to believe she had not felt the heat or passion he had felt. He wanted to beat down the door. He straightened his jacket, pulled at his cuffs and walked around to the waiting car. He had forgotten his security team was waiting. He would have to do 10 km on the treadmill, or more, to get Maddy and that kiss out of his system.

Inside, Maddy leaned against the door and slid down to the floor. She touched her lips and wondered what might have happened if they had gone any further…he was leaving tomorrow and who knew when he would return. Making love to someone who would disappear from your life for months at a time…that would be worse than wondering. No, she wasn't ready to lose her heart to another man just yet. On the other hand, she did feel heady.

She stood, squared her shoulders and walked to the bedroom, alone.

COME SAIL AWAY

♥ ♥ ♥

The days were easy to fill but the nights were long. Maddy tried yoga and meditation, listening to calm readings, drinking hot milk - nothing worked. She would sit and look through the photos and memories of her brief but sweet time with Sebastian. Seeing his crooked smile always made her feel so lucky to have known him. She would touch a photo and whisper "Indeed."

There had not been a memorial service after the shooting as gatherings were restricted and it seemed overwhelming to say goodbye to dear Sebastian and young Henry at the same time. Maddy wanted to wait until friends could gather without wearing a mask, without social distancing and worries about contracting a virus from those who wanted to grieve with her.

Life was so fragile; you lived and laughed and then you didn't. You were confined to your home, your routines were curtailed, your friends confined to a computer screen. No one to hug, no one to cry with, no one to share a meal with…

The riff of the telephone ring startled Maddy.

"Maddy, I've just had the most marvellous bad news and I need a friend. Come sailing with me. I need a week away." Christian sounded as though he had been drinking.

"Christian, are you alright? Can we get to Montenegro anytime soon? I'm not sure it would be a good idea for me to go to Hamburg with you."

"Listen, I'm coming over and I want to leave right away. I have a plan. Can you be ready?"

"Of course. You ran away with me when I needed to get away…I couldn't possibly say no. I'll be ready." This was exactly what she needed. A diversion would be welcome.

Christian had arranged for a flight with an investor from the bank. He arrived in casual clothes with his laptop and an overnight bag. He walked in, tore off his mask, and paced the room.

"My wife has asked for a divorce. She can't stand to have me return to the house in Germany. She wants nothing but the house. The boys, my horse-loving sons, want to stay with her. I am finally free. Why do I feel so empty?" He continued pacing. "I don't remember caring about her - it's been years. Ever since the move to London. I knew she would want a divorce when I retired but the bank keeps extending my time. This bloody pandemic is screwing up my life in every way." He looked at Maddy, realizing she was sitting on the sofa, listening to his rant, with an amused look on her face.

"Let's go. I need to feel in control of something. Am I still the Captain?"

"Indeed." Maddy laughed as they walked out of the flat with overnight bags and a survival kit with the bare necessities required for a few days onboard the boat.

The *Destiny* was moored in Montenegro, where they had ended their last journey. The town of Kotor was deserted - no tourists strolling the streets, restaurants closed, no cars on the waterfront. It took longer than usual to secure supplies, but they were ready to sail just before dark.

As they ate a late meal on the boat, under the stars, they reminisced about the trip they had taken across the Indian Ocean, up the Suez Canal and across the Mediterranean. The gaudy blue shirts, Henry's enthusiasm, reconciling with Sebastian…neither wanting to talk about anything that may have happened after that amazing month away.

"You know, I haven't spoken to anyone about Henry. I can't. It's such a loss. Sebastian being gunned down was hard enough, but to see Henry on the steps, that was agony. He was too young, so promising." She let the tears fall, she felt she owed them tears.

Christian was silent. He lost his friend and his future sailing buddy that same day. He knew the pain Maddy was feeling - he hadn't known how to deal with the loss either. Then the virus crept into their lives and everyone stayed away, wearing masks, afraid to be the next statistic. It seemed natural that he and Maddy would be on the *Destiny* again, grieving their losses.

The next morning Christian waved to the harbour master as he motored out of the bay. Maddy came up on deck with a coffee. She had cried herself to sleep, the memories too raw. Today was a new day, a new chapter in her life. Christian knew she would be sad to leave the memories of Kotor behind. He pulled her close.

"It's a great day for sailing. Let's see where the wind takes us, shall we?" Christian wanted to see her smile.

"Maddy, you are truly my best friend. Do you think we could ever be more than that? I mean, I am free now and I could give you a comfortable life…" Christian asked as they gazed at the stars after a full day of sailing.

Maddy contemplated her response, reaching out to touch his hand. "Christian, you love the freedom of chasing young models and living like a surfer dude, you love the revolving door of relationships - you are an excellent friend and companion and I love you dearly…"

"I feel a 'but' coming on…" he laughed.

Maddy smiled. "I'm in a different place Christian. I want my *happy ever after.*"

"I was jealous of Sebastian and his love for you. I wanted my own Maddy. Someone who entertained and enjoyed life. Someone who made a little boy feel loved. Someone who was interested in every aspect of life." Christian wiped his eyes.

"The month we sailed was the best time ever. I've wondered over and over again what would have happened if I hadn't told Sebastian where we were. Is any of this helping me make my case?" Christian was hopeful.

"You will always be important in my life Christian. You knew Sebastian, loved Henry, worked with Michael Riley and the larger-than-life Texan, PC, you encouraged me to participate in CityScapes, which by the way, was appreciated. You let me work at the bank when I first knew you and I was in awe of the way you were able to appear so carefree and yet so absolute about investing. You are a genius. You're okay at chess but otherwise, strategically sound. Let's not ruin a perfectly wonderful friendship by wanting something more."

Christian squeezed Maddy's hand and nodded in the darkness. She was probably right.

"What about Adam? He's crafty and rich and hard, you know, difficult to figure out. Is he good to you? Is he the best match for you?"

"Who really knows. When I see him I enjoy his company and he certainly treats me well. He knows he has to deal with all of you if he doesn't…" She squeezed his hand. "He's an enigma, I agree. He's also very kind and very protective. It's not serious enough to worry about. Let's give him a chance."

"If that changes, you let me know and I'll beat him up." He laughed.

"If that changes, you'll know. Best not to beat him up though, he hangs out with unsavoury characters, called security. I'd be worried for you."

"Adam wants to meet with me about some investments. Is that alright with you?"

"Of course, you're the best and he seems to be a shrewd investor. Good for you."

"Maddy, you are good for me - my best clients have fallen in love with you." Christian laughed. "Thanks for coming with me. I needed this, my friend." He kissed her hand.

"Thanks for asking me, my friend."

Life at sea was inspiring - bringing a sense of calm. Laughter released into the wind was cathartic and fulfilling, as was fishing for your dinner. The stars were the reward for a great day of sailing - they were silent companions. The week was over too soon but the travel arrangements had been made and they had to report back for a fortnight quarantine in London.

"Christian, you keep the boat. I can't sail it alone and you're free now - you can take her out whenever you like. Leave your boat in Germany until you decide what you want to do."

"Maddy, what a lovely offer but the *Destiny* was meant for you - I am your Captain, when you want time at sea. I feel revitalized and I'm grateful that we were able to sail together, again. No decisions now. We have time. Ready to go?"

They boarded the plane, weathered faces and hair bleached from the sun, each thinking how fortunate they were to have a wonderful sailing companion - no strings, no commitments. Just a good friend who would escape at a moments notice.

THE LETTER

Returning home, to her London flat, Maddy dropped her keys on the entrance table and sorted through the mail. An envelope lying on the side table near the door caught her eye. There was no postmark so it had been hand delivered. This must be the letter she found on the floor when Oliver arrived….it seemed like ages ago. There was a typed page, neatly folded - the date two months past.

She read the letter and sat down, holding it in her hand. Tears streaming down her face, she dropped the page and dialled the number, waiting impatiently for a reply.

"Jeffrey, it's Maddy. I just found your letter. I'm so sorry for you and the Buttons. How sad. Was there a service? Did I miss the opportunity to say goodbye?" She stopped speaking, realizing she was sobbing. Audrey, although complicated, had been a good friend. Maddy never understood why Audrey had wanted to destroy her relationship with Sebastian - she had disappeared and Maddy had not seen her since that fateful night in Decades, so long ago now.

"Maddy, there was nothing anyone could do. They think Audrey slipped out of the hospital when a delivery man was leaving. She walked along the railroad tracks, in her dressing gown, and no one knows how long she was out there. It was instant, the train engineer said it was impossible to see through the fog that night. We haven't had a service due to the pandemic. The children are fine, doing well at school. My friend Clara and I see them every weekend - they don't know about Audrey, about her struggles and her death. I wanted to let you know what happened. You were a good friend and I'm sorry she tried to ruin your relationship. I was sorry to hear about Sebastian - I never knew a man who was so in love. He was lucky to have you." Jeffrey's voice petered out.

"Thank you for saying so. Is there anything I can do? May I see the children? I miss them. It's been such a long year - is it safe to visit them at school? Would you mind if I did?" Maddy's mind was racing.

"They would be delighted to see you…they have a free afternoon every Wednesday. I think they sometimes go horseback riding but the school has your name as a guardian so you should be able to arrange a visit. I'll call now just to be sure." He hesitated. "Maddy, is the house on the coast still available?"

"Belle's house? Yes, I haven't wanted to deal with it…I didn't want to lose the memory. Are you interested?"

"Yes, the children love the area and it would be ideal for summer holidays. I could actually work from there. Would you mind if we were to rent or purchase it?"

"Not at all. It means you would be nearby. I'm keeping the beach house and I would love for you to be there. It's free now, stay whenever you like. I seem to have accumulated several homes. Belle would be so happy to know you wanted to live there. Please stay the summer. I'll arrange for the keys to be sent to you." She smiled at the thought of the Buttons being so close and how nice it would be for a family to live in the house. "Oh, I should warn you - It may need some attention."

"We'll take a drive this weekend. Don't worry. Clara would want to tidy it up regardless. She's like that." He chuckled. "I want you to meet Clara. I think you'll like her. She's wonderful with the children. Maddy, I hope you will come by and spend time with us. The children will be ecstatic. I'm ecstatic. Thank you."

IF NOT FOR YOU
♥ ♥ ♥

Walking on the beach was calming, familiar and rejuvenating. As Maddy climbed the stairs to the house she considered her options for a late dinner. She reached the top step and turned to look out at the sunset, always incredible, always soothing. The sound of the waves comforting.

"Where is he?" The question registered, but only after a hard cold object was thrust into her lower back. Maddy held her breath, surprised by the intruder. She was being pushed closer to the edge of the deck. It was a long way down to the rocks below. Instinct told her to tread carefully - there was an armed man behind her, wanting something from her. She turned quickly and faced her intruder, who had stepped back, taken by surprise. Maddy saw he was unsettled but he still pointed the gun at her.

"What do you want from me?" She asked, willing herself not to show fear.

"Where is Hassan-Rashad?"

"Who? The name is not familiar to me. Anyway, how would I know?" Maddy responded, confused.

"When will he come?"

"I don't know who you are talking about. I think you've got the wrong house."

"You know him. Where is he?"

"Okay, you're annoying me now. You break into my personal space, you threaten me with a gun, trying to scare me, asking about someone I don't know. Is that a machine gun? Do you even know how to use it?" She frowned at the gunman.

"You look like you should be in the desert, not in town, not in England anyway. You look a bit ridiculous, dressed like that, if you don't mind my saying so. You look Rambo-like even. Next time you should try to dress more appropriately for the area - so you don't stand out. The neighbours will be getting anxious. You…"

"Stop talking. Just tell me where Hassan-Rashad is."

Maddy rolled her eyes. "You're not listening to me. I do not know who you are looking for. Wrong intelligence. You are clearly in the wrong place…" She was enunciating carefully, hoping the gunman would understand.

"Stop talking. If you don't stop talking I will have to hurt you and when he comes for you and sees you damaged…" the gunman sneered.

"Well you can't have it both ways. You can't ask me a question and then tell me to stop talking. Really. Think about it." Maddy shrugged her shoulders and slowly moved towards the door.

"You are forcing me to harm you. Maybe it's better to harm you and let him find you, damaged and sobbing. Then he will know I have been here looking for him." The gunman seemed to be enjoying the image. "Stop moving."

"You're not very good at this, are you? Have you had any training at all? Is this your first time? Have you ever had to use that big gun? Do you get to scare many women? Do you scare children as well? It must be heavy. Is it noisy or do you have silencers? I don't suppose…"

"Stop talking. Why do you talk so much? Can you not see I have a gun and you are going to die if you don't tell me where he is…just tell me what

I need to know…" He lashed out and punched her jaw. She could taste the blood on her lip.

Maddy reacted by slapping his face with all her might. She would not accept being hit by a man. He stepped back, shocked that a woman had hit him.

"Oh great. Big move, smacking an unarmed woman. Are you going to hit me again?" She was baiting him. "So now what happens? I tell you where someone I don't know is and then you just walk away? Is your plan to shake my hand, say thanks as you leave or do you shoot me anyway? You really haven't thought this through. Who's in charge? Should I be speaking to your superior?" Maddy had moved closer to the door as she ranted.

"Shut up. Just shut up. Stop your incessant talking." The gunman was unsure of his next move. His finger itched on the trigger. They had been sent to frighten her, to find out where Hassan-Rashad was hiding, hopefully to find him here. Should he kill her? Why was she so aggressive, taunting him…he had a gun, she had no way to defend herself. Why wasn't she begging for her life? Something was wrong. He had to do something. His face was smarting but he dared not touch his cheek.

"Why do you want to find this person so badly? What has he done? You can tell me, who's going to know? Did you lose him? Is that why you're here with your big gun?" She laughed.

"Shut up. Just tell me where he is. When will he be here?" The gunman was getting desperate, his voice shaking.

Maddy was now at the sliding door, away from the railing. If she could get inside…it was dark and she could negotiate her way to the entrance door and out to her car. She would have the advantage as she knew the layout of the room. She hoped he wouldn't fire blindly into the dark…she was rather fond of the furniture and dreaded having it damaged from gunfire.

At that moment the gunman fell, his gun flew out of his hands and landed on the deck before Maddy. Before she could reach the gun two men appeared, dressed in black with bulletproof vests. She held her breath, waiting…

Adam Khan walked onto the deck, the men held the gunman's face up for him. He nodded and moved his head slightly to the left. The men in black efficiently secured the gunman and prepared to carry him off the deck. Adam watched Maddy as he deftly picked up the machine gun and checked it. He tossed the gun to one of the men as they walked away and turned towards Maddy.

"Are you alright? Did he hurt you? Your lip is cut, let's get some ice." Adam whispered.

Maddy stared at him, her eyes bright. She was trying to make sense of what just happened. She noticed Adam was also dressed in black - it was a good colour for him. She shook her head - she had just been held at gunpoint and here she was assessing how good a man she hardly knew looked in black. Must be shock.

Adam moved forward, not sure if he wanted to hold her or kiss her. He swept her up in his arms and carried her towards the bed. He was in awe of how she had handled the situation. Only when she burrowed her head into his shoulder did he realize how frightened she must have been.

He laid her on the bed and sat beside her, turning the bedside light on. He gently removed her runners and placed the duvet over her.

"What you did was reckless. You were brave, I must say, but it was reckless to goad a gunman. I know you have questions - they'll have to wait. He and his colleagues will be interrogated. Right now, I'm concerned about you."

"I'm glad I didn't know he had friends. Why are you here?" Maddy tried to sit up.

"We were following him." Adam gently pushed her back down on the bed.

"What took you so long to react? What if he had shot me?"

"We had to be sure we had them all. Fortunately there were only three, one with you and two outside the van. We had to be certain before we moved in. The snipers had him in their sights so no shots would have been fired. I wouldn't leave you here if I didn't think it was safe out there." He placed a cloth with an ice cube on her lip. "You're fortunate he only hit you once. Were you frightened?"

"I think I was more angry than anything. Especially when he hit me."

"Imagine how he felt when you returned the hit." Adam chuckled.

"You were here? Did you enjoy watching him point the gun at me?" Maddy challenged.

"Not for a moment. I needed to know what he wanted. I told you I had an alarm installed. Why didn't you have it on?" Adam sounded like an angry parent.

"What difference would it have made?" Maddy mumbled, the cold cloth stinging her lip.

"All you have to do is touch a door handle and the alarm will go off if you don't deactivate within a few minutes. It's the only way I can be sure you are safe. Please Maddy."

Maddy wondered why he would need to know she was safe…but there were so many other questions she wanted answered.

"You will never be threatened or hurt again."

Maddy smiled. "Is that a pinky promise or a guarantee?"

"Both."

One of the men in black appeared and nodded to Adam, pointing at his watch. Adam nodded back and stood, ready to leave. Maddy wondered if they always communicated in sign language. Very 'secret-squirrel'.

"I didn't lie." She whispered.

Adam turned back. "What was that?"

"I don't know Hassan-Rashad or where he is."

"You might." Adam was moving towards the door.

"No, I don't know anything about this man of mystery."

"You know enough."

"I'm confused…"

Adam was suddenly beside her, leaning over the bed. He softly kissed her cheek, his lips finding hers, careful not to hurt her bruised lips. He traced her face as if committing it to memory, feeling her dimples and then moving a strand of hair behind her ear. He looked into her eyes and saw a mischievous smile forming. She was not frightened or fragile or even confused…he had to go before she made it impossible for him to leave.

"Will you be alright alone? Is there someone who can stay with you?" He asked softly.

Maddy contemplated his question. "I could call Rod but I don't need anyone here. I'm going to sleep."

"Who is Rod?" Adam asked, stopping in his tracks.

"Rod lives nearby. He's an old school chum of Sebastian's. Nice guy. He's a lawyer."

"Get some sleep. I'll set the alarm." He said gruffly and then he was gone.

Maddy woke with a start several hours later. She stretched and yawned, her jaw ached and her lip was still tender. The ice had melted, the damp cloth beside her on the pillow. She smiled. Last night had not been a dream.

In the Interrogation Room Adam and his team waited for the gunman to regain consciousness. Adam rubbed his forehead, weary of the chase. He closed his eyes and saw the image of Maddy, her hair splayed over the pillow, her arm over her head, her face so peaceful as she slept. He sighed, thankful he had something good to think about…the world wasn't always a nice place.

JUST THE WAY YOU ARE

♥ ♥ ♥

Oliver looked over at Maddy, tears on her cheeks, a tissue at the ready. They were on an Air Emirates flight to Dubai and Maddy was watching a classic movie. Oliver had legal briefs to read but he wished he was watching the movie with her. She had agreed, reluctantly, to attend the wedding in Dubai. In just a few days Angela would leave her father's home for a honeymoon in New York and San Francisco, before settling into her new life with her husband and best friend.

Maddy had given him several reasons why it was not a good idea to travel to Dubai - she did not know the bride or the groom, she was anxious about travelling so soon after the pandemic had ended, she didn't want to impose on his friendship with Adam…he was able to counter every concern and besides, he needed a dance partner. Angela had made him promise to recreate the *September Morn* dance she had seen on YouTube.

It had been a fairy tale dance - Maddy hearing the music, turning at the door to see Oliver, resplendent in his Marine uniform, on the dance floor waiting, her tentative walk towards him, how everyone else left the dance floor, watching them, how they danced so well together and then she walked away. He smiled, recalling how disappointed Dermot, his friend, hosting the ball in the Embassy, had been when the video went viral. It was in the past. Dermot was settled in Washington, Maddy was dealing with the death of her husband and Oliver had only seen her twice since then…this was his chance to turn their friendship into something more…

The flight attendant touched his shoulder and offered a drink, startling him. Dubai was not the place to test your moves - the laws were strict about unmarried couples, sex before marriage, drinking liquor - he took a deep breath and sipped his bourbon. Patience.

The heat was oppressive in Dubai. Oliver immediately left the hotel to meet Adam and Angela at their home. Maddy booked a quad bike tour to ride the desert dunes. She asked about a camel ride and an overnight to the oasis, saying she would consider the tours after the dunes.

Angela, radiant in her excitement, was delighted to see Oliver, her western uncle, and disheartened that Maddy was not with him. Adam hoped his disappointment was not evident.

"You can't leave a single, white woman alone for a night in Dubai…Father, surely we have room for her at dinner this evening." Angela pleaded. "As a matter of fact, I will invite her myself. I have to see about the karaoke setup so I'll stop at the hotel. You two visit - but not too much whisky, please. There may be speeches tonight and I want you both at your best." She leaned over and kissed her father, and then hugged her uncle. It was always fun having him here.

Before either of the men could respond she was out the door, calling for Kaleed. He would know how to identify Maddy. Angela giggled as she gathered her oversized handbag and sunglasses. In two days she would be married…she was so ready.

The *tagelmust*, wrapped around her head, was most welcome when the sand pelted her face. Arriving at the hotel, Maddy unwrapped hers and waited for her key. The quad bike tour had been wonderful - she was the only participant with the guide, who soon realized Maddy was an experienced rider. He confessed he had not had such a fun ride since beginning to guide. Maddy had been willing to try anything he recommended. When she tried to tip him for a great tour he refused, saying he should be tipping her.

A beautiful younger woman, dressed in designer clothes with tasteful jewelry, approached Maddy and introduced herself as Angela Khan. Her wavy long hair reached her waist, her nails were impeccably manicured, complimenting the large diamond on her finger. Angela suggested Maddy take a quick shower and join her in the lounge, where they would have a chai before heading home for dinner and karaoke with a few friends. She would not leave the hotel without Maddy. Angela pointed out she was the bride-to-be and everything revolved around her very happiness for the next two days. Maddy laughed and went to shower. The girl, in her early thirties, was convincing and very likeable.

Kaleed bowed his head in greeting when he opened the car door for the two women. Maddy asked if he wanted her to drive - Kaleed looked up and smirked, shaking his head before closing the door. He wouldn't let that happen twice.

Angela was enchanting - talking non-stop, reaching over to touch Maddy's arm when she was reinforcing a thought. They agreed on a song for karaoke, as a surprise for Oliver and her father, before they arrived at the house.

Angela's enthusiasm meant Maddy didn't have time to think about how awkward seeing Adam and Oliver together would be. The house was modest from the outside but the interior was a design Mecca, tastefully decorated and yet Spartan - like a gallery. Guests were gathered around the outdoor pool, enjoying cocktails as Angela burst into the group and announced she had found Maddy. She quickly introduced Maddy to her bridal party and then dragged a handsome man over to her - proclaiming this was the lucky man she was marrying. Ahmed was shy but very gracious, welcoming Maddy and asking if she had enjoyed the quad bike tour of the desert.

Oliver appeared at her side with a flute of champagne, toasting her. "Angela can be very persuasive. I'm glad you decided to join us."

Maddy smiled and felt his presence before she saw him. Adam was beside her, his hand out to take her hand. He bowed and kissed her hand.

"Welcome to our home. It's lovely to see you. I hope you will enjoy Dubai. If there is anything you wish to do while here, please let me know." Finally, eye contact, and his dark eyes were staring right through her.

Adam remembered to breathe when he saw her smile back at him. Her eyes were as blue as the cloudless sky. Were they sparkling? Her skin rosy from the sun and wind, freshly scrubbed. She wasn't wearing make-up. How long did he stand there looking at her…he wasn't sure.

Angela was beside him, impatiently asking him something. He turned to give her his full attention.

"When can we sit down for dinner Father? Maddy has had quite a day in the desert, I'm sure she's famished. I'm sooo hungry. We all are."

Adam nodded and touched Angela's face tenderly. "Then we shall move into the dining room so you don't faint." He nodded to the wait staff and suddenly, the glass doors opened into a candlelit room; the table elaborately set, soft music wafting through the room.

Angela, Ahmed and Adam stood at one end of the table as the guests were invited to be seated. Oliver and Maddy allowed the friends to move into the room, taking the last seats, across from each other. Maddy was pleased to have a moment to herself. She had planned a quiet night with room service, in her air conditioned suite, overlooking the city.

The young man sitting next to her was keen on hearing about her day in the desert - he had never gone out on the quad bikes. Basheed, Angela's cousin and childhood friend, insisted on providing great adventure trips she could not miss while in Dubai. Did she ski? Did she golf? Had she been to an oasis on a camel? He was relentless. At one point he asked if he could touch her hair - everyone he knew had dark hair, he had never felt light hair. He was a lovely dinner companion - entertaining and certainly not demanding. Basheed insisted Maddy join him for tennis at the Club - he needed a partner - Maddy would save him from forfeiting the morning game.

Ahmed stood up and asked everyone to move places so the guests could meet new faces. Uncle Oliver sat next to Angela and Ahmed motioned to Maddy to sit next to Adam, who he felt needed a distraction from their animated friends.

"Angela is lovely and she looks so happy. You must be very proud of her." Maddy smiled at Adam, who seemed uncomfortable with her being so close.

"Thank you. She's very caring but also very spoiled. My fault, I'm afraid." He tried not to look into Maddy's eyes.

"That's what fathers are for…daughters and fathers have a special bond. I miss my father." Maddy looked away, her eyes misting.

"Were you and your father close? I don't mean to pry but I'd like to know."

Maddy nodded. "We were very close. My father travelled a fair amount and I was his travelling companion. He would go to work and leave me with an envelope of currency. My mission was to learn about the city, learn some phrases, eat local - no burgers allowed." She shook her finger. "I was to find something unique and report back that evening. I was so excited to tell him about my day. Then we would have ice cream." She smiled at the memory.

"What about your mother?"

Maddy sighed. "She lost a baby boy and stopped travelling, stopped being interested in us, stopped living. She disapproved of my travelling with my father but didn't offer any alternate so he continued to make it an adventure for me. When he passed away his friends continued to look after me." She looked over at Adam, believing she had said too much. She was touched by his tender look. She felt his hand on her thigh.

"There's so much I want to know about you. Do you realize how difficult this is? Being in the same country, same city, same room with you and not being able to kiss you." He moved his hand and sat back in his chair.

"There are so many things I want to share with you." He sounded tired as he looked around the room at the young group of friends, laughing and anxious to leave the table.

"Come on Maddy, karaoke is starting in the next room. Our songs are queued up..." Angela grabbed her hand and started for the door.

Maddy was happy to move away from the intensity of being near Adam. Neither had mentioned the beach house incident. Maddy was bursting with questions.

Angela and her friends sang several songs, not all of them on key. When Angela and Maddy sang their duets the crowd screamed their approval. Adam and Oliver sat at a table nursing their whisky, both applauding a job well done, both appreciating Maddy and how easily she had won the heart of Angela.

Hours later, after karaoke and dancing and storytelling. Maddy stood and said her goodbyes to Adam, Angela and Ahmed, thanking them for including her. Ahmed insisted she join them for his family dinner the next evening - it was to be family and a few older friends, a more traditional Muslim celebration. He was so sincere in the invitation she found herself accepting. Oliver was pleased.

As they walked out to the car Kaleed reminded Maddy she and Basheed were playing tennis in the morning. He would call for her at 9:30 am at the hotel. Whites and a racquet would be provided. Oliver was golfing with Mr Khan and would be called for earlier. They would meet at the the Club for lunch. It was all arranged.

THE WAY YOU LOOK TONIGHT

♥ ♥ ♥

Maddy and Basheed were well suited for tennis against their opponents - winning easily. They joined the golfers and enjoyed a light lunch overlooking the pool. Basheed introduced Maddy to his sister, Sofi, a student of design who was opening her own fashion house, with the help of her father. Sofi invited Maddy to her workshop to choose a gown for the wedding…she knew what everyone was wearing and her designs were one of a kind so no worries about anyone else wearing the same thing. As if…

Maddy had confessed to Basheed that she wanted to take a camel ride to the Oasis - she had a fantasy about being in the desert under a full moon. Basheed had relayed this to Adam who arranged for camels and a late night visit after the dinner that evening. It was not appropriate to book just he and Maddy so he invited Oliver and another female friend.

Maddy was pleased she had accepted the invitation to Ahmed's family dinner. Ahmed had been raised by his grandparents as his parents had worked abroad. He explained Adam was more of a father to him - he and Angela had been inseparable since they started school. Here they were, mature, well-educated and finally ready to start their lives together as scientists. Although neither needed to work, they were anxious to move on from being students.

The dinner was an exceptional experience - Maddy realized Ahmed and Angela wanted to be less traditional and more American - there would not be many more opportunities to sit with their elders and enjoy the culture.

Adam excused himself, professing he had promised to take his visitors to the Oasis - when in Dubai…he explained. After much nodding and hand clasping they were finally enroute to the camels. They were given long robes and turbans, introduced to their camels before slowly travelling, caravan style, under the star-studded night sky, with the moonlight illuminating the way across the desert.

"This is more amazing than I imagined it would be…thank you Adam. This was perfect. Camels, moonlight, chai, almonds, olives, dates, lamb kofta…it's unbelievably wonderful. Thank you." She hugged him, realizing too late, public affection was frowned upon. She stood back, embarrassed.

Adam laughed. "I'm delighted it met your expectations. I never know if this is just too Hollywood for most people to digest. It is an ideal time to be in the desert. No tourists."

"Adam, when you appeared at the beach house and took your prisoners you asked me if I was alright staying alone. What would you have done if I had said no?" Maddy had so many questions about that night.

"Given the option I would have stayed with you until you fell asleep. You were so brave and you didn't seem at all nervous or frightened. You were amazing." Adam stopped, not wanting the others to hear their conversation. "Are you warm enough? It can be cold in the desert at night."

Maddy nodded, took one last look at the palm trees, moving softly in the breeze, the bright moon and the camel awaiting her mount - it was like being in a movie. She waited for her camel to amble upwards and follow the guide. She looked over at Oliver who had seemed quiet and standoffish all evening. Adam's female friend was chatty and had a nervous laugh which seemed to annoy Oliver.

How could Maddy know that Oliver sensed the tension between herself and Adam - he wished she had embraced him the way she had easily hugged Adam. Perhaps he was imagining there was anything going on but in trying to make Angela feel special he had neglected Maddy. He would have to be more attentive tomorrow.

The wedding was picture perfect - blue skies, beautiful people gathered to witness a truly handsome couple commit to their sincere vows, endless food and drink, laughter and tears in all the right places. The toasts were eloquent and heartfelt, the father/daughter dance was magical; the newlyweds looked smitten with each other as they danced their first dance. Maddy noticed the fresh flower trestles and the elaborate flower arrangements throughout the room, between the fountains and overflowing food tables. It was splendid.

Sofi was a brilliant designer and Maddy felt elegant in her gown - the soft fabric layers seemed to float as she walked. The pastel blue would have delighted Sorento. The sash was beaded with diamond sparkles and Sofi had provided a matching sash for her hair. The gown was exquisite in its simplicity.

She was startled by the presence of an elderly man in traditional Arab garb. He pushed her forward and motioned to the door. He was an uncle of Angela's, she recalled.

"Excuse me." She was beginning to feel as though his nudges were less than friendly.

"What do you want here?" He asked, when they reached the lounge, not making eye contact. "Why are you here interfering? This is not your world. You only add distraction."

Maddy waited for more. She needed to control her breathing and her anger.

"You take my armoured car from the driver and you release a security team. What do you want with Hassan-Rashad el Sharif? Why do you distract him from marrying my second daughter? I cannot allow you English to ruin another life. His mother took him away but you will not." The older man was pointing a finger at her, his face red, his body shaking.

"I'm afraid I don't know what you are talking about." Maddy raised her chin in defiance.

"You must go, you must leave Dubai. Do not see Hassan-Rashad el Sharif again. Do you hear me?" He was shouting now.

"Uncle, this is not how we treat our guests. Angela is looking for you. Please, this is her wedding. Dance with Angela." Adam was standing in the door, his voice cold and controlled, his body rigid.

"You mark my words Hassan, she is going to destroy you and your happiness, just as your mother destroyed your father." The older man moved slowly out of the room, shaking his head, his shoulders hunched over.

Adam walked quickly to Maddy and wrapped his arms around her. "Are you alright? I'm so sorry, I had no idea the old man had pushed you out of the room. Basheed alerted me."

Maddy looked up at Adam, his face tight. "Why was he so worried about me being here? I don't understand. Who is this mysterious Hassan-Rashad and why does he keep coming up? I'm not sure what just happened. Why was he so upset about your mother?" She waited for Adam to speak. He didn't respond immediately.

Maddy shook her head and rubbed her forehead. "You are Hassan-Rashad."

He paced as he thought about how he would explain. Finally he perched on the arm of a leather sofa. He looked over at Maddy as though seeing her for the first time.

"Maddy I'm sorry that just happened. The old fool feels it necessary to control my life - his daughter was my wife. Now he pushes his other daughter on me. He hated my mother, she was English, she changed my name to Adam Khan, her maiden name, when we moved to London. My father was from a wealthy Emirates family. He met my mother at Cambridge, where they both studied. When she became pregnant he insisted she come to Dubai and live here with his other wives."

Adam stood and then absently fell into an oversized chair. He leaned forward, his head in his hands.

"He was cruel to her, she cried many nights. She had a friend in London who arranged for us to leave - I was five or six - he took us in and my mother changed my name so I would be accepted as an English boy. My father terrorized us, he wanted my mother to return home - he wanted me to be involved in the family business. Oil was needed by the world and we had oil. I was the only male heir in his large family. He was losing face, a fate worse than anything for an Emiratis." He stopped, looking over at Maddy.

"I told you there was much to share. I just couldn't risk telling you. I was enjoying being part of your world. I hoped there was a future…for us." He dropped his head, wiped his eyes and stood. He slowly walked towards her. "You were so brave at the beach house - I thought you had figured it out."

"Adam, you are so in control of everything, including your feelings. We all have a past, but we can't let it stop us from having a future." She threw her arms around his neck. Before she could move her face to look up at him she felt his lips on her eyes, her cheeks and then his lips touched hers and she found herself totally lost in his kiss. His arms around her, his body so close she could feel his heartbeat. She was breathless, ecstatic, but breathless. She thought she might fall if he let her go.

"Have I told you how stunning you look tonight? Do you have any idea how I've longed to hold you all night? How I hate to be away from you?" Adam whispered into her ear. "We have so much to talk about…"

Maddy stepped back. "Adam, we do, and believe me, I have questions, so many questions, but right now you are the proud father of the most beautiful bride celebrating her big day and she needs you to be present and happy for her. I'm not going anywhere. When the time is right, we'll be there for each other. Now go…"

Adam kissed Maddy on the cheek and walked towards the door. He looked back at her, knowing that he had found the woman he had dreamed of for so long. His life had been controlled by others, choices taken away from him - he was forced to marry, suffer the shame of having his wife disappear, leaving him with a daughter who needed his attention. Now he thought he might have a chance at happiness after all.

He heard Maddy thank him for rescuing her as he turned towards the reception. He paused, every instinct telling him to turn back and take her in his arms. Maddy was right, tonight was about Angela and Ahmed. He pulled down on his shirt cuffs, angry once more at the words he had heard the old man deliver. The old man had no right to badger Maddy. What might have happened if Basheed had not alerted him? She hadn't seemed frightened but she would need time to digest the words. He would have to protect her. It was becoming routine, his desire to protect her.

Ahh, Angela was motioning him to the dance floor. She did look happy - beautiful and happy. She was going to have a good life with Ahmed - he adored her. He smiled and joined hands with his lovely daughter and her new husband.

Maddy slowly walked back into the reception, her mind whirling with the words and anger spoken by the old man, warnings given, intentions voiced and the visions of Adam, as a boy, as a man, not sure where he belonged; so confident, yet so vulnerable.

Angela was beside her, begging her to do it again. She looked up and there was Oliver on the dance floor, in his Marine uniform, looking tall, handsome and distinguished. The music was starting and the crowd had been moved to the side. Maddy sighed and smiled, resigned to please the bride.

Walking slowly to the dance floor she felt removed from the evening. All she saw was an anxious Oliver, his hand out, waiting for her. She took his hand, placed her other hand on his shoulder. He held her in his arms as if he was afraid to lose her. They danced, looking into each others eyes, floating across the floor, trying to recreate a perfect moment. When Maddy placed her hands on his chest he took her hands in his and held her until the music ended. There was a moment of silence and then the crowd exploded in cheers, whistles and applause. The music began and the dance floor filled with couples anxious for their own magical moment.

Angela and Ahmed rushed over. "That was just as romantic as the first video…thank you. Uncle Oliver, that was the best wedding present ever. Maddy, when I hear that song I get chills."

Oliver looked at Maddy, wondering why she looked distracted. "Let's dance, shall we?"

Maddy smiled as she heard herself reply, "Indeed."

IN TOO DEEP

Morning came too quickly. Maddy groaned as she grabbed for a pillow to cover her eyes, attempting to keep out the bright sun. Her head was aching and she was glad to be in her own bed in her own room at the hotel. The wedding was probably still going on - it certainly seemed as though everyone in attendance was there for the long term.

The men had retired to a lounge with a billiard table and it seemed like the ideal time to escape. A long shower and several glasses of water later, Maddy had fallen asleep on the bed, dreaming about sailing. She really should check on the boat. Maybe when she woke up…

Waking up a second time, to the sound of her phone ringing. Maddy rubbed her eyes and reached for the instrument of destruction. She cleared her throat and said hello.

"Good morning, you are awake. I am holding a chai for you in the lobby. Will you come down or should I send it up?" It was Oliver and he sounded quite cheerful.

"Can't you leave it at my door? I need a moment but that was sweet of you." She tried to stand and fell back on the bed.

"Will do. It'll be at your door in jig time. Enjoy. We are off to the racetrack. Wish us luck. See you for dinner at 8:00 pm in the lobby."

Maddy spent the afternoon at the pool, reading and dozing. It felt decadent to be without an agenda but she was feeling much better - her neck was actually holding her head up now.

She walked into the lobby feeling well rested and in need of a sparkling water. Just as she settled onto a bar stool she heard Oliver and Adam behind her. They had been lucky at the racetrack and from the volume, they had consumed much forbidden alcohol. She stood and turned towards them. She could tell from the look on their faces she had made an error coming to the bar alone. They herded her into the dining room and after being seated explained that it wasn't prudent for single women to be in the bar alone.

"Then how do they meet handsome strangers? I need to go home where I can be a carefree, living, breathing member of society. I'm sorry. I was just anxious to see you both so I came down early." She tried to look repentant. "Shall I go up and order room service for one?"

Both men reached out to touch her and assure her they were all fine now. Oliver reminded Maddy they were leaving at noon the next day and the evening continued to be sombre as they each dealt with the reality of saying goodbye. Adam asked why they were hurrying away.

"I have a trial to prepare for, unfortunately. I didn't think to ask Maddy if she wanted to extend her stay. She is heading to the Villa Mirage in Italy. You really should see the place Adam, it's rather a renaissance piece, like you." Oliver laughed.

Maddy excused herself early and didn't return to the table. She left the men to talk about their next golf game and when they would go sailing again. It was a relief to be back in her room, alone.

Waking early to get a swim in before breakfast with Oliver, Maddy had packed and was ready to walk out of the room when her phone rang. She didn't recognize the number and answered tentatively.

"Good morning Maddy. Will you come for a walk with me? My car is downstairs. I would like to see you before you leave. Please join me." Adam sounded very businesslike.

Maddy stepped out of the elevator and saw Kaleed standing by the car. He opened the door for her, nodding a greeting. Adam was in the car. They drove past the Atlantis Hotel when Kaleed stopped the car and opened the door. Adam motioned to the sand and they started walking.

"I hope you enjoyed your short stay here. I'm sorry you are leaving so soon. I would have enjoyed showing you more of Dubai." He was walking with his hands behind his back. Soon it would be too hot to be out here.

"It was a lovely wedding. I hope Angela and Ahmed will be happy and live a long life together. Thank you for being such a wonderful host. How are you doing?"

"Fine. I need time to stop thinking about wedding plans and parties. I need to sort out so many things before I get back to London. May I see you when I am in London?" Adam sounded very businesslike.

"You know where I live. I'm going to spend a few weeks at the Villa in Italy. It appears the pandemic is not over everywhere and I may not be able to get back there for awhile." She sighed. "How fortunate we were to come and go as we pleased before the world got sick."

"Maddy," Adam stopped and looked at her, removing his dark sunglasses, "are you in love with Oliver? Am I wasting my time? I would like to know of your intentions?"

Maddy was taken aback. "He's my friend, an old friend. Why would you ask me…" She kept walking, angry that he felt he could ask, angry that it should matter. He and Oliver were friends, how could she respond without hurting one of them. This man waltzed in and out of her life when it was convenient for him, why would he care? Waste of time, to be sure.

"I have no intentions Adam. None. We should get back." Maddy turned towards the waiting car.

They walked to the car in silence. As they arrived at the hotel Adam looked at this watch and announced he had a meeting to attend. He wished her safe travels. He reached across the seat for Maddy's hand, squeezed it and then touched his lips to her knuckles. Maddy said goodbye and repeated her thank you's. As she watched the car drive away she realized Adam had not taken his sunglasses off.

"Intentions indeed. Pft." Maddy shrugged and went to collect her luggage.

LA DOLCE VITA

Villa Mirage was ablaze with lights and music, people laughing and celebrating the return of their beloved Maddy. Anza, no longer a puppy, was running circles around Maddy, so excited to have her back. The long outdoor table was covered with large bowls and platters of food, wine bottles and candles. Maddy had not been back since her wedding and the shooting - everyone was anxious to give her their condolences and show their love. She looked over at Father Dom and he winked, making her smile.

Father Dom was delighted to see Maddy. It was his habit to ask if she wished to go to Confession each time she arrived. Both had fond memories of their first meeting, in the confessional, so long ago, it seemed. As they walked the vineyards Maddy asked if it was wrong to harbour murderous thoughts against the gunman who had shot Sebastian and Henry.

Father Dom responded as a friend, not a priest. "Normally yes, but I know you have more good thoughts than bad. Concentrate on the good. And say at least two Hail Mary's." Maddy squeezed his arm and leaned into his shoulder.

Giselle and Philippe had managed to keep the Villa going through the pandemic - offering quarantine for wealthy guests from Rome and Naples. The village had been a safe haven - no cases, no deaths, just isolation. Everyone was talking at the same time - it felt wonderful to be back.

The group was careful not to mention Henry, the young man Maddy and Sebastian had cared for - it was still raw for Maddy. Henry had been gunned down by the shooter as he ran up the stairs to congratulate Maddy and Sebastian on their wedding - just minutes before. Maddy had lost both of them in the span of two minutes. She was not ready to talk about that loss, even after a year had passed. They respected her reluctance, wanting the Villa to be a happy place for her.

Giselle and Maddy spent several afternoons driving to wine outlets, enjoying lunch in Florence, walking through the markets, not yet crowded with tourists. Giselle was curious about Adam, the wedding in Dubai and the handsome Oliver. They laughed and cried together as they redesigned the gift store and agreed on decorating changes. Giselle missed her friend.

Late night visits with Father Dom, playing cards and catching up on the village news; long walks with Anza, business meetings with Giselle and Philippe, assuring the investors all was fine, kept Maddy occupied for the month. If not for the scheduled meetings in London, Maddy would have stayed on - the lifestyle, the weather and her friends were too comfortable to leave. She promised to return for the harvest. The visit had been therapeutic…Maddy felt the Contessa would have loved to see the Villa bathed in such happiness.

She would never tell her Villa family that when she returned to the Mayfair flat in London, alone, she closed the door and felt loneliness envelop her.

COME FLY WITH ME

London was slowly recovering from the health scare and it seemed everyone had a burning desire to have lunch at the club or host a dinner party or arrange cocktails in the garden. Maddy was busy with social engagements and business meetings, most dealing with the coffee shop/bookstore and the charity foundation. Christian, in his role both as banker and friend, kept Maddy involved. They talked of returning to the sailboat in Kotor and sailing from Montenegro across to Italy or even back to London.

Maddy walked around the corner to the flat, carrying her groceries. It seemed therapeutic somehow, to walk for your food and carry it home. She was listening to a podcast and had stopped to wave at an elderly neighbour across the street when she saw the car parked in front of her landing.

Adam stepped out of the car and walked toward her. He looked so fit and handsome she had to remind herself he was like the wind, blowing in for a night or two and then gone. They had not spoken since the wedding in Dubai.

He reached for her grocery bag and brushed her hand. He smiled at her and it was impossible not to return the smile. He took in her white teeshirt, short skirt and the red bandana holding her hair back. She was wearing sandals and again he noticed she had no makeup on. She looked like a fresh flower. They walked side by side in silence. At the car he reached in for a large wrapped package and a small leather bag.

"You should know I am without security. They've been released. I am a free man."

"Good for you. Are you scared?" Maddy asked with a smile.

"Not now."

Inside the front door he carefully set the parcel and bag down beside the groceries. He placed both hands on her face and kissed her. Maddy leaned against the wall as he kissed her neck, her ears, her eyes, her lips. Then he started over, kissing her with an urgency, leaning into her, his hands now pulling her into his arms.

"Hello." He stepped back, confused at her tears. She had kissed him back. They were attracted to each other. Was he moving too fast? He leaned over to tenderly wipe the tears from her cheeks. He could lose himself in those blue eyes.

Maddy closed her eyes, cleared her throat, collecting herself. "Would you like a drink? We should be celebrating your newfound freedom."

Adam laughed and carried the groceries into the kitchen. "I just landed. I have a few days in London and I hope you will allow me to spend them with you." He waited for a response. Maddy poured them both a drink and walked over to the sofa, kicked off her sandals, and sat with her legs folded under her, her arm across the back of the sofa.

He followed her, removed his jacket, folded it over another chair and sat beside her.

They were polite, catching up on the last two months, laughing over shared stories and embarrassing moments. Angela and Ahmed were fine, they hoped to hear about work in New York. Ahmed was waiting for his work visa. They agreed on dinner and sat out on the terrace enjoying the sunset with a nightcap.

"Pick a star. Any star." Maddy was looking up at the night sky.

"I don't understand. Aren't they all accounted for?" Adam laughed.

"No, really. Pick a star. We'll decide on the same star and when you're not here I'll look up and know that wherever you are, anywhere in the northern hemisphere anyway, we'll be looking at the star we chose. It'll make me feel connected to you." She looked over and smiled. "If that's too weird for you, you don't have to humour me."

Adam looked up and pointed to the star on Orion's belt. "I'll think of you when I see that sword." He didn't need a star to think of Maddy but it was something.

They danced to slow love songs, on the terrace and then inside. Adam was holding Maddy close, he bent to kiss her neck and she moaned. He kissed her with such passion she felt dizzy.

"Are you ready to let me love you?" He whispered in a husky voice. "I want to please you. Let me please you." He stepped back and took her hand, then turning suddenly he gathered her in his arms and walked towards the bedroom. He laid her on the bed, unbuttoned his shirt, letting it fall, he reached over and removed her skirt, loosened his belt and dropped his trousers, he placed his hands under her shirt and moved it over her head. He lay beside her, running his hands up her thighs, her stomach, her breasts, and down again. He leaned over and kissed her softly as his hand traced her body and found her pleasure spot.

Her body had a mind of its own - it was moving to his touch, her mind had checked out, her body was responding and it felt so good. When she thought she might explode she wrapped her legs around him and pulled him close. He moved her arms up over her head and kissed her breasts. Maddy cried out, not sure she could stand anymore.

He was gentle and when he shuddered, Maddy felt her body quiver yet again.

They lay silent and still for some time, recovering. When they faced each other on the pillow, looking into each others eyes, they both smiled and suddenly they were laughing. Adam reached out and pulled Maddy closer, she rested her head on his chest. They fell asleep that way and as the morning sun washed the room with pastel light-beams, they started over.

The warm water felt soothing as she lay in the bath, her eyes closed, her body aware of the lovemaking, it had been so long since she had felt like this. Maddy tried to stop her mind from ping ponging in every direction. Was she dreaming that someone had lifted her arm and was tenderly soaping it? She opened her eyes and saw Adam, intent on bathing her, sitting on the edge of the bath.

"Good morning. What are your intentions?" She asked, wondering why she was whispering. She wasn't sure she wanted him to stop stroking her arm.

"I'll take a shower and wait for you. You look so peaceful." He bent down to kiss her forehead, watching as she lazily smiled and then, to his amazement, and hers, he stepped into the bath - his intentions clear.

"An acquaintance in the city owes me a sizeable favour - he has recently acquired a Learjet, which will nicely take us to the island you want to check in on. Are you available to go on the weekend?" Adam asked as they drank coffee and checked their phone messages.

Maddy's eyes widened. "Really?"

He nodded and was pleased when she jumped up and threw her arms around his neck, kissing him and thanking him.

"It must have been a big favour." She couldn't stop smiling.

"It was."

"Like, really big?"

"Really big."

He obviously wasn't going to contribute more information so Maddy began making a list of the supplies they would need. She looked over at his business attire and asked if he had casual clothes with him. He seemed confused by the question so Maddy got to work ordering L.L. Bean striped shirts and chinos, wick wear tee shirts, deck shoes and an oilskin rain jacket, suitable for walking through the woods. She assured Adam the clothes were wrinkle resistant but he didn't seem to care. The items were to be delivered within the week.

They had not spoken about last night or this morning or the bath lovemaking - there were no awkward moments or discussions to be had. They both seemed comfortable planning the day, choosing workspace and being together. Maddy had given Adam the office as she found it had no distractions for her - she needed to see movement and the office was entirely too confining; Adam preferred the cocooning effect of the office, offering to change space after lunch. Maddy declined, she had to walk around and she might disturb him if he was in the front half of the flat. Adam held out the large parcel he had carried in and presented it to Maddy. She had admired the framed tapestry on the wall of his Dubai home. They hung it immediately, agreeing it fit perfectly.

SAY YOU WON'T LET GO

♥ ♥ ♥

Humans are adaptable. Adam was convinced. He was the perfect example - he had a simple life in Dubai, worked hard, doted on his daughter - then, he met a woman who didn't chase after him, a woman who was independent and so easy to be with. A woman who made him want to come out of the office every hour, just to see her.

He lowered his book and looked over at the woman reading beside him, her profile strong against the light. Watching her push her hair back behind her ear, turning the pages, reacting to the written words, smiling or shaking her head. He enjoyed the way she looked at him, the way she smiled with her eyes, how she cocked her head when she asked a question… he felt his body react to the thought of her, wanting to making love to her, again and again.

When his phone rang he reluctantly stopped thinking about Maddy and answered, sitting up in the bed.

"Hello Father, sorry to call you so late, early for us, but we are taking Maddy's advice and walking the Brooklyn Bridge before we leave. I just wanted to check in with you. Are you okay? We have some great news and we wanted to share with you first." Angela was excited.

"It's good to hear from you. Let's hear your news. Maddy is right here, may I share the news?" He looked over at Maddy, sitting up in the bed, her hair messed, shaking her head, not wanting to interfere.

"Of course. Hello Maddy. Your friend was wonderful with the housing recommendations. We found a lovely neighbourhood - it's perfect. Thank you."

Maddy smiled and expressed her delight.

"What's your news?" Adam held his breath, wondering, were they pregnant?

"We both got offered jobs in the Research Department at Princeton. We have to be back in a month. Maddy was so right, New York is exciting and Princeton is awesome - it's just across the river from Manhattan. Father, are you being nice to Maddy? She's exactly what you need…be nice. I recommend you make this relationship work. She's not a business venture, she's your future."

"Newly married and already giving advice. Don't worry, I'm working on it." Adam smiled as he looked across at Maddy. "I'm so proud of you and Ahmed. You'll be wonderful and the university is lucky to have you both."

"Gotta go, our cab is here. Watch for the photos. Bye Maddy. Love you both."

Adam held the phone for a few moments, wondering where the time had gone - when had the little girl become a scientist, in America? He must be getting old. Angela was right. It would be nice to have someone to share life with…he felt Maddy's back against his side and slipped under the covers. This was going to be so nice.

"Maddy, is this a relationship? Are we in a relationship?" He asked as they lay in bed, spent. Maddy turned towards him and sat up.

"It depends if the word 'relationship' frightens you or makes you uncomfortable. You might want to think of it as a merger, where both parties have something they bring to the table and both have something to lose. They work towards a common goal so the amalgamation can be successful and show annual growth." She wrapped her arms around her knees.

"If you need time or space, it's allowed. The partners are free to share, consolidate or take convergent paths to create a mutually respectful culture." Maddy looked over at him, a smile starting to spread across her face. "What that means is the partners need to be honest to each other, they need to share information about what they want and what they need. Maybe they share secrets that might be harmful at some point and they promise never to hurt the other knowingly. Does that help?"

"Come here, I need you. Tell me what you want." He pulled her over and kissed her.

"I just want you to be honest, to yourself and to me." Maddy whispered between kisses.

"What do you dream about Maddy?"

After a moment Maddy responded. "I've had such a great life it would be selfish to dream about more."

"Everyone has dreams. What's yours?"

"You'll laugh at me if I tell you."

"No, I promise. I just want to know what it looks like, your dream."

"I want the *happy ever after*. I want to grow old with someone who loves me; who I love. My parents didn't get theirs - I wonder if it's even possible." Maddy sighed.

"Everything is possible. You've told me so." Adam kissed her forehead. Happy ever after. Who didn't want that?

"What's your dream Adam?"

"You."

STAND BY YOU

Adam signed off on the reports, rubbed his eyes and rolled his neck, surprised to hear shouting in the kitchen. He pushed back from the desk - this was unusual. Maddy always spoke on the phone hands-free, but her conversations were usually friendly.

He could hear a man's voice, speaking rapidly and with passion in Italian. Maddy was preparing lunch, chopping vegetables and tasting a sauce with her finger, listening, clearly unfazed by the lecture she was receiving. She continued to add flour to a bowl, carrying the bowl over to the phone, mixing it with a spoon as she walked around the kitchen. This was not unusual, Maddy couldn't stand still, not even when she was brushing her teeth. Adam smiled. She never sat still, she always had one leg swinging…

There was a long pause, a dead silence, as Maddy methodically separated an egg into the batter. He watched her slowly walk over to the phone which was sitting up against the teapot.

"Hai finito?" She asked in Italian. *"Abbastanza."* She leaned against the counter. "When have I ever given you bad advice?"

Again, silence. Maddy continued adding ingredients to the bowl. She leaned over and spoke in a soft voice.

"You have to be the man who sees potential in new designers. You have to broaden your line. This girl is young, she uses bright, bold colours - she is creative with her fabrics and her fashion sense. She needs a mentor, a

European God. *Ti amo ancora* but you need new blood. I like her designs and after this past year in lockdowns women will want something that makes them feel bright and happy. What have you got to lose? *Mi amore*, what have you got to lose?" Maddy poured the batter into a pan and opened the oven door.

"*Va bene, va bene*, but only because you think I am a God. I will look at the work. But you must come to Milan if I meet her. *Si?*" The caller seemed pleased with himself.

"You are the best. Of course I will come to Milan…when you agree to work with her. *Quando?*" A timer sounded. Maddy moved over to the stove, leaning over to take in the aroma of the sauce.

The man on the telephone assured her it would be soon. He was anxious to see Maddy in Milan - he had many new ideas for her.

"*Baci, mi amore. Ciao.*" She blew an air kiss and ended the call. She did a little dance at the counter and moved back to the sink, catching a glimpse of Adam from the corner of her eye.

"I'm sorry. Did I disturb you? Sorento always shouts. I'm used to it."

"Not at all. I just thought you needed reinforcements but it appears you handled everything." He couldn't help but be distracted by the aromas in the kitchen. "It smells amazing in here. What's cooking?"

He stepped towards her, smiling at her flushed cheeks and the traces of flour across her forehead. She looked lovely.

"I'm making dinner and some meals for my elderly neighbours. It's a good excuse to check in on them, especially now, when they are afraid to go out. We could also take something with us - there aren't any restaurants on the island."

He wiped the flour from her face and kissed her. "Are you promoting Basheed's sister - the young designer?"

"Why not? Sofi is brilliant and Sorento needs to rebrand his design house if he wants to stay relevant." She bit the inside of her cheek. "Do you think I'm interfering?"

"Not at all. I think it's delightful that you want to help a young person in their career. We should do it more."

"Are you hungry? My banana bread is ready."

"You made bread from bananas? Well, well, well - this will be a first for me." He laughed.

Adam sat back, touched Maddy's hand and realized he was as comfortable as he had ever been, sitting here, having lunch with her. He announced he should go to his penthouse, just to check in.

"Do you have everything you need for the trip? Is there anything at your flat?" Maddy asked as she watched him stand and prepare to leave.

"No." He responded abruptly and turned away.

"I'm sorry, I just thought you might want to bring your things here." Maddy shrugged.

"No. It's not necessary." He stopped moving, considering how cold he must sound.

Adam turned to look at Maddy, walked toward her and sat down. "Maddy, I purchased a penthouse in London for tax reasons. I was collected at the airport, driven to the building, taken up an elevator and whenever I left, it was in the company of the security team. I don't even have a key. I only ever entered through the parking garage. I'm not sure I even know what the building entrance looks like. Sad, isn't it?"

"Do you want to go there?" Maddy asked.

"If it was possible. However, since I don't have a security team here, it's impossible."

"Maybe not." Maddy grabbed her phone. "Describe the building to me."

"It's a glass penthouse overlooking the Thames. I think it's Canary Wharf." He noticed Maddy's face change. She gripped the table and looked up at him.

"When did you purchase the property?"

"It must have been at least three years ago…"

Maddy quick-dialled a number, pacing the kitchen as she listened to the ring tone.

"Hey, Maddy, so good to hear from you. I trust you are calling to have lunch with me…how are you doing? I was just thinking about you." Lambert, Sebastian's longtime assistant, sounded delighted to hear from Maddy.

Maddy continued to pace as she covered the pleasantries and then asked if Lambert had ever found the lost key to the Canary Wharf penthouse suite. She explained it might be on the market again and she wanted to see it before the agents listed the property. It's empty at the moment so they wouldn't be trespassing. Adam smiled as he realized Lambert had no qualms doing Maddy's bidding. He was a willing accomplice.

Lambert, pleased he could help Maddy, agreed to meet her at the building in an hour. He had enjoyed working with Maddy - she was such fun - so different from Sebastian. He had watched Sebastian fall in love with Maddy, head over heels in love with Maddy, and his heart ached when their love story was cut short by a gunman, on their long overdue wedding day.

Adam watched Maddy and Lambert embrace, excitedly talking at the same time and laughing as they finished each others' sentences. Lambert was cautious as he shook hands with Adam. They entered the building, agreeing Maddy should do the talking.

The building Concierge was very talkative, remembering Maddy and expressing his condolences - he was horrified by the news - Mr Walker had been very kind in all his dealings. When Maddy told him they were going up to check out the saleability of the penthouse, he was generous with his information. The other tenants would be glad to hear the penthouse would be free of those foreign men, he assured Maddy in a conspiratorial whisper. Their tech team had arrived early in the week to remove all the devices, they were very rude. He hoped there wasn't much damage.

Adam stood with his hands behind his back, uncomfortable with the discussion. He was concerned that Maddy looked worried. As they ascended in the elevator they did not speak.

When the elevator door opened at the penthouse Maddy covered her mouth and nose with her sleeve. The smell was overwhelming. The windows and the walls had been covered with excrement, racial slurs across the glass. The furniture had been overturned and the lamps broken. Bare wires hung out of the electrical outlets, as if they had been ripped out…

"Adam, get what you need and let's get out of here. Lambert, can we get the cleaning company in here right away? Let's go down to the car, if it's still there. The valet should have the keys."

When they had driven out of the garage, Maddy stopped the car and looked straight ahead. "I don't know what we just saw but once it's cleaned up you can decide what you want to do. Right now, I think we all need a drink."

They sat on the terrace at the flat, nursing their drinks. No one had the appetite to start a conversation. Adam cleared his throat and thanked Lambert and Maddy for getting into the building, apologized for the scene they encountered and realized he owed them more - he wasn't sure where to begin. What he did know was that he was indebted to Maddy and he was not going back to the penthouse.

He didn't see judgment in their eyes, he saw something he was beginning to understand as friendship. He would tell his story someday, hoping Maddy would forgive him. He had been impressed watching Maddy convince the valet she needed the keys as she was the leasing agent and the car was in arrears. She had oozed authority - she had taken over and solved the problems - taken everything in stride and decided on the next moves. Adam and Lambert had merely accompanied her.

Standing at the door of the terrace, before he went into the flat, he looked up at the stars, searching for Orion.

WHERE HAVE ALL THE FLOWERS GONE

"Maddy, all good at the penthouse. It was quite a job, but it's sparkling clean. Are we ready to get it on the market?" Lambert asked as he drove them to the airport.

Maddy looked over at Adam, who nodded solemnly.

"Oh, before I forget, am I to keep sending the flower cheques?"

"Yes please. Mrs Bing is sure to tell us when she's too busy. I'm just going to run in for the packages Grace has prepared. Won't be a minute." She jumped out of the car, turning around to collect her shoes from under the seat, and ran into the bookstore.

"Lambert, what are the flower cheques?" Adam was curious.

"Well, Maddy would be upset with me for telling you this because she feels good deeds should be low key. This was her neighbourhood when she lived with Sebastian. Mrs Bing has the flower shop over there. She is a crusty old girl, but she and Maddy are great pals. When the pandemic started Maddy had to stop volunteering at the hospital. She used to visit with the chemo patients, but suddenly she wasn't allowed in the hospital. Mrs Bing would surely have lost her business except that Maddy has a contract to deliver an arrangement every Monday to the chemo floor, to brighten up the area. She also gives me a list of random addresses to have flowers delivered…you know, just to check in on folks." Lambert shook his head and smiled, watching for Maddy.

"Maddy has always given business to Mrs Bing, she's a widow and this is her life. I used to think she was ungrateful because she's so nasty, but then I realized she adds one Gerbera daisy to every arrangement. That's Maddy's favourite flower. Maddy always has fresh flowers around. She misses her garden. It was just around the corner from here. So many great memories in the space she created. Not to mention the house…" Lambert jumped out to open the boot for the packages.

Adam was touched by the story. Maddy seemed to be involved in so many good things, things that made others feel special and loved. When she returned to the car he squeezed her hand, not sure what he could possibly say.

Looking out the small window of the jet Maddy was reminded of the excitement she felt the first time she had flown to the island. No communication had taken place since the pandemic - Maddy tried to be positive about what they might find - yet her heart was heavy.

As they approached the island the pilot banked over the village. Adam had warned Maddy to expect things to be different. The village looked deserted - the hotel balconies were disintegrating, steel rods standing where concrete had been. The building materials had been substandard and the years of burning sun and wind had not been kind to the structure.

Two jeeps appeared on the runway - no one had responded to the radio. The men in the jeep wore military uniforms and carried guns over their shoulder. They pushed a crooked set of stairs to the door and waited for the passengers to emerge.

Maddy stepped out first, hoping to recognize a friendly face. She smiled as she saw the man in charge greet her with a wave. The General, of exactly what army was difficult to determine, offered to take Maddy and Adam to the village. As they drove on the bumpy road, hitting large potholes and rocky areas, Maddy asked where the villagers had gone.

"A ship take them away Miss Maddy. Nothing here. Water not good. We wait for next boat now. You be sad to see my village now." The General spoke directly at Maddy, shaking his head.

There was nothing to see, nothing to say. They were too late. The island would soon be a wasteland of bad roads, crumbling structure, piles of garbage and smelly water. The once beautiful beach was covered in dead palm leaves and plastic bottles. It was beyond a weekend work party - no quick fixes here. Soon the gas would run out and the vehicles would be abandoned. Maddy wanted to scream at the injustice of what had been done.

Adam and the General watched Maddy as she walked through the village, stopping at certain huts, standing in the doorways, as if waiting for the children to appear.

"The Boss Man wanted her to stay." The General wiped his eyes, not wanting Adam to see his tears. "She walked across the hot gravel, no shoes, muddy from the dig, holding the water bottle - she wanted to test the water. He told us she cannot get on the plane. She kept walking. It was so hot. Her tall Englishman was waiting on the plane, he wouldn't let the plane go without her." The General looked away.

"The Boss Man was yelling and telling her to stop but she kept on walking. When he picked up the gun we knew he was losing his mind. He tried to shoot her and it was the signal to fire. We fired. Miss Maddy fell on the steps but he was dead. We were free of him." The General shook his head. "Look what freedom brings."

Maddy found her way back to the jeep, the tracks of her tears visible on her muddy face. She was barefoot and mud had caked on her legs, the mud on her hands drying in the sun. She didn't seem to notice. As they drove back to the dilapidated airport Maddy asked to stop at the beach where she had played with the children. She walked into the water, scrubbed the mud from her face and legs and watched the waves for several minutes, wondering what became of the children. Adam and the General watched in silence, leaving her to grieve alone.

It was not possible to take the remaining soldiers to the mainland - they were afraid of the small airplane and there were too many of them. Maddy left food and fresh water and wished them well. The General assured her they too were leaving soon, but he was grateful for the supplies.

As they taxied to the end of the runway Maddy thought back to the glossy brochure filled with promises and progressive plans for development. How could this happen? How could there be no accountability for the devastation left behind…how could this be stopped in the future? As they reached their cruising altitude Maddy realized Adam had been holding her hand, careful not to disturb her thoughts but wanting to show his support and understanding for her sadness and her helplessness.

"Thank you Adam. I hoped we would be able to make a difference. I'm sorry."

"Why are you sorry? You tried to help…" He put his arm around Maddy and pulled her close.

She smiled and fell asleep in his arms, dreaming about the possibilities she had imagined.

Adam was disappointed for Maddy - she wanted to help the community and her dream was shattered by the ruin on the island. Adam hoped Maddy would find another cause - he admired her passion and would do whatever it took to help her. He had taken samples of the clay, believing the texture was a natural pozzolan, used to strengthen concrete or mortar. He had studied various clays for his water installations. He would wait for the lab report before suggesting an alternate opportunity. All might not be lost. Adam shook his head, surprised he had seen the possibility of enterprise in the fallout.

The First Officer approached Adam, announcing there was a storm ahead. Would the passengers have an alternate destination in mind for the night? Maddy stirred and looked at the chart on the wall.

"Let's overnight in Casablanca. The regional airport, Tit Mellil, is easy to find. I'm sure we can land there, it's never busy. I could do with a little time in the Medina." Maddy responded enthusiastically. She looked over at Adam to see if he needed more persuasion.

"Casablanca it is." Adam nodded to the First Officer, smiling. Maddy was resilient and resourceful. He was looking forward to seeing Casablanca with her.

I GOT YOU (I FEEL GOOD)

Laughter, long walks, visits with Grace and Davi (and of course, little Chance), selling the penthouse for Adam, reading the many requests for the Charity mentorships and following up with cheques, dinner parties with old friends and of course, glorious sex with Adam…the months were merrily slipping away.

Adam seemed to dominate Maddy's time, much to the chagrin of Christian and Lambert - neither felt entirely comfortable with Adam. They discussed whether to mention their concerns with the man to Maddy, but decided it was best not to interfere, especially since Christian was busy with Adam's investment portfolio. Maddy was committed to including everyone in celebrating life after the pandemic.

Lambert had solicited Maddy's help for the annual holiday party at the firm - Maddy had turned a drunken disaster into a family party several years ago and the change had been embraced by the office staff.

The party was held in an indoor skating rink this year - it was impossible not to get into the Christmas spirit while skating to carols and having elves and Mrs Santa greet you with hot cider. The food was served as a kebab - turkey with sage bread, potato and Brussel spout - it was wonderful watching the children deconstruct their dinner. Everyone was invited to keep their skates, in the hopes they would return to the rink for future family days. As he did every year, Lambert declared this the best party ever!

Maddy had offered Lambert the beach house for the holidays. She was looking forward to decorating a tree in the front window of the flat, sharing Christmas dinner with her friends, perhaps having Angela and Ahmed join them. She wanted to celebrate a traditional Christmas with Adam.

Adam was attentive and caring, generous and kind to Maddy. Friends believed him to be distant and aloof - he was intense, which Maddy realized was how he reacted to being insecure and feeling out of place. He didn't waste words and never spoke of feelings, except when talking about his daughter Angela. Maddy was comfortable with his long silences - she was able to work on her writing projects without feeling guilty. They prepared meals together and spent many evenings sitting across from each other reading. It was nice to have someone in the flat.

Maddy started walking, no destination in mind, removed from her surroundings. Just a routine check, they said. Blood tests and ultra sounds, routine, they said. Just one more test, to be sure. Could she wait for the results? One more test, no need to come back another day. Maddy sat through the tests, wondering why everyone was so sombre. She felt fine, so why worry? They said it was routine.

Finally, they sat down with her, a team of doctors, and got right to the point. She would be admitted to the hospital in the morning. Please leave an emergency contact number. She gave them Adam's mobile number. The surgeon was hopeful he and his team would be able to remove the ovarian tumour, no problem. She would be out in a week, cancer free, no discomfort.

She had nodded, pretending to understand. Appearing so brave and in control. *Just a routine check, lucky to find it so early. Good as new, before you know it. Nothing to worry about.*

Now, walking alone, in the drizzling rain, Maddy felt as though her life was in someone else's hands. She tried to decide if she was frightened or terrified or just angry that she hadn't seen it coming. How could something like this sneak up on you, without warning…without letting you fight back.

It was dark when Maddy walked into the flat. She was cold and wet and wanted nothing more than to have Adam hold her, and tell her it was going to be alright.

He was sitting in the dark, his overnight bag beside him, a drink in his hand. He stood when he heard her come into the room.

"Maddy, I tried to reach you but your phone is off. I have to go. They've found my wife. She's in Damascus. I don't know what I'll find but I have to go." He spoke quietly and precisely. He had just enough time to make his flight.

Maddy tried to nod, "I understand. You have to go." She moved closer to the fire, her back to him. She really didn't understand at all. She needed a friend. How did a dead wife take precedence over her needs? Was she being selfish? When she turned, realizing she had to stop feeling sorry for herself, Adam was gone.

Maddy fell on her knees and watched the flames for some time before running a hot bath. A hot bath her only comfort.

WICKED GAME

♥ ♥ ♥

"Why did you leave, Yasmin? Why did you leave your beautiful daughter and run away?" Adam asked the woman sitting across from him.

Yasmin, as a young girl had pursued Adam, who had been known as Hassan in Dubai. Her father was a powerful man in Dubai - Yasmin was wild, always in trouble. Yasmin and Hassan had been at the opening of a new office tower and she had followed him to the mens washroom, forcing herself on him. Hassan had been mortified when months later Yasmin told him he was the father of her baby. He did the only thing he could do to save her from her own traditional father and his wrath. They were married immediately - it was a volatile marriage - Yasmin did not want to be a wife, she did not want to live with Hassan - she wanted to be free. She constantly told him he was too old and boring. When she drank, she confessed she had accosted and seduced him in haste…she had no feelings for him. The conquest had been her only goal.

As soon as the baby was born she fled. Her father refused to acknowledge he had a daughter. Hassan was given many opportunities in business as long as he promised the old man he would dedicate his life to caring for the abandoned baby girl.

When his beautiful daughter and Ahmed, her best friend, came home from school and watched the newsreel of the twin towers in New York with Adam, they were all spellbound by the tragedy. Later that evening his daughter asked to change her name to Angela; she wanted to attend school in England, as her father had, and she wanted an English name. Just as Hassan-Rashed el Sharif had legally become Adam Khan.

"I heard the old man is dying and my lungs are not going to take air much longer - there are truths you need to know. Truths that will hurt you and make your perfect life shatter. I'm tired now, more tomorrow. Go now." She walked away, leaving him alone in the open air room. He dug his nails into the arms of the sofa, hoping to control his anger, to stop thinking about hurting her.

Each day, Yasmin shared stories, or truths, designed to hurt him and prove that he had been a fool. Yasmin seemed well informed on his life. When she spoke about Maddy he had reached over to choke her, stopping himself as she laughed and coughed.

Yasmin took great pleasure in announcing he was not the father of the baby. She was not allowed to marry the head of her father's security team, Kaleed, but he was able to stay and watch his daughter grow up. He drove her to school, he cared for her - his job was to be sure Adam did nothing against the family name. It was Kaleed who had vandalized the penthouse in London. He would soon be on his way to Damascus, to be with Yasmin. Kaleed hated Adam almost as much as Yasmin did, she assured Adam.

Adam found himself thinking about how he could hurt them both - how he had to protect Angela. When Yasmin went to her room he saw the vial of morphine on the kitchen counter. He searched the kitchen for more and found several vials in a cooler. His face clouded over and he leaned on the counter, unsure of his next move. He grabbed the cooler and walked out of the house.

The next day, when he was summoned by Yasmin, he arrived with a plan. He was not going to be the victim and Angela must never know how cruel life had been to them. He did not want his beautiful daughter to think she might have any of the hatred her mother had cultivated.

"Where is Kaleed?" He asked as he walked into the room. "Enough of your truths Yasmin. Where is Kaleed?"

Yasmin laughed and coughed, a hacking sound, she looked around for a vial of morphine. In between her coughs she claimed Kaleed was sitting beside a patient in a London hospital. He was making sure she stayed in a coma.

Adam hit the wall with his fist, not feeling the pain, wanting to hit Yasmin, wanting her to feel the pain she was causing.

Taking deep breaths he waited until he felt he could speak without lashing out. "Call him now and get him here, before his gambling debts get him killed. Do you hear me?"

Yasmin continued to cough and began to laugh at Adam. "He doesn't gamble."

"Yasmin, I have always been a computer nerd in your mind. Why would I not know about the surveillance equipment he installed? Why would I not reverse the process and watch him? Would you like to see who he brings home each night? Would you like to see what he does with other men in alleys? Would you like to see….."

"Enough," Yasmin was doubled over in pain. "You lie. He loves me."

"You pay him. You are his boss. Once the cheques stop, he will be gone. Surely you know this."

"Shut up. You liar. He loves me. He has always loved me. He will do anything for me."

"As of this morning he has no bank account. I made sure he was wiped out. He cannot pay his gambling debts and he will be beaten or killed if you don't get him out of London. Now."

"You don't know what you are talking about." She was frantically looking around for a vial of morphine. "Where is my medication?"

"No medication until Kaleed gets here. I need to see him. I need to know he is not at the hospital. I need to know the woman lives. Do you hear me?"

"You bastard. Where is my medication. I need my medication." She was coughing up blood into the cushion. "I'll call the doctor, he will bring more."

"No, I called your doctor and told him you were trying to overdose. He won't answer your call."

"When did you get balls Hassan? When did you get to be so heartless?"

"You have no idea what I will do to protect the people I love. No idea." He threw the phone at Yasmin. "Call Kaleed."

Adam would never forget the look of hatred in her eyes. He stood tall. He believed he would do whatever it took to protect Angela and Maddy. When had Maddy entered the equation, he wondered. Where had this cruel streak come from? He couldn't remember ever wanting to hurt someone he knew so badly.

"Now we wait. Any other truths you want to share?" Adam watched her, feeling no emotion.

"Give me the morphine. I can't wait to watch Kaleed kill you with his bare hands." The hatred in her voice was shocking. More coughing.

"Morphine when Kaleed walks in the door. If he leaves now he can be here in six hours. Flight leaves in one hour." He looked at this watch.

Yasmin spoke into her phone. She continued to cough and argue with Kaleed, finally throwing the phone across the room, she screamed at Adam. "He wasn't able to get into the hospital today - what did you do? He has no money and he doesn't want to come here. You've ruined my life."

Adam laughed, "That's rich coming from you. I am not a monster, I'll give you morphine, half a vial now, half when he gets here."

Yasmin greedily grabbed the vial from Adam and went to her room, swearing she would see him burn in hell.

Hours later Kaleed arrived, storming into the house, calling for Yasmin. Adam watched him throw doors open, angrily asking why she had cut off his money. It was clear he was not returning to his lover. Kaleed flipped his cigarette onto the sofa and watched, in a drunken stupor, as the smouldering became a colourful flame. He fell backwards, mesmerized by the fire, hitting his head on the glass table. Yasmin appeared from the bedroom, calling Kaleed's name. Her cough worsening as the smoke filled the room. She ran to Kaleed and knelt down beside him, slapping his face, hitting his chest, angry that he would not speak. She lay beside him, covering his body with hers, crying and coughing. She was unaware of Adam standing in the hallway, watching, frozen. Her only thought was to revive Kaleed and make him tell her he loved her, had always loved her. Her lungs were filling with the smoke but she would not move away.

Adam left the cooler bag with morphine vials on the counter and walked out of the house. His jaw clenched, his stride determined. He watched as the smoke engulfed the house. He felt a sense of calm overcome him - the truths had opened deep wounds and finally they would die here.

The sounds of mortar and sirens were usual background noise in Damascus. Wealthy Syrians resided here, in Al Mezzeh, away from the troubled areas. Adam waited for the fire trucks and the ambulance, surprised they were not here already. When assistance finally arrived it was too late. The fire had ravaged the villa. Charred bodies were carried out. Adam ran forward, explaining his wife was in the house. The paramedic held him back, advising him the couple in the house had not survived. Adam insisted he must see his wife.

Satisfied the bodies were Yasmin and Kaleed, Adam looked for the closest shrub and threw up. He wiped his mouth and sat on the stone wall, mesmerized by the lights.

The call from Christian had been less than friendly. Adam had not known why Maddy was in hospital, had not known he was the emergency contact. His repeated attempts to call Maddy, just to hear her voice, had not been returned. Christian had been concerned about the hospital visitor who claimed to be Adam. Maddy was not recovering as they hoped. He suggested, in an icy tone, that Adam not return to London. Adam realized after sitting perfectly still for some time that he was responsible for what happened next. It was the turning point for him. He had to protect Maddy.

He was asked to report to the local police in the morning - they had questions, naturally. He heard neighbours telling the investigative team they knew nothing about the woman who lived in the burning house; she never came out because she had a breathing problem. The man who arrived this evening had been seen before, always arriving intoxicated, always shouting at the woman. The poor woman was better off now, they said.

Adam had imagined Yasmin leaving him and the baby to travel the world, free and unencumbered, but instead, Yasmin had been a prisoner in a sealed house, in a troubled country, away from her family and friends, believing the hired man loved her and cared for her. She had missed seeing Angela grow up and become a beautiful woman, she had missed the wedding of her only child, she had missed…living a wonderful life. All because she desperately wanted the one thing she could not have…the one thing her father forbade her. She had made the decision to leave her home, her child and a husband who did not love her for the freedom to love another man, a man beneath her social standing. She had sacrificed her life for a man who deceived her until she died.

He slowly walked away, feeling sorry for a life lost but lighter than he had in years. He called Angela, just to say he loved her. Then he called the hospital in London, to be sure the woman he wanted to start a life with was alive and on the mend.

The authorities in Damascus were not interested in keeping Adam - the fire was ruled an accident; caused by a cigarette. The house was worthless as Kaleed had borrowed against it - there was nothing for Adam here. He was escorted to the airport. He did not look back as he boarded the aircraft for London.

I WANNA HOLD YOUR HAND

Rushing to the hospital was the only thing on his mind as he walked through the airport. He was tested for the virus as he boarded the plane and again, as the plane landed. Adam was anxious to be at her bedside when Maddy regained consciousness.

He shaved and changed his shirt in the lounge, picking up a London real estate publication on his way to the cab queue. He had called Lambert about flowers but was told the room was like a greenhouse already.

He met with the doctor in charge and assured him money was no object - Maddy must have the best care. The doctor smiled and sat down with Adam to set him straight. No one would receive better care than Maddy - she had encouraged the young doctor to go to Africa and work with Doctors Without Borders. She had arranged for his placement and had suggested he travel alone so he could meet like-minded medical workers in the field. He and his Kenyan wife were expecting their first child, having returned to London to raise their family. Maddy was to be the godmother.

The doctor explained that a strange man, identifying himself as Adam Kahn, had visited Maddy each evening, administering a counter-productive drug in her drip line. It was Maddy who found him out - waking one evening, disturbed by his ranting. The man had placed a syringe on the bed as he told Maddy of the horrors the drug would do - he was trying to disable one of the tubes. Maddy grabbed the syringe and plunged it into his neck, which made him fall back into the monitors. All the alarms sounded as his fall disconnected the wires - it was seconds before the room was filled with nurses and security staff. It was brave but reckless, so like Maddy. It took the team some time to replace the monitors and calm her - adrenaline rush, no doubt. She should be waking soon, the effect of the drugs wearing off. The doctor assured Adam she was getting the best care possible.

Adam rubbed his forehead and then started to laugh, a chuckle becoming a full belly laugh as he imagined the scene and how they had both been fighting the same battle, in different countries, with different people. He laughed for the freedom he now knew, he laughed for the love he felt and then closing his eyes, he laughed for the future with Maddy.

He reached out to hold her hand in his and stopped laughing when he saw her eyes flutter. She was coming back to him. She had told him once he should laugh more. She was right.

"What are you doing here? Kaleed said you were dead." Her voice was soft and frail, but so sweet to hear.

Adam squeezed her hand, bending over the bedside to touch her cheek with his lips. "I'm right here, waiting to take you home. Please forgive me, I was so caught up in my own world I didn't protect you. That will never happen again. I promise you."

Maddy smiled weakly as her eyes closed and she fell into a deep sleep, her hand in his.

"I missed you." Adam whispered. He sat beside her, listening to her breathe, holding her hand, until the bright light of dawn.

I WONDER WHAT IT'S LIKE TO BE LOVED BY YOU

♥ ♥ ♥

A month of healing, with long walks and afternoon naps, was as much as Maddy could endure. It was time to celebrate - she had missed Christmas and New Year's so she invited her friends to Sunday dinner.

Come and celebrate the new year, wellness and friendship.
Bring a friend, good cheer and delightful stories
of what you intend to do next.
My flat, Sunday 7ish. Casual dress.

Adam was concerned it might be too early but Maddy was determined. She had food and drink arranged; an area of the front room cleared for dancing and he had to admit, she looked healthier just thinking about hosting an event.

Maddy ran to the door and welcomed Grace, Davi and Lambert, followed by Christian and his date, a younger tennis instructor. Sam and Deirdre arrived with Oliver, just returning to London for a few days before heading back to his assigned ship. No sooner had they settled in when the door was thrown open by Giselle and Philippe, arms laden with wine.

Maddy was in heaven, surrounded by friends and laughter, chatter and clicking glasses. Adam watched her come alive with the crowd - she was smiling that golden smile, the smile that started at the corners of her mouth, moving to her cheeks, making her dimples deep, then lighting up her eyes. He found it distracting to speak with others when all he yearned to do was touch her face and bask in her glow.

When everyone was seated at the table the food was passed - the conversation was loud, interrupted by the many toasts made by friends, expressing their love for Maddy and for the end of the pandemic with its restrictions and uncertainty.

Oliver reached for Maddy's hand and asked her to dance, wanting to be alone with her. He was quiet and Maddy felt he wanted to say something, but was hesitant. They returned to the table, Maddy flushed with the wine and dancing.

Deirdre raised her glass in a toast. "Here's to Maddy, who planned the greatest event ever in memory of my brother. We had a rocky start and you stole the heart of my childhood sweetheart but Sebastian did love you best. Maddy, here's a toast to you and your charmed life. You just seem to go from one good thing to another. From one good man to another."

Maddy blinked, feeling the words sting. Although she smiled to acknowledge Deirdre she was frantic to leave the table.

Flushed from the wine, Deirdre continued. "How do you do it? You aren't thin, you could lose a stone or two, you wear those tunics, you hardly wear shoes, yet you have all these men fawning over you. I don't get it. What is it about you?"

She was interrupted by Sam insisting she stop talking and sit quietly. Deirdre folded her arms and sat perfectly still.

Sam turned to Maddy. "Sorry about that."

Maddy nodded, excused herself and walked, forcing herself not to run, out of the room and out to the terrace. The evening breeze felt cold against her cheeks. She crossed her arms and let the tears fall.

Adam had followed her out, concerned at her reaction. Christian and Sam also followed her. They hoped to show support but instead felt awkward, standing on the terrace watching her sob.

"Maddy." Adam stepped forward. "What's wrong?" He was whispering, afraid of disturbing her. He hadn't understood what Deirdre was on about.

Maddy turned to the men gathered. "Charmed life, indeed. Is that why the people I love die and leave me? How is that charmed?" She moved closer to the railing, wiping her tears away.

"We love you…" Christian started.

"No, stop. You can't love me. Don't you see?" She held her face in her hands, wondering how to make them go away so she could be alone in her sorrow.

"That's ridiculous. I can't imagine another woman I would want to sail with for a month. Of course I love you. We miss Sebastian and Henry too, but we still have you to love." Christian stepped forward.

"Maddy, Sebastian was the one you chose but we were there for you because we loved you too. You are an amazing friend and none of us can imagine not having you in our lives. You must know that." Sam reached for her hand.

"I've never known anyone like you. I fell in love with you the first time I met you. People will always come and go in your life but you have this amazing group of friends who love you and who count on you for your friendship. I'm sure that's what Deirdre meant." Sam wrapped his arms around her. "Besides, when I thought I was going to lose the nightclub you saved me. I'll never forget that."

Lambert joined the group on the terrace, anxious to know his friend Maddy was alright.

The group closed in and Maddy giggled as she realized they were all embracing her at the same time.

"I'm sorry. I guess I'm just oversensitive. I am definitely the luckiest woman I know. I have the best friends and my life is full. Charmed, hardly. Fortunate, absolutely. Thank you all." She smiled and looked at their anxious faces.

"We better go back in. I hope I haven't thrown a wet blanket on the party." She motioned for them to go. "Thank you."

The group returned to the table, feeling they had salvaged the evening.

"It was time for a group huddle - we decided not to play party games." Sam announced, breaking the solemn mood. Within minutes the group returned to boisterous conversation.

Deirdre leaned over and touched Sam's hand. "Did I screw it up? Did I say something wrong? I'm famous for saying the wrong thing…should I speak to Maddy? I wouldn't want to upset her. She said she doesn't have a maid. Should I send mine to clean up?"

"Leave it be. Just eat something and drink less wine. Be sure to send her an over-the-top hostess gift tomorrow." He patted her hand and poured a glass of water. "Not everyone has a maid, my dear."

The group sat at the table for hours, changing seats, catching up on the last year and sharing their plans for the next year. When Adam and Christian walked out to the terrace with a whisky in hand, Oliver followed them. He had not spoken to Adam since the wedding and was anxious to know how Angela and Ahmed were enjoying their new life in America. He hoped to see them soon.

Christian was relating the story of travelling with Maddy on the sailboat. Both men had known Michael Riley and the sailboat had slipped into the conversation earlier in the evening. Adam was keen to know the details as Michael had required his contacts to purchase the boat.

They cut short their discussion as Oliver was not familiar with the boat or the back story. Christian exchanged pleasantries and left to refill his glass.

Once the men caught up on news of Angela and work, Oliver cleared his throat and asked Adam which hotel he was staying at. He had not seen the car outside - where was Kaleed? He seemed intent on knowing when Adam would be leaving.

"Kaleed is no longer with us. I don't have a driver at the moment." Adam responded, uneasy with the conversation.

"Perhaps Christian can offer you a lift. I understand Uber is available again." Oliver moved closer to Adam. "I think it's time I made my move on Maddy. Tonight is the night. I'll stay over, I'll tell Maddy I don't have a room elsewhere. I've been thinking about this for a long time. Maybe you could be a good friend and suggest to the others that it's time to go."

Adam shifted. "I don't think I would do that to Maddy. She has been planning this evening for some time. She misses her friends and it's been difficult since the surgery. Let her be."

"What surgery? What am I missing? Are you playing house with my *Dream Girl*?" There was no playfulness in Oliver's voice.

"You've had a great deal to drink tonight. Perhaps we should talk tomorrow." Adam was trying his best to sound reasoned and calm.

"Don't patronize me. I'm your friend. Tell me you didn't know I wanted to be with Maddy." Oliver started to move forward, his words slurred.

Philippe walked out onto the terrace, oblivious of the tension between the two men. "Ah, Adam. I meant to tell you, your irrigation system is efficient, clean and just what we needed. I can't wait for you to see what we've been able to accomplish in the vineyard with your plan. Maddy says you hope to be our way within the month. Father Dom is anxious to see you both." He realized both men were glaring at each other - he had walked into a situation best left alone.

"Well, it's been a lovely evening. Good night." He bowed and walked back into the room, concerned about what might transpire on the terrace.

Neither of the men spoke as they watched each other warily. Adam moved towards the sliding glass door, hoping to get back into the party without incident. Oliver stopped him with a hand against his chest.

At that moment Maddy appeared at the door. She looked at the two men, moving her gaze from one to the other. "Everything okay out here?"

Oliver dropped his hand, moving away from Adam.

"Maddy, why him? Why Adam?" His voice cracked. "Did he promise you everlasting love? Did he tell you he was married? Did he tell you how he made his money? Did he? Did he promise that he would stay? Did he promise that he would never hurt you? Did he tell you he knew I was crazy about you? Did he? What did he promise you?" He was shouting now.

Maddy concentrated on her breathing. How could this possibly end well… she clapped her hands together under her chin, closed her eyes and pursed her lips. "No promises were made." Adam had been so patient, not rushing her, afraid of hurting her.

"He'll run away as soon as he hears from his wife or his family. They hold the purse strings." Oliver moved toward Maddy. "I'm just concerned for you Maddy. Why couldn't you wait for me? I waited for you."

"Oliver, you were my first heart throb. I was a teenager and you made that summer the best ever. When I saw you in Italy you were so…so…brotherly. You stayed here for two weeks during your quarantine and then you just left. There was no indication… I had no idea…"

"Please tell me you are not so naive you didn't know how I felt for you? Did you need to sleep with the first man…"

"Hey, that's enough." Adam stepped forward, placed his arm around Maddy and motioned for her to leave the terrace. "Oliver, if you are angry with me, that's fair, but you have no right to talk to Maddy this way. It's time to go."

Oliver kneaded his forehead, aware that he had overstepped. "I'm sorry." He said weakly, feeling miserable.

Maddy turned to look at him, a tear slowing rolling down her cheek. "I'm sorry too, Oliver. I wouldn't want to lose my friend and you don't want to throw away your friendship with Adam, do you?" She wiped her cheek and composed herself, pushing the incident to a corner of her mind, to be revisited later, when she was alone. She turned and returned to her guests.

Embracing departing friends, committing to get together soon, Maddy closed the door, flicked her shoes off and walked wearily into the kitchen to assess the mess. She smiled as she scanned the room - surprised to see Adam loading the dishwasher, all surfaces clear. The dining room table was tidy and ready for the next event. Her friends were the absolute best.

She leaned against the wall, suddenly feeling tired, aware there were many conversations still to be had. "Thank you." She wasn't sure she had spoken out loud.

Adam walked towards Maddy, a towel in his hand, stopping to polish a spot on the counter. "I hope you were pleased with the evening. Your friends seemed to enjoy themselves. Lovely group of people. You must be tired." He moved her hair behind her ear, touching her cheek. "Would you like me to go?"

Maddy looked up at him, not sure why he would think she wanted to be alone. What a night. She blinked, suddenly feeling too tired to think.

"You have to do what your heart tells you to do. I don't know what you want. I have no expectations. None." She stifled a yawn and made her way to the bedroom.

ONE IS THE LONELIEST NUMBER

The morning sun was warm on her face as she stretched, not ready to open her eyes, not ready to face the day. Maddy could feel she was alone in the king size bed. Maybe if she rolled over and fell asleep she would rejoin the dream - the dream where she was floating and holding the hand of someone, feeling content and safe. She never saw the face attached to the hand that gave her such comfort, she only knew she felt genuinely happy.

She threw one leg out from under the duvet, touching the floor. It was time to get up. She contemplated going to the beach house - who could blame her for running away?

Maddy padded through the flat, thinking back to last night and how lovely it had been to see her friends and hear laughter again. She made a chai and checked her phone messages as she ran the bath water. Photos and thank you's popped up on the screen, making her smile. A curt apology from Oliver, suggesting they talk soon, made her wistful.

As she sat in the bubbles, listening to rock and roll hits, she suddenly felt very sad and lonely. She shook her head and started talking to herself - *get over it - you need time alone - you don't need a man in your life - you have friends and work and people depend on you to be positive...come on Maddy, let's go.*

A visit with Grace, Davi and baby Chase proved to be the perfect tonic for Maddy. Grace didn't ask why Maddy was alone, but she sensed something happened last night - Maddy would tell her when she was ready. Reading to Chase at the little library table always made Maddy happy.

She left her friends assuring them she was fine. She would go to the beach for a few days and visit with Jeffrey and the Buttons - they had settled into Belle's house and were hoping Maddy would sell it to them. There was no reason for her to hold onto the house now - she had several residences - Jeffrey and the children needed a home to start their new life with Clara, who would soon marry into the family. It seemed like ages since Audrey had passed - Maddy was filled with sadness as she walked home thinking about Audrey and how things had worked out. By the time she opened the door of the flat she made a decision to stop dwelling on the past; she could miss Audrey, Michael, Sebastian and Henry but she couldn't stop living. She owed them time to remember warm memories - never letting them go completely.

After a week at the beach house, walking with the children, who now wanted to be called 'Kiddos', Maddy was ready to return to London and continue her work on the book. As she walked the beach with Rod, a schoolmate of Sebastian's, she described the outline of her book. She had been struggling with how best to tell the story of Michael Riley. Rod was a good companion and a good listener - they had dinner most evenings, inviting Jeffrey, Clara and the Kiddos to join them for outdoor barbecues and stargazing. Maddy was pleased to see how easy Clara was with the children - they obviously adored her. That in itself was comforting. It seemed only right they should own the house. Belle would be pleased.

Rod looked forward to spending time with Maddy, although he had come to realize she considered him a good friend, nothing more. He called her each week, just to check in. If she needed anything, anything at all, she was to call him. Maddy thanked him for being such a good listener and promised to see him when she returned to the beach house. He had offered several well thought out options for the book.

London was beginning to start up again, after a long year of lockdown and caution over the virus. Theatres were slow to open and large gatherings were limited. Lambert and Christian found excuses to visit with Maddy, concerned she might become depressed if left alone for too long.

Maddy travelled to Italy for the investors meeting at the Villa Mirage, much to the delight of Father Dom, Giselle, Philippe and Anza, the dog. The irrigation system Adam had designed was working perfectly and it appeared the vineyard would produce a fine vintage this year. Villa Mirage was a popular quarantine destination - the program offered just the right amount of mental health care necessary for those who could afford the stay. Maddy felt relaxed in the gardens, with her friends. She also had fond memories of her first visit, the Contessa, developing the concept of a retreat, events in Florence with her American friend Dermot, and always of her time with Sebastian. She tried to make sense of Oliver and his visit… turning to long hours of physical work in the vineyard to forget.

Advice from Father Dom:

Time passes and wounds heal, laughter and good memories fill the sadness around your eyes better than botox injections. Life is challenging enough looking forward, don't forget the past, enjoy the best parts and learn what you want to keep; what you don't want, throw away. Be content with your friends and the rich life you have. Salud.

YOU'VE GOT A FRIEND

The sound of a harp playing filled the room. Maddy opened her eyes, blinking several times before she realized it was the phone. Unknown callers had been assigned the harp chords. Slowly Maddy reached for the phone. No good ever came from a call in the dark.

"Hello, Maddy here." She yawned.

"Hi Maddy, I'm so glad I got you. It's Angela. Sorry, did I wake you? I'm frantic. I have not heard from my father for three months and he's always in touch. I'm hoping he's there with you. Sorry, I'm starting to panic." Angela finally took a breath.

Maddy sat up in the bed. "Oh dear Angela, I can't help you. I haven't seen your father for months, haven't heard a word. I understand, well, I don't understand, what happened, but he left, without a word and although I'm getting better with that, I can't forgive him for worrying you."

"Oh Maddy, I'm such a child. We love Princeton and our jobs and our life here, but I'm homesick. There's nothing left in Dubai and no one there has seen him for months…do you think something happened? Do you think we should call the authorities? I don't know what to think." Angela sniffled and sighed.

"Why don't you come here and stay with me. London isn't home but you both went to school here so you'll have time to meet old friends and I'll take care of you. We'll have movie nights and karaoke and maybe shop."

Maddy hated to hear the distress in the calm, cool voice of Angela. "Listen, a friend of mine handled some investments for your father - maybe he can help you. Will you come over?"

"Ahmed is nodding. I think he would like a night out with his schoolmates. It's very kind of you to offer. Are you sure you want us to descend on you?"

"It would be my pleasure. You were both so welcoming to me in Dubai. I could use some company. Just let me know your flight details and I'll meet you at the airport. I assume you are both vaccinated and safe to travel." Maddy was already planning what they would do.

"If you are seriously offering, we would love to see you and get away. Thank you Maddy. I'll send you a text message. Anything you want from New York?" Angela was laughing. "Mr Gold says he wants to send you pastrami on rye. Such a weird gift."

"I'll tell you the story when you get here. Excited to see you. Safe travels. Don't fret, we'll see what we can do to find your father."

"Thank you Maddy. Oh, Maddy, I'm so sorry he left you. I know he cared for you."

Sadness covered Maddy like a blanket. "Indeed."

After a whirlwind week with Angela and Ahmed the flat seemed so quiet and empty. Maddy smiled as she thought about the way Angela had settled in immediately - her clothes strewn around the flat, her handbag always spilling out on the hall table, her constant hugs and her enthusiasm for everything Maddy suggested. Ahmed was the perfect husband - he adored Angela and picked up after her, laughing at her carelessness. She was meticulous in the science laboratory, he assured Maddy.

Maddy invited Lambert and Christian to dinner, suggesting they may know how Adam could be reached. When the conversation regarding

Adam began Maddy excused herself. She had decided there was no room in her heart to mourn another man.

Angela and Ahmed were sensitive to the hurt Maddy must have felt, not knowing why Adam disappeared. They avoided any talk and did not report back on whether they had found him or not.

Maddy wistfully said goodbye to the couple and promised to visit them in America. Angela confessed she had never been close to another woman - Maddy was what she imagined a mother would be like. She hoped Maddy didn't mind her saying so.

Alone in the flat, on the terrace, with the stars for company, Maddy wondered how life with Henry would have unfolded - would he have been a Chef? Would he have become a naval officer? Would he have wanted to get married and have children? Would he and Sebastian have argued about school?

Maddy knew in her heart it would not have mattered…she would have enjoyed every moment with him. She and Sebastian had never talked about growing old or watching Henry become his own person. They never had the chance to talk about the future - the future was taken away that fateful day on the steps of the Registry Office.

One day you have it all - a wonderful lover and husband, a delightful boy with such potential, a new home, time and resources to enjoy life…and a random shooting takes away your dreams and hopes…why? Why am I still here? Why was I spared? Why both Sebastian and Henry? Enough. I'm still here - I better make my life count. No more tears, no more regrets. This anger isn't healthy. Come on, Maddy, get on with writing the book - you promised Michael.

Maddy tried not to look up at the stars - she didn't want to see Orion.

IF THE WORLD WAS ENDING

♥ ♥ ♥

Turning the corner, Maddy waved at her neighbour. The podcast she was listening to was just about over - she slowed her steps to hear the wrap up. A small dog ran past, two children chasing after the dragging leash. She smiled as they screamed the dog's name. Anza had never had a leash and she would never run away, more likely to lick you and make you run away.

No use trying to listen now - her mind was flipping back and forth to Italy and the Villa, seeing Anza, the beautifully tempered dog, lazing in the sun. Now she was thinking about the success of the meeting this morning…Grace had mentioned there were several organizations trying to get mothers back into the workforce now that the lockdowns had been lifted. Maddy met with the social work agency administrators and suggested several 'cottage industry' opportunities for moms who were not able to commit to a rigid work schedule. She offered funding and support.

As she left the meeting Maddy contacted Lambert and asked if he would do a session on staging a property for sale - of course he was delighted. Maddy had appealed to his thespian alter-ego…he would enjoy performing and imparting his wisdom. Her next call was to Deirdre, who had the means to sponsor a workshop on where her crowd would go to look for accessories - did the ladies of London who lunch shop online? Would they have business clothing they wanted to donate? Sam was pleased to offer the venue as it was a daytime event. His club, Decades had been a ghost kitchen during the pandemic - he was ready to have people back in the club. Maddy hoped he would offer a dance class, just to set the mood for the serious work of engaging the women.

Her last call had been to Grace to arrange a cooking class for women who needed to prepare quick healthy meals for their families - meals that could be frozen and pulled out when time was short. Grace was keen and had several ideas for options that would allow children to help with the creation of a fun dinner.

Everything was set - now all they needed was a room filled with enthusiastic women who wanted to be their own boss. Maddy smiled at the thought and almost missed her front door. She stopped, seeing a pair of legs on the steps. She stopped and turned.

He was sitting back on the stoop, leaning on his arms. He sat up abruptly as he realized Maddy was standing in front of him.

"I don't think you left anything here." Maddy tried not to make eye contact. He looked so fit and handsome - even better than she remembered. Her heart was pounding and she was desperately working on controlling her breath. She was sure her face was flushed.

"I deserved that. I know you think I'm a monster but I need to tell you what has transpired since that fateful evening. Will you please hear me out? Please Maddy. I want to show you something. Will you come with me?" Adam reached back and produced a take-out cup of chai - her favourite. He held it out for her, his face creased in a shy smile.

Maddy smiled, knowing it was useless to pretend she was angry. She looked down at his puppy dog face, his rolled up sleeves, holding out the cup as a peace offering. She looked away, afraid she would forgive him without making him squirm.

Adam watched Maddy's face, delighted to see her dimples, her smile, her blue eyes, wondering what she might do next. "Come with me, it won't take long, I promise. I want to show you something." He stood and resisted folding her into his arms, she was so close and she smelled so good.

"I'm sorry I ran away…" he started.

"Whoa, no explanation required. I know all about running away. It's what I do best." Maddy interrupted, recalling how many times she had run and wasted valuable time with Sebastian.

He took her hand and led her to the sedan, opened the door and waited for her to be seated. He felt lighter walking around the car - Maddy hadn't slapped him or screamed at him to go…he was hopeful.

They drove in silence; Adam enjoying her presence, Maddy wondering where they were going. She knew they were driving westward but she resisted asking, knowing somehow he wouldn't say. She sipped her chai, thankful she had something in her hand.

"Maddy, that night, when Oliver had his meltdown, I realized he was right - I wasn't being fair to you. You deserved to be with someone in a relationship - *all or nothing*. I stayed up most of the night fighting with myself and I finally decided you were worth it all - I left that morning with a mission. I was determined to clean up all the loose ends in my life and come back to you when I could give you everything you deserved." He looked over at her, wanting to touch her cheek, move her hair behind her ear, kiss her.

"You took a risk. How did you know I would still be here? That I hadn't moved on?" Maddy whispered.

Adam smiled and reached for her hand. "Maddy, you are the wallpaper in my mind. Your image is tattooed there. It helps me get through the days when I'm not with you. Your face allows me to do what I have to do. Sometimes I have to stay away to heal before I come home."

"But that's what home is for…for healing." Maddy squeezed his hand. "Are you coming home?"

Adam felt as though a weight had been lifted from his shoulders. He cleared his throat, hoping his voice didn't crack. "I checked in with Christian and Lambert, they kept an eye on you for me. They kept you busy enough.

Believe me, it was hard to imagine you might give up on me. I wanted to come home."

Maddy turned to look at him. "Have you called Angela? She was frantic. She was worried about you. That wasn't cool." Her voice was firm as she scolded him.

Adam laughed. "Yes, I have been in touch. Angela told me you were marvellous. Your invitation was so appreciated by both she and Ahmed. Don't worry, any anger you may have towards me cannot be worse than the acrimony my daughter expressed towards me. I have been admonished properly and again, I'm sorry."

Maddy sat back. "Wallpaper. I'm trying to imagine what I look like as wallpaper."

"You look wonderful."

They laughed and suddenly the colours of the world around them were brighter, more vivid.

They were nearing Henley-on-Thames, a lovely town in Oxfordshire. Maddy had travelled there with Sebastian enroute to Oxford to watch the regatta. Maddy smiled as she remembered how wonderful the day had been - lunch on the Thames, the regatta and then a walk to Marsh Lock before leaving for Oxford, Sebastian's alma mater.

"Close your eyes. Trust me. Just close your eyes until I tell you to open them. Please Maddy."

Maddy stared at Adam for a moment, bit her lip and closed her eyes. The car turned off the main road for a short while and stopped. Adam ran around the car, opened the door, took Maddy by the hand and guided her along a fragrant walkway.

"Alright, open your eyes."

Maddy took a deep breath, her senses were bombarded with fragrance, colour and the most beautiful little Tudor cottage she had ever seen. The garden was overflowing with flowers - lupins, fuchsia, foxglove, delphiniums, red and yellow roses, bellflowers, black hollyhocks, peonies and primrose. Adam named all the varietals and pointed out the clematis vines, then ran his hand over the lavender. The herbal infused walkway curved around jasmine shrubs, opening up to several seating areas, leading to a pointed wooden door. The cottage had a sloped slate roof, the walls were covered in ivy, the windows framed with wooden shutters and window boxes. Maddy expected to see fairies in the windows - it was a delightful cottage.

Adam directed Maddy around the side of the cottage - against the fence on either side of the lawn was a wild flower garden under a grove of trees, overlooking the Thames. Maddy gasped. She turned to Adam, speechless.

"This is so lovely. How did you find this place? Who lives here? It's magical." She gushed.

Adam watched her. He was pleased with her reaction to the cottage and the grounds.

"If you like it, you live here. It's yours. It's ours."

He wasn't prepared for the full body slam of Maddy throwing her arms around his neck.

He embraced Maddy who was crying and laughing and asking him over and over if he was crazy. He held her, not wanting to let go…hoping she would accept his offer.

Maddy pulled away, taking his hand and leading him down to the water's edge. There was a love seat on the bank of the river. Maddy pulled Adam along and sat on the seat.

She wiped her face and stared out at the water. She noticed the boathouse hidden in the trees and turned to Adam.

"What is going on?" She asked, confused by seeing Adam again, the cottage, the setting…it was all too much.

"I went away vowing to be back when I could give you everything you deserved. You missed your garden, you missed being outdoors and it was killing you living in a flat, in the middle of the city. I thought this cottage might make you happy. I found this old cottage and gutted it, modernizing and rebuilding it myself. I thought we could start our chapter here…now I know it was presumptuous of me, but I'm ready to fight for you and make you the happiest woman in the world. If you give me a chance. I want this to be our h*appy ever after*. What do you think?" He kissed Maddy before she could answer. To his absolute delight, she did not turn away.

The interior of the cottage was white with thick, majestic Turkish carpets on the hardwood floors. The sun was streaming through the many windows, creating a soft pastel glow. Maddy visualized the baby grand piano in the open room. The kitchen overlooked the river, copper pots hanging from the centre rack, a ceramic island with six stools, a Dutch door to the back deck.

Adam explained the carpets were from his house in Dubai - the only things he kept when he sold the house - if Maddy didn't love them they could go…he would leave the decorating to her. The only room with furniture was the bedroom. He had shopped for the bedding, surprising himself at how rewarding the experience had been. He had wanted a cloud bed, fluffier and more inviting than the beach house bed, which he had found so inviting.

He had purchased thick white bath towels for the bathroom and had tried to stock as many items as he could recall Maddy having in her bathroom. The bathtub was free standing in front of the window, the shower open to the room. Twin sinks and large mirrors, modern light fixtures and candle holders completed the inviting room. Adam had spent hours on the details - he had done much of the work himself, working to a deadline only he had determined.

The work had been cathartic - he had laboured and sweat - wondering if the callouses on his hands would always be a badge of honour. His reward for the manic schedule and manual labour was presented now - watching Maddy smile as she touched the surfaces he had lovingly sanded and stained; as she noticed the details and admired his choices of texture and colour.

Adam produced a picnic basket with deli foods, baguettes and wine; he flipped a plaid blanket on the floor in front of the fireplace, inviting Maddy to join him. He touched the floor, pointing out the radiant heat - no radiators or duct work. It was rewired and insulated for cool summers and warm winters. The garage was under the cottage, suitable for two vehicles. He was about to describe the nearby village when Maddy reached over and touched his lips with her hand.

"Please stop. Let me enjoy this. It's overwhelming. We'll have time to explore and get settled. Right now I want to hear what happened. This cottage is absolutely wonderful. That you found it and did all the work and wanted it for us…it's too much to fathom. I need time. I need to know what you had to give up. Can you share that with me?" Maddy was whispering.

She rested her head on his chest, hoping he would feel less vulnerable if she wasn't looking directly at him. Adam lay back, holding Maddy in his arms and took a deep breath. Once he started, there was no turning back. He had to trust her. He closed his eyes and wondered where to start.

ONE FINE MORNING

Laughter and chatter interrupted his dreams. Adam opened his eyes. He was alone on top of the duvet in the king-sized bed, fully dressed. He tried to remember why they hadn't christened this wonderful bed last night. They hadn't had too much to drink. Maddy had listened to him, asking only if he had ever killed anyone. He had hesitated and answered honestly. He might not have another chance to tell her everything - he decided she could handle whatever he confessed.

He sat up, hearing more laughter and shouting. The voices were outside the bedroom window, in the garden. He stood up and went in search of Maddy - surely she hadn't left. He felt a wave of panic as he realized she might have gone…

He walked out into the garden, towards the voices. He stopped as he saw Maddy and several older couples sitting on wrought iron furniture in the garden, sipping coffee and chatting as if they were old friends.

"Ah, good morning Sleepy Head." Maddy stood and walked over to greet him. "Coffee and a cream danish?" She smiled sweetly. "Come and meet our lovely neighbours. They've brought us furniture for the garden. Isn't that wonderful?" Maddy handed him a coffee mug and a danish wrapped in a napkin.

Adam was speechless but he noted Maddy had said "our neighbours." He nodded at the group. "Good morning. It's not gone eight yet, has it?"

The couples snuck a look at each other and laughed. "We're early birds. We saw Maddy admiring the garden and boldly introduced ourselves, you know, to welcome her, to welcome you." The elderly man stood and extended his hand. "I'm Bernard and this is my fair bride, Marianne. We run the local brew house, The Stag."

Bernard was wearing a brown tweed jacket with patches on the elbow and an ascot, his wife was dressed in a long medieval gown, holding a silk fan in her hand.

"Nice to meet you Bernard. I'm Adam Khan. Thank you for the hospitality." Adam was warming to the moment. "Marianne." He bowed his head.

"Are you Jewish?" The fair bride asked. "We haven't had a Jewish person here before."

"Sadly, no." Adam smiled at the question.

"Are you an Arab? You have that Middle East mystery about you." Marianne was not giving up.

Adam was uncomfortable, he was a private person. "I am British but I have roots in the Middle East. My mother raised me as a Christian. I do speak Arabic, if you should ever need a translation."

"We've been watching you work away but we thought you were a foreign worker so we didn't come over. What a wasted opportunity. We could already be friends." Marianne waved her fan and smiled demurely.

"Excuse my wife, she loves culture clashes and she has no filters. I say, old man, you handled that well." Bernard chuckled. "You'll get used to her, I did." He moved away, amused.

"Let me introduce you to Gillian and Fred, they operate the bakery and make these delicious danish, David and Chelsea have the Vintage Shoppe on the High Street. We are invited to Annual Afternoon Tea in the Common on Wednesday afternoon. Isn't that just the best? I love

Afternoon Tea." Maddy was obviously amused by the welcome committee and their strangeness.

Adam nodded, realizing words were not necessary.

Adam surveyed the couples. Gillian and Fred were middle aged, wearing jeans and golf shirts, they looked very active, despite their pale faces. David and Chelsea, perhaps in their late fifties, were dressed as if on safari, in khaki shorts and vests with knee socks and hiking boots. David had a gruff voice and Chelsea just smiled prettily. He looked at Maddy, comfortable in her white tee shirt and short denim skirt, no shoes, her hair loose and uncombed, and wondered what they thought of her.

The eclectic group was dispersing, heading to their perspective venues, ready for the London tourists who would soon be arriving. With goodbye waves and reminders of the various offers, they were gone.

Alone in the garden, which was even more pleasant than Adam had intended, he looked over at Maddy and asked how she was doing.

Maddy took his hand and assured him she was feeling content. Her face glowed and she seemed lost in thought. She asked if they could zip into London for a few things, although Chelsea had suggested she take a look at the vintage clothing - Chelsea believed Maddy was an old soul.

Adam was encouraged - Maddy seemed content here, in her garden, with new friends.

"I'll stay here. I'm expecting deliveries and I have a few repairs to complete. You go ahead. Don't be long." Adam hated to see her go.

Maddy smiled mischievously. 'I hope I can find my way back."

"I set the navigation system in the car - just touch 'Home' and it will bring you back."

Maddy turned and fell into his arms. "Good to know." She was having difficulty putting a name to the feeling - was it happiness, was it comfort, was it a sense of security? She kissed Adam on the cheek and quickly left to collect her things.

Davi delivered the sofa and chairs, some artwork and a desk from Maddy's storage container - Grace had a cooler of food and drinks - Lambert brought a wine rack and filled it with a selection of bubbly, red and white vintages. He had also retrieved the rolls of twinkle lights Maddy had strung around the garden at Bellmere. Christian stopped by with two bicycles and set up a hammock on the back deck, adding a barbecue and a hamper with steaks, potatoes and salads - hoping he had enough for everyone.

Maddy was surprised to see her friends at the little cottage when she returned. Adam had planned this - he was trying very hard to convince Maddy this was their new home.

He was encouraged when Maddy asked him to hang the tapestry he had gifted her immediately; to christen their new home.

Adam sat back and took in the scene before him - Maddy's friends had transformed the colourful garden into a delightful party area. As the evening wore on the neighbours dropped in with bottles of wine and gift bags. Maddy welcomed everyone with such sincere warmth, he wondered if this would be a regular happening.

"You certainly did the right thing to win the fair maiden. Maddy loves a garden and she loves to have her friends around. Good on you." Christian raised his glass to Adam.

"I never thought I'd say this, but this garden is more impressive than Maddy's garden at Bellmere. She will love living here. Adam, I hope you're a good dancer. She loves to dance in the garden." Lambert added as he walked towards the bar set up.

"This is lovely Adam." Grace had said. "Just don't keep her away from us. We need to see her - Chance will miss her. The Coffee House is getting busier and Maddy always has great ideas to keep us ahead of the crowd. I understand what you're trying to do but please, don't take her away from us." Grace looked at Adam, seeing a confident, handsome, yet dangerous man whose dark eyes softened when he looked at Maddy.

"Grace, I just want her to be happy. Happy with me. Her friends are too important. Only a fool would stand in the way of her friendships. I hope little Chance will visit and enjoy the gardens with us." Adam responded in a soft voice.

Grace hugged his arm. "Thank you. We all want her to be happy. She deserves it."

Bernard and David, their new neighbours were deep in conversation with Maddy, gesturing and expressing anger. Adam approached the triad, hoping to lighten the mood.

"Well, enough of that. I'm sure you don't want to hear more about this now. We'll talk later." David pushed Bernard's arm and they nodded at Adam as they walked away.

"What's that about?" He asked, watching the men walk away. He leaned over and kissed Maddy. "Having a good time?"

"Yes, I am. You?" Maddy turned to Adam. "There seems to be trouble in paradise…a large developer is trying to buy up the homes on the river to create a high-rise condo project with high end boutiques. It will certainly change life here. The locals are up in arms."

"I'll look into it. Now go and mingle, have fun. We can save the world later." Adam pointed towards the garden.

Maddy laughed and kissed his cheek. "Thank you. Thank you for this…" She looked around the yard, her arms outstretched.

When the last guest had waved good night Maddy and Adam stood alone in the garden. The lights were just right, creating a misty backdrop - the heady floral scent was wafting through the space and the music, soft and seductive seemed to surround the garden. Adam held Maddy in his arms and they danced, under the moon, under the stars, losing track of time.

"This was lovely. Thank you." Maddy whispered into his neck. Her warm breath making him shiver.

Adam led her into the cottage, turning lights and music off as he closed the door. He held her hands and moved them above her head, leaning into the wall. He kissed her neck, encouraged by her soft moans and her body responding to his. Both of them were breathing erratically and when he touched her lips with his, he felt faint. He wanted her and he felt Maddy was ready for him. Still holding her hands above her, he moved her arms slowly down the wall, pulling her even closer. He could feel her heartbeat. Her breathing was fast and he couldn't wait any longer. He moved his hands down and pulled her up, her legs wrapped around him.

Maddy found his mouth and kissed him, her arms around his neck, one hand running through his hair, pulling him closer. She could feel his hands under her tee shirt, the coolness of his hands soothing her burning skin.

Suddenly Maddy was on the bed, her tee shirt and bra lifted over her head, thrown hastily on the floor, her skirt and panties pulled off and Adam, naked, was above her, kissing her with an urgency that took her breath away.

"Maddy, I've waited so long for this moment." He whispered into her hair, inhaling the musky scent of her.

Maddy responded by pulling him down, her hips raised, ready, welcoming him.

Adam moved slowly, not wanting to hurry the passion he felt with his whole being. He had never been this aware of every movement, every heartbeat, every pleasurable feeling. When Maddy shuddered he released all the passion he was so carefully controlling. How had he never felt like this before? How had he never let go so completely. He rolled away, worried he might hurt Maddy with the weight of his exhausted body. He reached for her, not wanting to let her go. He turned his head, still breathing hard, and saw her beautiful eyes watching him. He touched her face, afraid his trembling hand would scare her. He wasn't sure he could speak, but if he could, he would tell her that he loved her, that he had spent the last few months hoping for this night.

"Can we do that again?" Maddy whispered, a smile on her lips. "I mean, could we ever do that again?"

Adam wrapped her in his arms. As Maddy snuggled into his embrace he could hear her even breathing and he realized he had been given a gift. An amazing gift. A woman, a partner he could grow old with, a companion to share life with - someone to protect and watch over. He fell asleep holding the gift in his arms.

HAVING THE TIME OF MY LIFE

♥ ♥ ♥

The sound of the rain was soothing. Maddy sat on the front step, protected by the entrance portico, cradling her tea mug, enjoying the smell of the earth as it absorbed the rain. The flowers, anxious to drink the welcome drops, were dancing with glee.

Adam woke, alarmed that Maddy was not beside him. He had hoped to start the day making love to her. Last night had been prodigious…amazing and totally unexpected, but worthy of repeating. He smiled as he stretched and rolled out of the bed. His life had taken a turn for the best and he would work hard to keep this feeling alive.

He found Maddy sitting outside. He quickly donned his sweatpants and walked out, his coffee in hand.

"May I join you?" Adam sat beside Maddy, kissed her cheek and looked out at the rain.

"Good morning. I didn't want to wake you - you looked so peaceful lying there." Maddy leaned into him.

"You look good in my shirt."

"I feel good in your shirt."

"Are you flirting with me?" Adam was getting aroused, just being beside her, knowing she had nothing on but his shirt.

"If I say yes, will you take me back to bed?" She batted her eyelashes and hid her cheek in her shoulder.

Adam stood and reached for her hand. "Let's go before the neighbours stop by for a visit."

"What a way to start the day." Adam whispered. "I hate to wake up without you beside me."

"Tell me what makes you feel good. You are so unselfish with me. I want to know what to do for you." Maddy turned to look into his eyes.

Adam was taken aback. He had no idea what to say. No one had ever asked him. He didn't know himself. He was hypnotized by her eyes.

"Do people talk about this?" He asked, averting his eyes, shaking his head, embarrassed.

"I don't want to make you uncomfortable, but yes, we should talk about it. I want to please you the way you please me."

"Oh Maddy, you do please me. In so many ways, you please me." He stroked her cheek. "We have so many things to talk about. Is this where you want to live? With me?"

Maddy rolled back and stared at the ceiling. "The cottage is lovely, the gardens are magnificent, you are wonderful…you worked so hard to make everything perfect and it is. I want someone to grow old with someone I can share my life with. Where isn't as important as who. I'm tired of running away. I'm tired of losing time and people. If you want to take a chance on me, I will do my best to make it work. I can't promise it will always be easy…"

Adam pulled her over into an embrace, stopping her. "I'm new to this as well, we'll work at it together. After everything I've told you, the person taking the chance is you. The last months have been hell for me - you told me to follow my heart - but you already had my heart." He kissed her, hoping everything he wanted to say would find its way into that kiss.

"Hmm. You have two choices - feed me or make love to me again. Full disclosure - I'm really hungry." Maddy sat up, laughing. "Let's get started on our future. The rain has stopped." She leaned over and kissed him.

"Bagels and cream cheese with smoked salmon, sir." Maddy presented a plate. "Let's take the bicycles into the village when we're done. Just have a look around."

"No bicycle for me. Thanks." Adam was firm. "I'm enjoying breakfast."

"We don't have to go for long. The bikes are ready. There aren't any hills and they're electric-assist anyway."

"No biking for me. You go ahead."

"I'd rather go with you. Do you want to walk instead?" Maddy was anxious to get out and do something.

"Listen, children in Dubai don't go bike riding when the pavement is scorching hot. I never learned to ride a bike, if you must know." Adam sighed.

Maddy reached over and touched his face. "Oh Adam, I didn't know. I'm sorry."

"You find this amusing, don't you?"

"No, I just see an opportunity for a trade-off. You teach me Arabic and I teach you to ride a bike."

"Why would you want to learn Arabic?" Adam was now interested.

"Well, what if you have a nightmare and shout out in Arabic…I need to know what you're afraid of, don't I? What if you dream in Arabic?"

Maddy asked, her eyes wide. "What if we have an accident and you give me instructions in Arabic?"

Adam laughed. "That's crazy, but you win. You can try to teach me to ride a bike."

"You go to the gym and work out. Haven't you ever taken a spin class? This is easier."

Adam just stared at Maddy.

"Come on. It's easy peasy." Maddy reached for his hand and pulled him out to the garden.

Adam was a quick study and Maddy was a patient teacher. Soon they were ready for a ride. By the time they reached the Common Adam could not feel his bottom. He was shocked, but pleased, when Maddy reached behind him and massaged his backside.

They sat on the grass and Maddy jumped up to get ice cream cones, trying to guess at his favourite flavours. Adam could not remember when he last ate ice cream - it was too hot in Dubai to sit outside and enjoy a cold treat. Adam laid his head on Maddy's lap and closed his eyes, relaxing as she ran her fingers through his hair. He was experiencing so many new, wonderful feelings with Maddy.

Adam drifted off to sleep as Maddy visited with the locals, finding out where to eat, where to shop, when the tourists came, who to avoid, who to call for various fixits.

When he sat up there was a crowd around them, sitting on the grass, laughing and sharing a blender of drinks. Maddy was one of the gang and they were sad to see her leave. Adam hobbled over to the bikes, aware he might never sit again. Maddy patted his bottom and kissed him, hoping to encourage him and take his mind off the pain. She promised a bath when they got home.

The weather was fine enough for dining outdoors - Maddy carried a tray laden with their meals, wine and scones out to the garden. They had turned on the twinkle lights when the phone rang. Angela was calling with news. She and Ahmed were having a baby. It had been planned for a December delivery so they would be off work. Would Adam and Maddy please come to America and spend Christmas with them? There were tears of joy and some apprehension as Angela revealed she was worried - she was thirty three years old, having her first child. Maddy's assurance seemed to calm her. Maddy asked if they wanted the baby to be born in America or in England. The couple said they felt American now so they would stay in New Jersey. Angela sobbed when Maddy offered the cottage as the birthplace.

When Adam told Angela he had ridden a bicycle, eaten an ice cream cone while sitting and then falling asleep on the village green, she laughed until she cried, again.

"I feel so much better knowing you will be here in December. We love you both and we can't imagine not having our family here to welcome little Adam or Andrea - we don't want to know the sex before the baby comes." Angela had exclaimed. The call ended with air kisses.

Maddy reached over and touched Adam's hand. "Congratulations Grandpa."

Adam seemed disoriented. Maddy left him alone with his thoughts. He would talk to her when he was ready. She was thrilled - planning what they would need in December. She immediately emailed Mrs Bing to wire flowers for the excited parents-to-be. She would have time to help with the harvest at Villa Mirage before heading overseas. She was bubbling with questions for Adam.

"Maddy, do you think Angela should know who her real father is?" Adam was pale as he walked into the cottage.

Maddy ran to him and put her arms around his waist, resting her head on his chest. "Oh Adam, you are her father - you were the dad who sat with her, who loved her and gave her away at her wedding. You said he died. What good would come from opening that door? Especially now?"

Adam buried his face in her hair, feeling grounded in her arms, inhaling her scent. "Doesn't she have a right to know?"

"Maybe she already knows. Kaleed told me when he was trying to kill me at the hospital. How far would Yasmin have gone to hurt you?" Maddy asked, afraid to know the answer.

"I don't know. Everything was lost in the fire. Angela hasn't said anything." He tried to think where Yasmin might have kept important papers or personal effects. He shook his head. He would not let this dominate his thoughts.

"Let's go down to the river, the moon on the water is quite nice." Maddy took his hand, hoping to distract him.

As they sat by the water, watching the boats slowly move up and down the river, it occurred to Adam that he had lived in some part of England, on and off for sixty years and yet, he could not remember eating outdoors or enjoying good weather - he looked over at Maddy, waving at the boats, swinging her legs, exuding energy - he felt warm and realized she was the difference. Maddy made life better, in any country.

He reached over and pulled her close. "Are you happy here?" He asked, hoping she responded positively.

"I love it. Oh, Adam, who wouldn't be happy here? It's wonderful. I don't know how you did it, but you made it magical." She stopped. "Are you happy here?"

"Of course I am. It was a risk but you've reacted so enthusiastically to everything - more than I had hoped." He kissed the top of her head, tightening his embrace.

She pointed up to the stars. "It helped, you know." She had looked up to find Orion most nights, finding it soothing. "You probably thought it was silly."

Adam smiled. He had also looked to the night skies, thinking of Maddy.

"Would I sound spoiled and ungrateful if I asked for speakers in the garden?" Maddy asked wistfully. "I think soft music would make it heavenly. They make speakers that look like rocks - they have lights so they could light the pathway." She leaned away from him so she could see his reaction.

Adam was quiet for several minutes. Maddy squirmed, closing her eyes, wishing she hadn't spoken. The garden was wonderful and asking for one more thing seemed so ungracious. "I'm sorry…"

Adam turned to her. "Not at all. Why didn't I think of it when I was planning? Good thought. I'm just figuring out how much wire I need." He was lost in his calculations.

"Good collaboration. Hopefully next time we'll do the planning together."

Maddy stood and pulled him up from the seat. "Come on, I want to show you how appreciative I am of your efforts."

TAKE ME TO THE RIVER

Adam was digging a trench for the speaker wires when his phone rang. He wiped his brow and pulled the phone from his back pocket. The connection wasn't very good so he struggled to hear who was calling.

"Adam, it's Maddy. I don't want you to worry but I went down to the river to feed the ducks and a barge went by. I asked them if they were going to London and they stopped for me. The family live on the barge and they have a garden and I'm hitching a ride. I'll take the train home later. I hope you will help them with their water system."

Adam ran to the back of the cottage, along the pathway, looking out at the river. Could she really have stepped onto a barge with strangers? He sat on the stone wall and wondered what to say. "Where are you now?"

There was commotion and she laughed. "We seem to be rounding the bend to Westminster. You wouldn't believe how lovely this is. No tourists. I'll jump off at Millennium Bridge and visit with my friends at the Pub and then I'll head over to see Chance and Grace. Do you need anything in the city?"

"Maddy, I've ordered some security equipment. I'll collect you at the Coffee House. We can have dinner in the city if you like."

"Great. Oh look, I have to go. It looks like Florence is about to eat the flowers." There was more screeching noise.

"Florence? Who is Florence?"

"The goat. Oh oh, gotta go. Later. Bye." Maddy was gone.

Adam sat on the wall, leaning on his knees, wondering if Maddy realized how reckless it was to jump on a strange barge and head for the city. What if…

"Trouble in the Garden of Eden, Adam?" It was their neighbour Bernard. Adam looked up and almost laughed. The man was wearing full HAZMAT gear, his face shielded behind the beekeepers hat and veil, a fogger in his hand.

"Good morning, Bernard. I didn't know you had bees."

"Down to one hive - might have to split the hive now that your garden is here. Everything alright?"

"Maddy just called me. She went to feed the ducks and hopped on a barge for London. I'm to meet her there later today." He shook his head, wondering why he felt he had to tell his neighbour.

"Plucky girl, that Maddy. Good for her. I've always wanted to take a barge into London but I've never had the nerve. Look forward to hearing about it. You got yourself a little firecracker there." He chuckled. "Best get on with my queen. Ta Ra." Bernard disappeared around the hedge in a cloud of smoke.

Adam rubbed his forehead and smiled. His life had certainly changed - here he was digging in a garden, talking to a bee keeper, his love interest had just hopped on a barge with Florence, the goat. Life in Dubai, with the perpetual air conditioning, social rules, business suits and fine restaurants seemed light years away. Given the choice, he would stay in this garden, with Maddy, his little firecracker.

Late afternoon, Adam found Maddy sitting on the floor reading to Chance in the children's room at the Coffee House. Chance was falling asleep in her arms. He could imagine her reading to his grandchild, providing love and warmth to the child.

Dinner with Grace and Davi, at their home, was busy - the kitchen was chaos, Chance was energized after his nap, Davi was baking, Grace was singing with Maddy and everyone had a task. Adam was given orders to create an epic salad with a tray of produce. When they finally sat down to eat Adam could hardly stay awake. More wine, more laughter, more tears…it was, without a doubt, the craziest evening Adam had ever known.

As they walked out to the car, shouting goodbye, Maddy took Adam by the hand and ran towards the road. She put her finger to her lips and kept walking. They walked up a long drive, to the backyard of the house. The garden was overgrown, the wall of the house was glass, softly lit so the rooms were visible. There was limited furniture in the house; the dining table was covered in dishes; there was no art on the walls - it looked as though a party had just ended. The guest house in the garden was closed up - Maddy walked over to the deck and tried to open the sliding door. It was locked. She sat on the deck, her head in her hands, and sobbed. Adam sat beside her, not sure why they had come to this place. Suddenly Maddy stood up and wiped her eyes.

"This is Bellmere. This was my garden, our home. It was beautiful, really it was." She looked around, resting her head on his chest. "Not as lovely as the garden you created. Not by a long shot. Let's go. I want to go home. With you."

Adam looked around the unkept garden and tried to imagine how it might have looked. He kissed Maddy, placed his arm around her and started walking back down the long drive. They drove in silence, the happy mood of the evening dampened.

As they arrived at the cottage Maddy whispered, "You can't go back. You just can't go back. I'm sure I knew that…"

Adam agreed.

SAVE YOUR TEARS

The music wafted through the garden, as if an accompaniment to the birdsong. It was, as Maddy suggested, magical. Adam had fallen asleep on the sofa, reading. They had returned to the little cottage late in the day, had dinner in the garden and Adam had watched football on the television, while glancing back at a report on water systems he had written years ago. Maddy had mentioned the water on the barge had an odour and she asked if there was a way to help her new barge family friends with a system for clean drinking water. It seemed collecting rain water was not the best solution.

Maddy strolled out to the garden, watching the fly catchers at work, inhaling the scents of the various bushes and flower beds. She caught sight of a rogue weed and bent to pull it out by the roots.

"Maddy, I need to talk to you. Alone."

She stood quickly, her heart beating fast. She turned to see Oliver standing in the garden.

"Oliver, you gave me a start. What are you doing here? It's late. Come into the house. Can I offer you anything?" She kept talking, trying to calm herself.

"No. I just want to talk to you. Alone."

"Are you alright? Has something happened?" Maddy was concerned.

"I want to know what you see when you look at Adam." He was staring at her, his voice calm, eerily so.

"Oliver, what's this about?" Uneasy now.

"Just tell me. What do you see when you look at Adam?" He wasn't giving up.

Maddy sighed and thought for a moment. "I see a kind, generous, giving man who put his life on hold to raise a daughter, a beautiful daughter. I see a man who was forced to make drastic decisions for his own survival. I see a man who needs to be loved."

Oliver nodded, not in agreement, but in disappointment. "And you think you're the best person to love him?"

Maddy whispered. "If he lets me."

"Hmmm. So, what do you see when you look at me?"

"Please Oliver, let's go inside."

"No Maddy, what do you see when you look at me? I think I deserve to know."

Maddy took a deep breath, looked around the garden and hoped she wasn't doing the wrong thing by responding. "I see the handsome and confident young man who stole my heart, so many years ago. I also see a man who has spent his life hating his career, wanting to please others, wishing he was sailing in the America Cup. I see a man who is lost." She touched his cheek. "I see a man who has not been true to himself."

Adam had been listening to the voices in the garden, not wanting to interrupt or disturb the conversation. He sat up, ready to run out, should Oliver do something extreme.

Oliver was silent as he mulled over Maddy's words. No one had ever spoken to him with such thoughtfulness. He did hate his job - he saw the worst of humanity every day and he was charged with defending people he hated to the core. He did want to sail, he couldn't remember ever telling anyone he coveted that America Cup. He was never able to love anyone because he didn't love himself. He sat down on the small bench and held his head in his hands.

Maddy stood still, watching him, wanting to reach out and touch him, to let him know he mattered. She felt a tear slowly roll down her cheek.

Oliver raised his head and looked over at Maddy. His voice was soft, "How did you know?"

"You're my friend and I care about you." She moved to the bench and sat beside him. "When we were in Sicily you talked about the past and losses but you never talked about the challenges of your work. You seemed to have lost the passion for sailing, for competition. Oliver, it's not too late. You don't have to continue to defend the law, you don't need money, you need to live - for yourself. I'm not what you need, I'm not what you want. I'm just the only thing you can hold onto in the dream. Get out on the water, start sailing again, start competing, start owning your life." Maddy put her arm around his shoulders. "I want to be there when you hold up the America Cup. I'll be so proud of you."

"You know you are my *Dream Girl*."

"I'll always be your *Dream Girl*. The girl you wanted me to be. The dream will always be there and so will I. Go and find the love you need, the love you've denied yourself all these years. No one is going to judge you. Just be honest with yourself. Be happy."

Oliver stood and reached for Maddy's hand. "Are you happy?"

"Yes, very." She smiled at him.

"Good." He turned to go. "I'll let you know when you can take that photo." He closed the gate. "If he doesn't treat you right, if he ever hurts you, call me. I'll come right over and straighten him out." He laughed. "If I can't be your lover, I can surely be your big brother." He stopped for one last look, waved and walked into the darkness.

Maddy stood in the garden until she heard the car drive away. When she turned towards the cottage she saw Adam standing in the door. He held out his hand for her.

TRUST IN ME

The music in the garden seemed louder, somehow. Adam ended the call and gently placed his phone on the desk. He sat back and drummed his fingers on the file he had been reading. He rubbed his eyes and pushed away from the desk, ready to move forward with his plan.

He walked to the door and smiled as he watched Maddy dancing in the garden. He would have to be careful initiating his plan. No emotion. He could not afford emotion.

"Is dancing as effective as talking to the plants?" He asked Maddy as he wrapped his arms around her.

"No complaints so far. Have you come to dance or are you still working?"

"I must go into the city." He moved over to the bench. "Maddy, I have acquaintances who require living quarters for a short time - a few months. Would you consider letting out the flat? They would pay, of course."

"If they are friends of yours, just let them have it. Grace and Davi have lots of space if we need to stay overnight. The house is so big and they would love it if we visited more often. Wouldn't it be lovely to wake up and have Chase join us for breakfast?" Maddy was already staying over in her mind.

"The tenants are not friends, they just need a safe place to stay. Is there anything in the flat you cherish?"

"Well, they are just things but I would like to move the piano. Mr Simpson, who owned the bookstore, found it for me and I sold my stand up paddle board for the large chair in the dining room. The gallery said they would take the mural back - it's too big for the cottage and I'm sure someone would love to own it. That's about it."

"Are you able to meet me at the flat later this morning and remove any other personal effects?" Adam was sounding very officious.

"Sure. Should I leave some food and drinks in the kitchen for them? It's always nice to have something when you first arrive."

"No. Not necessary. Remove any alcohol as well." Adam was walking into the house. He turned, realizing he had been brusque. "I'm sorry. That was very thoughtful and considerate of you, but not necessary."

He saw the contrite look on her face and felt badly. He had not meant to be harsh, he was getting short on time. He would make it up to her, somehow.

As he drove off Maddy wondered what Adam might be involved in. She knew about his past and she thought, well maybe she hoped, the past was behind him. She wanted to believe he was happy here with her. She sighed and got ready to collect her things from the flat in London.

When Maddy arrived at the flat she was amazed to see the piano and the oversized dining chair she had bought Sebastian, were gone. Empty boxes had been left for her personal things.

The wine and liquor had been removed and the large mural which had once hung over the fireplace at Bellmere was gone - a framed print had been placed on the wall. She smiled as she recalled the day she and Sebastian had chosen the mural at a gallery - paparazzi had followed Dermot, then the U.S. Ambassador to London, forcing him to flee, leaving Maddy alone in the gallery, unable to leave without creating a scandal for Dermot. Sebastian had been in a meeting when Maddy called, yet he had rushed to the gallery to protect Maddy. Almost everything she touched as she walked through the flat reminded her of Sebastian, although they had never lived in the flat together.

She packed her things and carried the boxes out through the back door, to the garage, avoiding any queries from the neighbours. One last walk though, she told herself, just in case. Sebastian had never spent the night here with her - it was to be their honeymoon escape - a new beginning for their married life. She had no regrets leaving the flat and knew she would not return. Lambert could sell the flat - she didn't need another residence.

Maddy was just about to start the car when her phone rang. Adam asked her to meet him at Grace's house as soon as possible. She drove off, never looking back.

Chance and Davi were pleased to see Maddy when she arrived. Adam had not been to the house. They enjoyed a tea party with Chance and his stuffed animals, on the outdoor patio, waiting for Adam.

Several hours later Adam called from a number Maddy did not recognize. He apologized and asked if Maddy could meet him at the beach house. He would be there just after dark. He ended the call before Maddy could ask him any questions.

The drive to the beach was usually so enjoyable for Maddy - a soothing prelude to the sound of the waves. This evening she was angry as she drove, not knowing what was happening, why Adam was being so secretive. She hit the steering wheel with her hands, damning him for playing games with her.

It was dark when she walked into the beach house. She felt for the light switch and heard Adam's voice. "No lights."

She was shocked to see Adam in full traditional dress - a long white thobe and headdress.

"What's going on? Why are you…" Maddy started to ask.

Adam stopped her from speaking by raising his hand. He pulled her close and whispered, "I have to go away for a while. I'll be back, I promise. I can't tell you anything more - for your own safety. It's better if you don't know so you don't have to lie."

Maddy's eyes were tearing. She had so many questions. "Where will you go?"

"I don't know. I just have to leave. I have to disappear for awhile."

"Go to my boat. It's in Montenegro, in the harbour in Kotor. It's called *Destiny*. I'll give you the code. The harbourmaster is Victor, he'll look after you."

"I know the boat." He took a long look at Maddy, his eyes were boring through her, as if he was memorizing her face.

"What about your grandchild? Will you be back?" Maddy didn't want him to go.

"Of course. We'll go together. You must not worry." His voice had taken on a foreign accent. He turned to go, walking in the dark, towards the door. "Turn on the alarm."

"*Allah yohresak*." Maddy whispered to the shadow. She hoped she was saying it correctly. *May God protect you.*

Adam stopped. He turned and strode back to Maddy, placing his hands on her face. Maddy thought he was angry, his eyes were flashing. He kissed her with an urgency, his lips hard on hers, trying once again to put all the words he wanted to say to her in that one kiss. Then he was gone.

Maddy felt weak, her knees were shaking, her lips felt swollen, her mind numb.

She walked out to the deck, fell onto the lounge chair and curled up, wrapping her arms around her knees.

There were stars in the sky, the sliver of moon hanging over her, the sound of water lapping against the rocks was loud - the world was as it should be. Except Maddy was sitting alone, filled with trepidation, worrying over someone she thought she knew.

The sounds of a music riff woke her. She looked for her phone and for a moment wondered why she was asleep on the deck and not in her bed. She was stiff and felt damp. The sun would soon be up.

"Hello." She cleared her throat, wondering where her voice had gone. "Hello."

"Oh Maddy, you're alright. Oh my God. I've been terrified ever since I saw the news. Where are you? Tell me you're alright." Lambert's voice was frantic.

"I'm fine. I'm at the beach house. What's the matter? Are you alright?" Maddy stretched and stood.

"You haven't heard? The flat in Mayfair - it's gone. A bomb was thrown through the window last night and it's gone. I'm so glad to hear your voice."

"Was anyone hurt?" Maddy held onto the door frame, feeling faint.

"They haven't reported body counts yet. No one has taken responsibility - it's just breaking on the news. Again, I'm so pleased to hear your voice. Listen, go back to sleep, we'll talk later. I've already contacted the insurance firm. Don't worry, I'll take care of everything. Good night dear Maddy. Hell, it's just a building - thankfully you weren't there. Kisses."

Maddy walked into the beach house and sat on the bed, her mind whirring with questions. Surely the authorities would want to know why she had moved her things out - who had moved into the flat? Had they survived? How did Adam fit into this picture? Why did he have to leave? Where did he go? Why was he in traditional Middle East dress?

She fell back on the bed, craving sleep, hoping to wake up and find she had imagined the whole affair.

MY SWEET REFUGE

Christian drove to the cottage in Henley to speak with Maddy about the loss of her flat in London. He was concerned she might be distraught. She had asked several questions about the incendiary device used - she also asked him to research what type of device was used in the Michael Riley boat bombing. Christian knew she would not be pleased with his findings. She had returned to the cottage, feeling too far away from London at the beach house.

As he drove he mused about Adam Khan. The man was reputed to be ruthless and yet, when he was near Maddy he was most solicitous. He appeared to be totally in control, but in an intense manner. Adam had involved Christian in his latest venture and although he found the man unscrupulous, he had to admit he was capable and cunning - too cunning for Christian.

Christian sat in the car, looking over the stone wall at the little cottage, wondering how much he should reveal to Maddy, wondering how he could protect her from Adam and his world. He heard music and smiled. Maddy loved it here - the garden, the community, the solitude…he wished she was closer - he missed her. He braced himself and headed through the brilliant colours and scents of the garden, to the door.

Pleasantries were exchanged, drinks poured and finally they were seated on the back deck, overlooking the Thames. Christian reported on the damage to the flat, how the investigation was proceeding and then asked questions of his own. Maddy was confused when he said the insurance settlement would be huge for the damaged mural over the fireplace. She was sure it had been removed. She had been surprised to see the piano and oversized chair here in the cottage when she returned.

According to the reports, neighbours witnessed several men removing furniture early in the day; they saw no one else enter the flat until later in the evening when several people were dropped off in a white van. The neighbours believed the flat had been vandalized and the late arrivals had broken in, this was confirmed by the police report. The white van drove by slowly just after midnight, stopping only to toss several items through the front windows. No vehicle numbers were recalled. The explosion lit up the street shortly afterwards. The fire brigade contained the blaze to the one unit, although the smoke damage was extensive in the flat next door. There was no way to identify the bodies in the flat - the fire had been intensely hot and damaging.

Maddy closed her eyes and rubbed her forehead, hoping to erase any thoughts that Adam had been in the flat.

Christian stopped and waited for Maddy to digest the news. When she looked up, he knew she was ready to hear more.

The incendiary devices in both accidents - Michael Riley's boat and her flat - had been identical. No connection had been made, at this time, due to the time lapse. Christian had followed up, based on Maddy's hunch and his working relationship with Michael Riley and now Adam Khan. Somehow both men were connected in business and now it seemed, in death. Christian had spent a great deal of time looking for connections - he was not trained in forensics but he did find enough links and anomalies to construct a plausible scenario. If only he could speak with Adam…

Lambert and Sam, no longer teaching, no longer called The Professor, arrived for dinner and the mood lightened. The friends enjoyed a barbecue, drank too much, danced in the garden under the twinkle lights, sang along as Sam strummed his guitar. Later they moved into the cottage and Sam played the piano. Laughter and friendship filled the little cottage, blocking out everything and anything beyond the garden walls.

Maddy could hear voices in the garden when she opened her eyes and stretched. Her neighbours were having coffee with her friends in the garden - Christian was apologizing for any noise the night before but Bernard insisted he was thrilled to hear such raucous laughter. His only regret - he had not been invited.

David and Fred, dressed in cricket whites, invited the men to their match - they were playing another village on the Thames, not as quaint as Henley, but still, on the water. Marianne said she had never touched the hair of a man of colour, would Sam mind if she ran her hands through his hair? Maddy smiled as he laid his head in Marianne's lap. Lambert was holding court with Gillian and Chelsea, emoting his favourite stage monologues.

"I love it here." She hadn't realized she had spoken out loud.

THE TRACKS OF MY TEARS

"I need your help Maddy. You are the creative one and Sammy says whatever you suggest, he will deliver at Decades." Deirdre stirred her martini with her swizzle stick, contemplating eating the olive. "I will beg if need be."

"You don't have to beg. I know it's an important fundraiser. Does Sam know you call him Sammy?" Maddy smiled. "Any thoughts on what you want to do?"

"None. I just know the date and the goal. I leave it to you - you were brilliant last time." Deirdre looked around the room and sighed. "I never had the opportunity to say how much I appreciated all your hard work on my family fundraiser. It was spectacular and everyone talked about it for months. My parents were thrilled and the foundation is doing well. All because of you and your ideas. Can we do it again?"

Maddy closed her eyes, recalling the western theme and how Sebastian had walked away with Audrey, her best friend, breaking her heart and causing her to flee.

"Give me the details and I'll get back to you." Maddy needed time to separate the memories.

"Where's your dreamy Sheik these days?" Deirdre threw back her drink and motioned the waiter for another. "It's a shame he won't be asked to join the Club."

"Adam won't mind at all." Maddy had never spoken to Adam about joining the Club Sebastian had belonged to for years. She knew there was a sensitivity to his being of Arab descent, even though he believed he was British. It didn't seem important.

"What's your secret Maddy? You don't follow the rules of society, I've told you before you should lose some weight and you insist on carrying that awful bag - don't you have a designer handbag?" Deirdre was pointing to the colourful cloth bag Maddy had hung over the back of her seat.

Maddy regretted not having a wristwatch so she could fake a hurried goodbye.

"Seriously, Sebastian was crazy in love with you, despite having all of London society to choose from and then I heard Michael Riley had a thing for you, I mean really, Michael Riley - he had scores of young models but preferred to have lunch with you. I also heard you and the U.S. Ambassador had a thing going. The video of you and that uniformed Adonis was too much and then suddenly, there you are on the arm of Adam Khan, man of mystery, the man everyone wants to bed. How do you do it?" Deirdre was staring at Maddy. "I mean, I get it. I could fall for you, but not like that crazy friend of yours. Whatever happened to her? You know the one…" Deirdre waved her hand in the air.

"Audrey. She passed away." Maddy whispered, her eyes tearing. She had wondered, in her darkest moments, how she came to know such love with Sebastian and then a surreal friendship with Michael - how Audrey had turned on her and how Adam had appeared in her life with comfortable connections to her past, just when she was most vulnerable. Where was he now? Would she ever see him again? Her thoughts were interrupted by Deirdre.

"Sammy would leave me in a flash if he knew you needed him. Your banker friend is gaga about you and Lambert would slay anyone who said a word against you. Are you a witch?"

Maddy looked at Deirdre, gazed at her perfect raven hair, her diamond pendant, her red rimmed eyes, her expensive designer suit, her Bvlgari timepiece, her Céline bag, her manicure, the skin pulled tight over her boney structure - when she crossed her long legs the stiletto heels of her expensive shoes glistened. Yet for all her adornments she was lonely and continuously looking for a husband.

"Deirdre, you need to eat something. You don't look well. Maybe food will make you see things in a better light - make you a nicer person."

"You can never be too thin or too rich…don't you know?" Her words slurring. "I guess you don't. Stop eating those carbs, you'll thank me someday."

"I'm calling Sam to come for you. In the meantime, let's order something to eat. I'll help you if I can, but you need to eat."

Maddy felt sad as she looked over at the poor little rich girl who was still looking for love.

HE'S STILL A MYSTERY TO ME

London was ready to party, after a year of lockdown and *stay at home orders*. Sam reopened Decades, his nightclub, and invited his friends to join him celebrate the return to freedom, such as it was. He had sold the club but the new owners defaulted and here he was again, *Master of the Music Universe*.

Christian and Lambert were escorting Maddy and a few other friends to the event - recalling the good old days of dancing and drinking excessively. Sam had reserved a table for the group - joining them when he was able to relax.

Lambert grabbed Maddy's hand as a favourite song was played. It felt good to be back with her friends, dancing and pretending life was uncomplicated.

Above the dance floor, on the mezzanine, a tall, dark bearded man watched the group of friends as they danced, returned to the table for shooters and then back to dancing. He was only interested in one woman. She was surrounded by friends who took turns dancing with her. The bouncers were attentive whenever some poor unsuspecting fellow came to ask her to dance. The bearded man clenched his jaw, his nerves raw…it was time.

Maddy sat on the stool, hoping to catch her breath, lifting her hair off her neck, laughing at the antics of the group dancing. She felt cool hands on her neck, making it impossible for her to turn her head. She recognized the scent and was disoriented as a man whispered in her ear.

"Would you care to dance with me and let me take you home?" His voice was sultry.

"If you say yes, I will ensure you receive every pleasure a man can offer." He was kissing her neck with small pecks. "If you say no, after we dance, I will walk away and you'll never have to see me again." He continued to nuzzle her neck. She felt faint.

She barely had the strength to respond, every nerve in her body was electrified. "What's the third option? There should be three choices."

He continued to kiss her, lifting her hair from the back of her neck, his breath warm on her ears. "Of course. We dance, I give you a night of immeasurable pleasure and in the morning you can decide if I stay or go."

Maddy sighed, waited a moment and then lifted her shoulders, trying to move his hands. She turned her head and leaned back into him. "I'm going with the third option. I like the level of risk involved." She stood up and turned to look at him, her knees weak, her mind not prepared for what she saw.

Adam stared back at her, his dark eyes penetrating, his cheeks hollow, his skin tanned with a black beard covering his jaw and chin. He was wearing a crisp white shirt, unbuttoned at the collar, and black dress pants. Maddy checked to make sure he didn't have a gold chain on - he looked like a sun-kissed magazine idol. He had lost weight but the creases around his eyes and his straight nose clearly identified him.

Adam looked down at Maddy, her face flushed, her eyes shining, her lips parted as if she were going to speak - it was difficult to stand before her and not touch her. He was twitching with anticipation - he steeled himself not to reach out and pull her close, wanting nothing more than to cover her mouth with his.

Maddy was desperately trying to control her breathing. She wanted to reach out and hold him, to tell him she was pleased to see him, to tell him he had been missed. She also wanted to slap his face, tell him how angry she was not to have heard from him for months. As she debated whether she was angry or worried, Adam moved forward and in one motion swept her up in his arms and his lips connected with hers. Maddy felt her arms reach up for his shoulders and then his neck. She was floating, her feet off the ground.

When Adam released her he asked if she preferred to dance here or in the garden.

Maddy replied, shaken. "Here, for now. There, later." She flashed a lazy smile, her eyes closing.

"We better get started. Dancing, I mean. I have so many questions. Thankfully you are alright. I don't know if I am. Let's dance." Maddy started towards the dance floor.

A burly bouncer stepped forward and then continued on after Sam waved him away.

Christian and Sam exchanged glances. Adam was back. Both men wondered how Maddy would handle his return. Both men hoping she would proceed with caution - she didn't need any more drama in her life.

Adam hadn't told Maddy he had installed the security system in the country cottage so he could monitor how she was doing, from anywhere in the world. He had checked in with her daily, without her knowledge, justifying his actions as protective. He could not imagine how he would cope with not seeing her for months.

The garden had filled out and when the twinkle lights came on, it was magical. After several ballads Adam guided Maddy into the cottage and began his promise of pleasure by removing her clothing, and his - stroking and kissing her entire body, touching her with his hands and his tongue. When she cried out she couldn't take any more he lay back and waited for Maddy to take the lead.

The sun was nosily peeking across the horizon when they finally fell back onto the bed, side by side. Too exhausted to move.

Adam caught his breath and looked over at Maddy. "So does it look good for me staying?"

Maddy turned, her head on his chest, her leg over his hips. "It's not morning yet. Your option runs out in the morning."

Adam fell asleep holding Maddy in his arms, a smile on his face. For months he had dreamed about being here, with Maddy, planning for the future.

"You've had marathon sex. I can tell just by looking at you." Marianne, dressed like Norma Desmond in Sunset Blvd, was studying Maddy's face as they sat in the garden, enjoying a late morning coffee. "I hope it was with your Sheik." She reached over and touched Maddy's face. "I've got some salve for your face. Beards can be rough on the face."

Maddy sat back, wanting to laugh out loud, hoping Adam wasn't awake and hearing this conversation. He would be uncomfortable - Maddy certainly was.

As if on cue, Adam appeared at the cottage door, coffee in hand. He was clean shaven and although tanned, there was a difference in his skin tone. He touched his face, as if the beard was still there, bent over Maddy to kiss her and noticed the redness on her chin. He would have to apologize, when they were alone.

"Good morning Marianne. Where's Bernard this morning?" He tried to sound interested.

"He's with his bees. Listen, as much as I want to sit here with you and ask a myriad of questions, I can see you have some catching up to do. Adam,

Maddy's face is going to be tender for a few days. I'm sorry to have missed the beard. Ta Ra for now." Marianne floated out of the garden.

"Sorry about the beard. I should have shaved last night. Are you alright?" Adam sat beside Maddy, genuinely concerned, hoping she wasn't in pain.

"I'm fine. Thank you for shaving, although I must say, it was rather rakish." She touched his face. "I like this better."

He put his arm around her and pulled her close. "We have to talk. I owe you an explanation. Let's go in, shall we?"

TALK TO ME

Adam reached for Maddy's hand as they sat across from each other in the kitchen.

"There's so much to tell you. It goes back a few years." He looked around the room. "I am sorry about the London flat. Collateral damage." Adam dropped his head.

Maddy shrugged. "If you mean the apartment, it really didn't have any history or ambiance. It was just an address. Please tell me no one was killed there."

"No, it was set up to look as though there was a murder - mine. My DNA will be found, as planned. I left the gold bracelet I know you didn't like." He smiled. "Michael told me his wife, Francesca Bennett, gave him an expensive gold watch which you said was gaudy. He carried it in his pocket after that and left it on the boat the night before the explosion, knowing Francesca would identify his body when it was found."

Maddy bit her lip. "Oh dear, I should have been more gracious. But it was awfully big for his wrist and it was so bright it screamed Mafia. Sorry."

Adam smiled and continued. "I wore the *traditional thobe* so it could be identified in the fire, along with the bracelet. I left you in such a rush so I could arrive at the flat and set everything up. Lights were covered with moving figures, an Arabic radio station was on, there was a delivery of food so they could see me at the door. What they didn't see was me leaving by the parking area. I was on a helicopter to France before the explosion ever happened." He kneaded his temples, choosing his words.

"The boat was ideal. Thank you. I set sail early, wearing a cap, heading out into open water, no questions asked, no need to talk to anyone. When it was clear, I slipped back into the harbour and left the marina. She's a fine sailing vessel. There wasn't a moment I didn't wish you were with me." He looked away, surprised at the emotion he felt.

Maddy waited. "Why the elaborate plan, why did you have to go at all?"

Adam cleared his throat. He knew she had a right to know. "It's complicated."

"It always is. I thought we were sharing." She shook her head in frustration.

"Oh Maddy, you started this whole thing. You asked about the charity Francesca Bennett ran - your questions had a phenomenal effect on her. The charity was in the red and when you, or Sebastian Walker, on your bequest, stopped sending cheques, so did many of his acquaintances. Francesca Bennett was incensed. She could easily deal with Michael's mistresses - they took the money and disappeared, but you - you had more influence on Michael and his cronies." He smiled at Maddy.

"Michael and I had several business ventures which were doing well - Michael Riley was incapable of losing money. He was brilliant." Adam turned and stared at the garden through the window.

"Francesca was pressuring us to fund the charity. She knew we were making high risk investments and had the money. Michael heard about her plan to force him into investing - the destruction of the boat was meant to scare him, so he used the explosion for his own escape. The only other person he told was me. Francesca was shocked when it appeared he had died in the fire on the boat. She chased me down, insisting Michael had wanted our business ventures to fund her charity. When she found out I knew about the explosion she set out to destroy me. She couldn't know I had two passports, she only knew she had to be rid of Hassan-Rashad el Sharif. She didn't know Adam Khan." He stopped to refill his coffee cup.

The look on Maddy's face melted his heart. She looked so crestfallen - shouldering the blame for Michael's accident, for the explosion, for the series of events causing nothing but pain and destruction. He wanted to hold her, he wanted to see her smile again.

"Maddy, Francesca was evil - it was only a matter of time before she wanted Michael out of the picture. It was insensitive and wrong of me to suggest this was all of your doing. I'm sorry."

"Why are you talking about Francesca Bennett in the past tense?" Maddy asked, trying to make sense of the connection.

Adam hesitated before answering. "Ms Bennett has been arrested for fraud, embezzlement, larceny and murderous intent. I believe there are several other charges pending. She is ill and is not expected to survive the trials. Her father has passed away, having denied any knowledge of her wrongdoings. It appears the family was torn apart by the death of Michael Riley. Mr Bennett hired Michael Riley to marry his daughter and keep her out of the business. Francesca was struggling with her small corner of the empire, locked out of the day to day business. Bad blood, bad business, bad outcome."

"Are you safe?" Maddy looked up. "How can you be sure there won't be more attempts on your life?" Tears were welling in her eyes. "Am I just a part of the sting? Now that you've settled the mystery, where do I fit in? Am I expendable? I don't mean to sound churlish but what happens to me? To us? Is this over?" She stood, looking for an exit.

Adam saw the situation falling apart. He rushed around the counter to Maddy. "No, Maddy. No." He wrapped her in his arms, holding tighter as she squirmed, trying to get away.

"Maddy, please. I told you Michael refused to have us meet. Oliver mentioned you in conversation so I had a perfect opportunity to introduce myself. When I saw you at the theatre I felt I'd known you for a lifetime. When you turned to look at me, I knew I had to see you again. I was obsessed with your blue eyes and those dimples. I knew after that first dance that I had to have you in my life. Every minute I spend with you makes me want you more." He kissed her cheek, finding her lips, careful not to aggravate her chin.

"It's morning. Will I be staying to build a future with you or walking away, never looking back?" Adam hated to ask, not wanting to hear the wrong answer. He closed his eyes, wondering why Maddy wasn't responding. He felt a wave of panic as he realized Maddy might not want him. He had asked the question, perhaps prematurely. Maddy had asked him if she was part of the sting…surely she knew how he felt, how he had planned every detail of this cottage to please her, how he had changed his life to be with her, how he…he had to convince her.

Maddy waited for Adam to make eye contact. Her blue eyes searching for his. When he looked at her, he looked tormented, his brows furrowed. He was confused by her silence.

Suddenly he was drawn into her eyes, his face relaxing, a slow smile spreading across his face. He opened his mouth to tell Maddy how he felt but she touched his lips with her finger.

"Shhh." Maddy whispered, "Welcome home."

LIVING LA VIDA LOCA
♥ ♥ ♥

"Adam, are you asleep." Maddy whispered in his ear.

"Not anymore. Are you alright? What's the matter? It's the middle of the night." Adam sat up, alarmed.

"The fireflies are amazing. We have to go out on the lawn. Come on."

"Let me get dressed." He sat on the edge of the bed, his feet on the floor, not sure what a firefly was and why he was going out, leaving his warm bed.

"No. Don't get dressed. Come on. Take my hand."

Maddy almost dragged him out to the back garden. She had placed a small solar fountain on the lawn to attract birds and the area was lit up with fleeting sparks of light.

Adam realized his feet were wet on the damp grass but the moving lights were fascinating. He was also aware he was naked. They were naked on the grass, chasing after the glowing lights. Maddy had a jar in her hand and she was intent on capturing a light. He watched her in wonder. It was a beautiful sight - a naked woman chasing a light beam under the light of the crescent moon.

"Here you go." She handed him the jar. "I got you a firefly. It's your very own firefly. Isn't it wonderful? The males don't glow - the females light up to attract the males."

Adam laughed at her enthusiasm. He took the jar and saw the light flash. He had never seen anything like this. Maddy draped her arm around his shoulder, watching the light show before them.

"My father always woke me up to see the fireflies. It was our thing." Maddy reminisced.

"I hope he wasn't naked." Adam whispered as he embraced Maddy.

"No. My mother would have been shocked beyond words." Maddy laughed.

They stood in silence watching the dancing lights.

"Let's go in. Shall I set her free?" Adam asked as he opened the jar. He pulled Maddy closer and kissed her. "Come to bed and let me show you how thankful I am you shared this with me."

YOU CAN COUNT ON ME

♥ ♥ ♥

"Good morning Maddy, I have a meeting in London this afternoon. Would you like to travel with me into the city to see Grace at the Coffee Shop? We could have dinner before heading home." Adam asked as he leaned over to kiss her neck.

"Hmm. I have a commitment tonight." Maddy frowned. "I would love it if you would join me." She stood and wrapped her arms around him. "Really, it's important."

"Well, if it's important I couldn't possibly disappoint you. Shall I collect you from the Coffee Shop?" Adam could tell no further details were forthcoming. He would have to wait.

Grace and Chance were sitting with Maddy in the kitchen area, watching Davi prepare a special order when Adam arrived. They were laughing and Adam hated to disturb the happy scene.

Maddy jumped up and kissed his cheek. "Ready to go? Here's a chocolate croissant and cappuccino for the road. Later folks." She kissed Chance, waved and they were on their way to the surprise destination.

As Maddy parked the car Adam stared at the grey building across the street and wondered why they were in this part of the city. There was a queue of ragged-looking men on the sidewalk - Adam wondered if it was safe for Maddy to be here. The men waved at Maddy and she joked with several before heading into the building.

"Welcome to the Mission. Grab an apron. We have work to do before that lot gets fed." Maddy squeezed his hand and left him to greet the others in the kitchen.

Adam looked out at the long tables, mismatched plastic chairs, stacks of melmac dishes and hand crafted signs on the walls - bottles of water were being placed on the tables by young volunteers, all cheerful and animated. Maddy was in the kitchen peeling potatoes and laughing with the elderly crew. She motioned to him, introducing him to the volunteers, who all greeted him with such bonhomie he felt embarrassed by his first impressions of the building.

"We have a lot of hungry men to feed Adam, what would you like to do?" One of the volunteers asked patiently.

"Tell me what needs to be done." Adam removed his jacket and donned the full front apron tossed at him. The rubber apron felt heavy as it settled on his white shirt.

An hour later Adam had buttered several loaves of bread. He looked over at Maddy and smiled. She had peeled enough potatoes and carrots to fill the large cauldrons, now boiling away on the range. The kitchen was warm with heat but also camaraderie.

It seemed in no time the meal was ready, set out in long warming trays.

The doors were opened and a steady line of men shuffled in to gather a plate and make their way through the line. Maddy and Adam stood side by side serving the vegetables. Maddy was known by several of the regulars. Some asked after Henry, some offered condolences, many just touched her hand and nodded.

A disheveled man with ripped leather gloves advised that the soldiers were all painted and accounted for - battles ready to be fought. Maddy smiled and thanked him, wiping away a tear. It was only later Adam would hear about the toy soldiers on the corner table. The men had reenacted battles for Henry at that table, making history come alive for him. Maddy had brought the little figures in and the men had restored them. It was a touching story. Adam learned more about the men and their stories throughout the evening.

Adam chuckled as the men snuck extra biscuits into their pockets, motioning for Adam not to tell, winking at Maddy.

The clean up was efficient as all the volunteers knew instinctively what needed to be done. Adam was given the task of wiping down tables. He rolled up his sleeves and tried to stay dry, eventually giving in to the chaos and scrubbing without worry. His white shirt no longer crisp and clean.

The tired crew sat for a cup of tea, laughing in mock amusement that all the biscuits were gone. Adam asked where the produce came from, had they considered hiring a cook and service staff, did they need funding - carefully considering the responses. He who had never worried about where his next meal would come from could surely help. He would ask Maddy how best to make a difference. If funding was needed he could certainly help - it seemed important to Maddy - to all the volunteers.

Finally the group began to disperse, closing the kitchen, ensuring everything was tidy for the next day. Maddy hugged many of the volunteers as they walked out. Adam couldn't remember being so physically tired. For a moment he wondered if the car would still be where they had parked but he shrugged the thought off, concerned Maddy would be disappointed in him.

Maddy stood on the sidewalk, breathing in the night air, her face flushed, her eyes bright. "Thank you for being such a good sport Adam. We fed over a hundred souls tonight. Isn't that wonderful?"

Adam looked over at Maddy and tried to think of a word that would express how incredible it was that so many people in the city, in this area, depended on the Mission for food; how incredible it was to have such committed volunteers; how beautiful she looked in the moonlight; how impressed he was with her good heart; how happy he felt that she had shared the experience with him.

"Wonderful. Yes, truly wonderful."

HARVEST MOON

The summer passed quickly - Maddy and Adam were popular neighbours in Henley, hosting several garden parties; they were invited guests at weekly events in the community. Maddy was able to hire a gardener who loved the space as much as she did; Adam purchased a small boat for floating visits on the Thames, enjoying the water and the characters who lived and worked the waterway. Maddy insisted on motoring into the city to see friends, shop for something special or to have lunch near the Tate Modern. She loved arriving at Westminster and seeing the city unfold before her.

Adam had to admit it was fun to travel into the city with her, watching her interact with the other boats and barges, stopping to buy fresh fish or items he was sure they didn't need. She usually gave away the trinkets, cakes or teas she bought, but she had such fun doing it and the recipient of the gift was always so pleased, he played along.

The grapes at Villa Mirage were ready for harvesting in the next weeks so Maddy and Adam sadly said goodbye to their village neighbours and headed to Italy. Financial reviews with investors kept Maddy occupied for a few days, so Adam spent time in the vineyards with Philippe, inspecting his irrigation system installation.

Father Dom was aging but his delight at seeing Maddy seemed to give him new life. He was anxious to hear of her garden, her charitable ventures and her friends in London. He had yet to warm up to Adam, who refused a good cigar, although they were worthy opponents at chess.

Giselle and Maddy travelled to Milan to visit Sorento and see the new lines - Maddy was thrilled to see Sofi and her influence on the collection. Sofi had been apprehensive about Sorento but his daughter had realized her talent and had become a good friend and mentor. Maddy insisted Sofi return to Villa Mirage for a few days of rest after the show. Adam would be thrilled to see her and hear of her success.

Sorento was delighted with the reviews and the renewed interest in his name. He declared he could not love Maddy more than he already did.

Tending the grapes in the vineyards was soothing, albeit hard work. Twice Adam found Maddy sitting at the end of a row, her head in her hands, her head filled with memories of the past - arriving at the Villa, the Contessa, Sebastian, the storms, Giselle and Philippe marrying, the harvests, Dermot and Oliver…there were so many memories. The dog, Anza, lying quietly at her side, her large paws on Maddy's knee. It was a poignant picture, sad but lovely. Each time, as Adam advanced to comfort her, Father Dom suddenly appeared to sit beside her, with a hand on her shoulder.

Angela called to report on her expanding baby bump and her new waddle walk. Adam and Maddy laughed as Ahmed trained the computer screen on Angela walking. They were thankful for the many gifts Maddy had sent for the baby's room - knowing full well that Adam had no idea what they were.

"Maddy, the dressing table is perfect in the space. You have such wonderful taste - this baby will love that room. Dad, I know Maddy just signs your name, but we do appreciate your thoughtfulness." Angela cleared her throat.

"Maddy, please stop signing things Auntie Maddy, we have so many wanna-be Aunties here and we've finally chosen the godparents - everyone says you simply must have godparents." Angela looked at Ahmed.

Maddy's face had fallen and Adam was aware she was hurt by the comment. She was so connected to the expecting parents and baby - she had enjoyed her Auntie duties. He looked at the screen, a questioning look on his face, not sure how he could let Angela know how important the baby issue was for Maddy.

"Maddy, Dad, if it's okay, we want Maddy to be 'Grandma'. We don't know what's going on with you two, but Dad, you look happier than ever and I know that's because of Maddy. Is it okay if we call you Grandpa and Grandma? Don't be offended Maddy, please. You have been the most motherly woman in my life and whatever happens between you and my dad, I still want you, we still want you, in our lives." Angela looked anxiously into the screen. Ahmed beside her, nodding enthusiastically.

Maddy wiped a tear away. "I would love that, thank you. Are you okay with that Grandpa?" She looked over as Adam wrapped his arm around her, nodding. He mouthed "thank you" to his beaming daughter and son-in-law.

"Great news. You better be prepared for even more deliveries. We can't wait to see you both in December. Maddy, that's Grandma, has a calendar with the days marked - it's getting closer." Adam looked at Maddy, then at Angela and Ahmed, who were both smiling broadly at him from across the world and suddenly he was filled with such love and happiness he felt he might burst. He hugged Maddy closer and said his goodbyes.

When the call ended Maddy leaned on Adam's shoulder. He reached over, moving her hair off her forehead, kissing her softly, feeling thankful. They sat in silence, looking at a blank screen, joyous to be included in the future, together.

DON'T STOP BELIEVING

Father Dom coughed and averted Maddy's eyes as they sat around the table in the courtyard, enjoying a delicious feast at the end of the day. It was cool and Maddy was wrapped in a colourful scarf. She moved away from the table and returned with another pashmina, for Father Dom. He fussed but pulled it close.

Maddy had arranged for Father Dom to accompany her and Adam to Florence for lunch the next day, under the auspice of delivering wine to the restauranteur. She had also invited Octavio Feldi, a doctor she had met during the receptions at the Embassy. Octavio was a fine chess player so he and Dermot had spent many evenings drinking bourbon and challenging each other. Octavio was meeting Father Dom as a favour to Maddy - she had always slipped him a bottle of the best wine as he was leaving the Embassy - it was a simple request. Dr Feldi could not refuse.

Adam expressed his concerns over the set up as he knew Father Dom did not believe he had a health issue. Maddy convinced her luncheon guests they were tasting the wine, which Paolo, who was pleased to see Maddy again, professionally poured as they sat at the table. Father Dom coughed into his handkerchief, making Maddy cringe with worry. Octavio eventually introduced himself as *el doctore*, insisting Father Dom come to his surgery - his shortness of breath was not to be taken lightly.

After lunch, which was entertaining and noisy, Father Dom succumbed to the spirit of friendship, adding his own stories of Maddy's arrival at the Villa. He was grateful for the consultation, especially when Maddy announced they had errands to do for the afternoon, and would gladly wait for him.

As they strolled over the Ponte Vecchio, shopping bags filled with beautifully soft gloves for Angela and Ahmed, colourful pashminas, shoes for Adam, gelato in hand, Maddy took the call from Octavio. He reported Father Dom was in Stage IV of COPD. Maddy sat down, disheartened by the diagnosis. Octavio expressed his condolences, understanding how sad Maddy would be - Father Dom would have to tell them in his own words. The doctor offered to provide any comfort he could.

Maddy was repentant when she saw Father Dom approach - greeting him and asking for his forgiveness - she had not meant to trick him but she was worried about her friend. Adam watched, uncomfortable, as Father Dom fell into Maddy's arms, quietly sobbing, moving his lips in prayer.

The drive to the Villa was quiet, Maddy holding Father Dom's hand. Father Dom relating the extent of his malady. Adam was amazed at Maddy's strength - she was providing solace to the priest, even though Adam knew she was devastated. He smiled as the priest suggested he return to his diocese in Rome, for his final days - Maddy arguing that the village would prefer to look after him. In the end, Maddy challenged him to choose between a church that had left him in poor conditions, never visiting or recognizing his work and his flock; and the people who loved him, had given him a will to live and serve for all these years. Did his God want him to suffer for his entire life? Could he not endure the kindness of strangers as his last sacrifice for the Church? Maddy eventually wore him down, taking over as his hospice director.

Father Dom fell asleep, realizing he could not argue with Maddy. He had so little time - he would spend his last days with his parishioners.

The usual harvest festivities were replaced with a celebration of life for Father Dom, the much loved anchor in the village. True to her word, Maddy had arranged for a rotating schedule of care for Father Dom, ensuring he was fed and made comfortable in his last days. No replacement had been named for the little Church, despite the many calls Maddy made to the diocese.

Another priest had been commissioned from Florence to perform the Last Rights and Sunday Mass. Father Benedict was stern and business-like in his approach to the healing of souls. He fussed over the dust on his black shoes, refusing to don sandals. The village elders took over the task of recruiting, hoping to induce former villagers who had joined the Church.

Sitting down at long tables the village enjoyed a feast. The evening was sombre and yet, poignant, a wonderful tribute to Father Dom, a friend and confessor to all. There were happy stories and memories shared, laughter and tears. No one could imagine life without Father Dom.

NEED YOU NOW

♥ ♥ ♥

Arriving in New York City, Maddy and Adam were met at the airport by Ephrom Gold's chauffeur. They had several commitments before heading to Princeton. Maddy declared she had last minute shopping in the city - Adam couldn't imagine what else she hoped to find but her delight at finding matching nightshirts for the family was contagious.

They settled into the hotel and set out for a walk, following Maddy's suggested route to see the Christmas displays and visit a few key stops - a rare wine shop, a specialty chocolate shop and a mens haberdashery shop where Maddy insisted on purchasing monogrammed shirts for Adam. She also stopped at several galleries to greet artists she had befriended over the years.

Lunch and dinner were booked with friends both days. Maddy felt tension between Adam and former US Ambassador to London, Dermot Matthews, even when she pointed out they both knew Oliver.

On the way to dinner with Harold and Ephrom Gold, at an exclusive seafood restaurant, Maddy gave Adam the background on the family and her first meeting with the daughter Rachel. The Gold men were effusive in their welcome of Maddy, who thanked them graciously for assisting Angela and Ahmed with the purchase of a townhouse in Princeton. Ephrom offered Maddy the model suite next door to the townhouse as the development was sold out and would be removed after the holidays.

Adam left the table to take a call and walked towards the washrooms. He felt hands running down his back, under his jacket. When he turned he was shoved against the wall. Rachel Gold stood close, her hands unzipping his fly, her hands sliding down into his groin. Her rings scraping the skin as she rubbed against him. "I've never made love to a terrorist." She smiled lasciviously.

Adam grabbed her wrists, jerking them out of his trousers. He could easily have broken her wrists. Instead he pushed her away, disgusted and feeling dirty. He composed himself and walked back to the table, waiting for the evening to be over.

Adam was quiet and distracted as they prepared for bed. Maddy came out of the bathroom humming and brushing her hair. She stopped in front of Adam, who was sitting on the footstool, leaning forward on his knees, still dressed. Maddy kneeled in front of him, her hands on his thighs. He didn't respond.

"What's wrong Adam." She touched his cheek, concerned.

After a moment Adam looked at Maddy. "Why did you take me back?" His voice was cold.

Maddy leaned forward, watching his face. "Why did you come back?"

Adam smirked, acknowledging she had answered his question with a question. "I thought of you every minute I was away. I wanted to hear your voice, I wanted to feel your touch, lie beside you, be with you. More than anything."

Maddy waited, wondering where the conversation was going. "What's changed?" Her voice soft.

With a sudden motion Adam stood and paced the room. "Your friends are uncomfortable around me."

"Then they can't be my friends." She replied, defensively. She shrugged and stood, watching him continue to pace. "What happened? Why would you say that and what does it have to do with us?"

"Maddy, don't you see the way people react to us? Today I was called a terrorist and my motives were questioned…"

"Are you a terrorist?"

"Of course not." He responded, angry at the question.

"Then why do you care? I'm sorry if that hurt you or offended you. I wish I'd known. I would have straightened the person out…"

"I don't need you to fight my battles. I just think…"

"Stop thinking and tell me what happened. You'll burst if you keep this inside." Maddy walked over to him, putting her arms around him, she whispered, "I'm so sorry. I didn't know."

Adam realized he was punishing Maddy for his foolish reaction to the attacks. He wrapped his arms around her, feeling safe and cherished. He would tell her - but not tonight.

Adam slipped out of the bed, careful not to wake Maddy. He opened his laptop, inserted his cryptic key and pulled up a search - he felt comfortable in this role of digging up the past of enemies or those implicated in unsavoury dealings. He soon found the information he needed. He posted the photo with a few questions and sent it to a dirt digging reporter he knew would follow it up. Adam closed his laptop knowing the damage would never be traced back to him.

Rachel Gold would be forced to run and hide.

He would deal with Dermot Matthews later. He didn't need anyone telling him how he should treat Maddy.

Adam slipped into bed, reaching for Maddy who flung her arm across his chest. He fell asleep immediately.

BABY, IT'S COLD OUTSIDE

Rock stars had never been welcomed with more enthusiasm than Maddy and Adam as they arrived at Angela and Ahmed's townhouse. The group finally made it in the door and into the kitchen where Maddy deposited the bags of groceries she had insisted on bringing. She knew Angela did not enjoy cooking so she was prepared to produce a meal.

Adam and Ahmed retired to the living room, wine glasses in hand, leaving the women to turn groceries into a feast. Angela sat at the marble island, rubbing her large tummy. She complained about her swollen ankles and her sore back. Maddy rubbed her back, soothingly whispering it would soon be over. Maddy suggested she take a quick nap before dinner and smiled as Angela hugged her on her way out of the room.

Adam walked into the kitchen and watched Maddy dancing as she wiped her forehead, leaving a streak of flour across her face. He smiled as he realized she was alone, creating several dishes, the aromas drawing him in. He wrapped his arms around her, nuzzling her neck.

"What can I do?" He asked, genuinely concerned she was on her own.

"Almost done. You can set the table. How's Ahmed doing?"

"He seems scared but he's fine." Adam stopped and looked at Maddy. "I know how he feels. I was terrified. I got through it and he will too."

"Yes, that's true, but he's fortunate to have you to help him." Maddy kissed his cheek and turned to retrieve the casserole from the oven.

Angela and Ahmed repeatedly thanked Maddy for the lovely dinner - they weren't much good in the kitchen so they ate takeout most nights. Angela commented on how special it was to dine with Adam and Maddy - her father had never brought another woman into their home while she was growing up.

Ahmed cleared his throat and suggested that was because of Kaleed and his comments. He recalled the day Kaleed, their driver, had told the youngsters they might not be together anymore after Adam returned from London. He was looking for another wife and the new wife would not want Angela around so she would be sent to boarding school and Ahmed would have to return to his grandparents. Angela and Ahmed had run into the house, sobbing, grabbing Adam around his knees, begging him not to bring back a wife from London.

Adam had been angry at Kaleed and had painstakingly explained to the children that he had no intention of finding a wife. His promised them his duty, his mission, was to see them complete a fine education and settle into a good life, together, if that was what they wanted. And he had been true to his word - providing guidance, support and love for the only things that mattered in his life. At some point it was just too late to change his life.

There were tears as Angela confessed she had cried herself to sleep every night Adam had been away. She also earmarked that day as the day she began to hate Kaleed. He was intent on creating rifts or doubt about her father and it was Ahmed who had convinced her Adam had their best interests at heart.

Here they were, decades later, together. Angela and Ahmed reached out and took Adam and Maddy by the hand, completing their circle. Maddy was touched by the bond the three of them shared and how that simple gesture now included her.

Over coffee and cheesecake Maddy asked if the couple had considered hiring an *au pair* to help with the baby and the cooking. She knew of a young woman, someone she had watched grow up, who was unsure of whether she wanted to attend university in Canada or travel. She was an accomplished cook as she had prepared meals for her family - her mother had been Maddy's assistant at the ranch in Canada.

Angela and Ahmed looked relieved as they had no idea when they would have time to look for such a person. Maddy suggested they discuss the idea and she would contact the girl to see if this was an option. The couple agreed it would be a brilliant solution - they would await word from Maddy. Adam merely shook his head at her ingenuity - she always seemed to know someone who would be perfect for any situation.

After dinner Maddy and Adam walked over to their own townhouse, unpacked and fell onto the bed. They turned to look at each other and started laughing. Here they were, too tired to move. Day One and they were exhausted - what would become of them in a month?

"Maddy, where is your phone? Oliver is desperate to speak with you. He's booked a chalet at his ski club and he wants us to spend the weekend." Angela sat at the kitchen counter watching Maddy unpack the groceries.

"I'm not sure where my phone is. Are you feeling up to travelling north for the weekend?" Maddy looked over at the very pregnant woman.

"Ahmed and I agree we need a weekend of *feet up by the fire* before our lives change. Let's go, please. You can ski and we can just relax and catch up on our reading. Oliver said it was a lovely chalet with a great view of the ski hill. Please, can we all go together - it'll be a family vacation." Angela was pleading.

Maddy smiled and hoped Adam would be agreeable. He had been quiet and withdrawn the past few days. This would be good for him…he and Oliver needed some time together.

The drive north through the snow was slow and quiet as everyone other than Maddy slept for most of the trip. Maddy listened to several podcasts as she drove, enjoying the snowfall.

Oliver was standing on the large outdoor deck when they arrived. As everyone piled out of the car he greeted them with steaming hot chocolate mugs on a tray. The group met around the stone fireplace in the main room after settling into their assigned rooms. Angela looked Madonna-like, wrapped in a colourful blanket, feet up on the leather hassock, Ahmed so attentive to her every need.

Oliver had dinner underway, the smell of garlic filling the room. When the doorbell rang Oliver asked Maddy to see who would be calling at this hour.

Maddy smiled as she opened the door. Before her was the most beautiful man she had ever seen. She knew she was staring - she took in his chiseled features, his blond hair, his height - well over six feet, and his sparkling green eyes.

"Hello. I'm Maddy…"

"I know who you are. I'm Nathaniel. Nate. You are Oliver's *Dream Girl* and I am the boy next door who grew up adoring him. He's my *Dream Guy*. You were the one who gave him permission to follow his heart. I owe you. We owe you." Nate embraced Maddy.

"Well, come on in and meet everyone. I am delighted to know you Nate." Maddy linked arms and walked into the main room.

Oliver stood back as Maddy introduced Nate to the group, observing the reactions of each person. Angela and Ahmed were gracious; Adam seemed surprised and Maddy was as welcoming as he had hoped. Finally Nate came over to greet Oliver and they embraced. Maddy clapped her hands under her chin, delighted to see the two men together. She felt insanely happy seeing Oliver with Nate. They were an attractive couple.

"Dinner is ready. Come and sit at the table." Oliver invited the group to the dining area as he placed large bowls on the table. "Adam, can you handle the beverages?"

Nate was a refreshing addition to the group. He told the story of how difficult it was to live next door to Oliver, as a child, adoring him, wanting to warn him about the dangers of marrying his sister, who Oliver had divorced in no time, and how happy he was that they had finally connected. His sense of humour and his mannerisms had everyone in stitches.

Adam retired early and declined the offer to ski the next morning, reminding Maddy he was from Dubai, surrounded by desert. Maddy, Oliver and Nate were out on the slopes early - returning late in the afternoon, tired and exhilarated with the ideal snow conditions and a great day of skiing. Oliver had rented a karaoke machine for Angela and she was anxious to get dinner over with so they could try it out.

Maddy was aware that Adam was disengaged through dinner. He said he had a busy day on the computer, attending to business, his mind elsewhere. Although Maddy was physically tired she made a note to spend time with him tomorrow - she didn't want him to feel left out because he didn't ski.

The music had started and Angela was singing with Nate in the main room. Maddy followed Adam into their bedroom, closing the door softly.

"Adam, what's wrong? You seem angry and agitated. I've never seen you so upset with work." Maddy touched his shoulder.

He turned quickly, almost knocking her over. "Why are you doing this? What do you want from me? Is it the money? Are you trying to ruin this family? Tell me why Maddy." His words were like daggers.

"I don't know what you're talking about. What have I done?" Maddy was genuinely shocked by his outburst. "Adam, what have I done?"

"Your threats, your demands, the photos on your phone…what do you want from me? Why are you here, pretending to be so concerned about

Angela and the baby? If it's money you want just name your price and go. Go away and leave us alone." He spat the words out and threw her phone on the bed. "The old man saw this happening - I was a fool to defend you."

Maddy could feel tears on her cheek. She was speechless. She had no idea what he was talking about. She was so tired and now she was angry. Angry that he was accusing her of something - something she was not aware she had supposedly done. She turned to go, realizing he was not in the mood to discuss anything. She had to leave before more hurtful things were said.

She walked into the main room, eyes brimming with tears, unaware the music had stopped and the group was staring at her. She grabbed her coat and pulled on her boots, not sure where to go, only certain she had to get out.

As she walked into the cold night, the stars bright and the moon shining on the snow, for a moment she noticed the beauty of the sparkling snowflakes as they came loose from the trees. She felt an arm around her and looked up, her tears freezing on her cheeks, to see Oliver. The look of concern on his face made her sob. She fell into his chest with heaving sobs. Oliver held her and whispered everything was fine, he was there for her.

Oliver took Maddy to the local bar, a large neon sign advertising *Coors Light* illuminating the entrance. The bar smelled of beer and peanuts, the jukebox was playing Willie Nelson and the men sitting on the wooden stools at the bar were hunched over, watching hockey on the television above the bartenders head. No one glanced over as they entered the sanctuary of the locals.

Oliver ordered a gin and tonic and a beer and directed Maddy to a small table near the dart board. They stepped on peanut shells as they pulled out the chairs, sticky from the beer and grease of chicken wings.

"You bring me to the best places, dear Oliver." Maddy smiled, drying her eyes.

"Only the best for you, My Lady." He bowed and sat down beside her.

"Maddy, I don't know what just happened but let's sit here or dance or talk, whatever you want to do. Nate will take care of Angela and karaoke - he loves it almost as much as she does." He was trying to keep things light.

An older woman with bright lipstick and caked make-up, dressed in tight jeans and a ripped sweatshirt delivered their drinks and left a menu, announcing the kitchen closed in half an hour. Her gravely voice and raspy breathing reminded Maddy of Father Dom and for a moment she felt she might begin crying again. She took a deep breath and bit her lip.

"I don't know what happened but I've been such a fool. I don't know where to go now. I don't even know what I did. What's wrong with me? Is happiness this elusive for everyone? Sorry. I'm having a pity party right now when I should be happy - happy for you and Nate, happy for Angela and Ahmed, excited about Christmas…" she stopped and hung her head. Another Christmas ruined - it was too much.

Oliver absently peeled the label off his beer bottle, not sure what he could say; he hated that Adam had driven Maddy away, that he now had Nate, that it was too late to hold her and make her smile. He knew he didn't want Maddy to leave - he was afraid she would disappear from his life. He reached out and took her hand in his, a simple gesture of friendship.

Maddy squeezed his hand and smiled. "Can best friends dance?"

Oliver laughed and stood up, took her hand and lost himself in a slow waltz. Maddy in his arms, needing him - wasn't this what he had dreamed about for years?

"Can I borrow your car? You better get back - Nate will be worried. Thank you for being…for being the best thing in my life right now." She reached up to kiss his cheek. He handed her the keys and she was gone.

Oliver walked back to the chalet, his shoulders hunched, his hands in his pockets, his mood improving. He would talk to Nate about having Maddy stay with them for awhile.

He hoped Adam would leave in the morning. His words had been harsh and had been heard in the main room - there was no mistaking his accusatory tone. Oliver took a deep breath and walked into the chalet.

The fire was crackling and the room was warm and cozy. Nate was sitting alone in the main room, hunched over, his elbows on his knees. He stood up when he heard the door open, anxious to see Oliver and Maddy return.

"Everything alright? Where's Maddy?" He seemed unsure of what to do, looking around for Maddy. "Did Adam find you?"

"Maddy needs time. She'll be back in the morning. If everyone leaves tomorrow would you mind if we asked her to stay with us, just for a few days…"

Before he could finish his thought Nate was nodding in agreement, "Of course, she will need to be with friends."

"Thanks. What happened here after I left?" Oliver looked around the room.

"Whew, it was explosive. Angela tore into her father - it seems it was all a misunderstanding. Someone is trying to blackmail Adam and he thought it was Maddy because he saw some photos on her phone - which he shouldn't have taken anyway - but the story is something out of a bad movie." He sat down and motioned to Oliver to sit beside him.

"Apparently Adam goes missing for long periods of time. Angela received a call and some photos from someone who would not identify themselves. She couldn't find Adam so she called Maddy. Maddy came over from London on a private jet, some Texan she knows had a government contract and his jet was returning to New York, anyway, she came over to help Angela. There was some indication that Adam was not her father so Angela, working in a lab, needed something to test. Maddy brought a few items they could test and as it turns out, Adam is not the father. *Quel drama.*" Nate paused and rolled his eyes. He touched Oliver's hand and continued.

"It seems some seedy bodyguard was the father but somehow they blackmailed Adam into believing Angela was his daughter…anyway, it was Maddy who figured it all out. She was the one who convinced Angela that Adam had willingly taken on the task of fatherhood, to the detriment of his own needs…anyway, there was a lot of crying and a lot of hugging and recriminations. In the end, everyone agreed Adam needed to find Maddy and apologize. They really believed you would bring her back here." Nate took a deep breath.

"Whoa. Let's call it a day. We can't do anything more tonight. Everything will look better in the morning. I hope." Oliver fell asleep immediately, dreaming of Maddy wandering in the snow, trying to make a decision, not sure which door to choose.

PLEASE FORGIVE ME

♥ ♥ ♥

The morning sun threatened to melt the snow as icicles dripped from the eavestroughs and the roads became slushy. Maddy parked the car outside the chalet, noting the sedan was gone - that meant Angela, Ahmed and Adam had gone. She sighed, relieved.

As she walked into the chalet she collected her thoughts, wondering if she could stay with Oliver and Nate for another night. She also felt it was time to break free - start over - get away from anyone involved with Adam. She had considered flying to the boat, skiing with Dermot or taking the long flight to Paradise and a warm beach.

Maddy opened the door and was immediately charged by Angela.

"Oh Maddy, we've been sick with worry. It was all a misunderstanding. I've explained everything to father, to Adam - he is being blackmailed but I think he got to the bottom of it - we can all go about our lives without worry. I'm so sorry you were caught in the middle." Angela kept Maddy in a bearhug. "I'm so sorry."

Maddy's heart was pounding as she watched Adam walking towards her. She felt faint. She wanted to run. Maybe it was over for Angela and Adam but Maddy had not expected to be accused of extortion from someone she had lived with, slept with, shared with.

At that moment Nate opened the door and he and Oliver swept in with grocery bags.

"Adam, that car is a beauty. Ah Maddy, you're back. I hope you've decided to stay on with us. We got your favourite wine." Nate was speaking over his shoulder as he put the bags on the counter.

Angela stepped back and Maddy moved towards the door. "Thanks Nate. Lovely offer. I just need a lift to the train." Maddy turned to open the door. She wanted to be outside, in the fresh air. Suddenly there was a shriek and Angela bent over, water gushing onto the floor.

"I'm not due for another two weeks. What is happening?" Angela was starting to hyperventilate.

Maddy ran forward, to stop Angela from falling over. Ahmed was frozen in place.

"We need to get you to a hospital. Your baby wants out. Breathe. Breathe." Maddy grabbed the colourful blanket from the sofa, placing it around Angela's shoulders.

The men, looked at each other, frozen. "Oh my. It's time for baby." Oliver threw the keys to Adam, suggesting he drive. He calmly gave instructions to the hospital.

"Ahmed, why don't you help Angela into the car?" Maddy moved away.

"No, Maddy. Please. I need you to come with me. Please." Angela was gasping and pulling on Maddy's sleeve.

Maddy blinked, torn between wanting to help and wanting to go.

"I'm here Angela. Concentrate on your breathing. Don't worry, we're all here. Everything is going to be fine. Breathe. Breathe. Breathe." Maddy puffed out the words.

Angela and Ahmed were taken to the birthing room at the local hospital. Adam and Maddy handled the admitting paperwork and paced the hallway. They still had not spoken to each other. They were directed to the waiting room by a nurse.

Maddy gazed around the room, not wanting to make eye contact. The waiting room was painted a pale yellow. There were chips in the wall where the chrome chairs with naugahyde seats had been pushed back by those impatiently waiting for news of their loved ones. The tile floor was worn from the pacing. Maddy was concentrating on how paint and new chairs would brighten up the room. Anything to occupy her mind so she would not have to speak to Adam.

"Thank you for being here for Angela. Oliver and Nate have called me an ass. Angela is disappointed in me. I don't know what to say. I am so sorry for my words and thoughts. You have only been wonderful to me, and to Angela. I blew it. Will you ever be able to forgive me?" Adam wanted to hold Maddy but he held his ground, waiting for her to respond.

Maddy sighed. "Adam, you should be thinking about your grandchild. You have a daughter who needs you. Your life will change as soon as that baby is born - you get another chance. Make the most of it."

Adam shifted uneasily. "Maddy, I can't see a future without you. That's the only chance I need." He touched her arm. "I need you."

Maddy turned to Adam, her hands holding her face. "I thought we had a good life, a grand future, a chance at happy ever after. But you tossed me out, no questions, no explanation. What we had meant nothing to you." She hugged herself. "I am worth something. I'm a good person. I'm not the kind of person who would destroy your family or cause pain to those I care about. I'll start over, I'll be fine. You won't have to see me again." She shrugged and moved away from Adam.

"No, Maddy. Please, come back to me. Let me explain. The phone calls, the photos on your phone, the constant messages suggesting someone close to me, someone I trusted, was responsible…I felt betrayed. I was angry. I should have handled it differently. I should not have doubted you. I know that now. You are worth everything to me. Please forgive me."

The tension was broken by the arrival of the doctor. He pulled his mask off and smiled. "Mr and Mrs Kahn, would you like to meet your grandchild? I've never known a baby more anxious to be born. Congratulations."

Adam turned to Maddy and wrapped his arms around her, holding her close. He felt tears of joy welling up and instinctively kissed Maddy. She was also crying, happy to hear the news, confused by the kiss.

They followed the doctor, donning gowns and masks before entering the birthing room. Angela and Ahmed were joined in an embrace around the beautiful baby. Angela looked up, so proud of the bundle in her arms.

"Grandma and Grandpa, meet Adam Sharif Zaid. Isn't he beautiful?"

SOMETHING

It was easy to fall in love with baby Adam. He was a happy, healthy little bundle of joy and his parents were mesmerized by his every move. Maddy rocked and held the baby to allow his parents to sleep, shower or get out for a walk. Grandpa Adam looked forward to his afternoon siesta with Adam Junior, on the sofa, in the sunshine.

Returning to their Princeton home, settling in, receiving friends and colleagues who came to call with baby gifts, prepared food, wine and best wishes. Maddy hosted the visitors, ensuring there was coffee and cake for all. There was a festive feeling in their home.

"We need to let Angela and Ahmed establish their own routine, without us. Let's take a break. I think you need a break. You've taken care of everything." Adam took Maddy by the hand.

"Adam, I know you want me to forgive and forget and I probably will, someday. This is what comes from keeping secrets. This is what happens when you don't trust enough to ask a simple question rather than let things fester. How could you even begin to think I would be so malicious? You can't know me very well if you thought, even for a second, that I would do something that sinister."

Adam bowed his head. "I know I hurt you. I wasn't thinking. I was so engrossed in the blackmail, everyone was an enemy. First the calls, then I saw the photos on your phone. I felt betrayed. It was wrong. It was heinous of me. If I lose you because of my inability to believe in love I don't know what will become of me. I cannot lose the best thing to come into my life… do you understand that?" Adam reached for Maddy, hoping with all his heart she wouldn't turn away.

"I need to tell you things I've promised to tell you before. I do trust you. I love you." Adam led Maddy to the sofa. He pulled her towards him, lying back, holding Maddy in his arms.

Maddy listened to the story unfold, wavering between wanting to hold him and wishing she could punch him. He was an Intelligence Officer, trained for combat and reconnaissance work. His specialty was cyber/counter-espionage. His computer allowed him to track enemies of the state. His long absences were due to clandestine operations - some more unsavoury than others. He had seen and participated in operations that gave him nightmares and made it difficult to share emotion. He could not divulge for whom he worked.

He and Michael Riley were involved in a covert operation involving the Bennett family. Adam was amazed at Michael's skill with manipulating funds and his financial wizardry.

The Bennett family had reneged on a multi-million oil deal - compromising the Saudi government and the Sheik. They had amassed a large sum of money by using the deal to entice investors. The operation was to destroy the Bennett family. Michael was able to infiltrate the family by marrying Francesca, who had no interest in men. Mr Bennett enjoyed watching Michael make money for the family, not realizing he was moving funds out of the Bennett holdings.

When the charity came into question Francesca became more greedy, wanting more of the company and less of Michael. She planned to have Michael killed - leaving her a wealthy widow. Michael had to disappear, he had to let her be responsible for the ruin of the empire. The boat caper was simple - blow it up, leave personal items, including the watch and a sanitized phone for identification. The money was already in the Swiss account, the Saudi operation was over, it wouldn't take long for Francesca to bankrupt the remaining funds.

When Mr Bennett, the patriarch of the family business, was diagnosed with pancreatic cancer, it was believed he committed suicide, rather than suffer from the effects of the prescribed drugs. Francesca pointed a finger at the Saudi group - hoping to blackmail the Saudis. The ruse at the flat in London was part of the plan - she hired a disenfranchised Saudi to place evidence against the Saudis. Unfortunately the operation was handed to Adam - known to Francesca as Hassan-Rashad el Sharif. Once the evidence, or alleged evidence, had been placed, rather clumsily by design, Francesca hired a local thug to eliminate el Sharif. The hired killer had worked with Adam on prior assignments - he approached Adam for assistance. The plan was to blow up the flat - leaving no survivors. It worked as planned but Adam had to disappear until the dust settled.

Maddy's offer of the boat had been serendipitous - Adam was able to disappear without a trace. Hassan-Rashad el Sharif was dead, burned in the flat.

Adam leaned forward to kiss Maddy's neck. "I couldn't stop thinking about you on the boat - the pillow on the bunk smelled of you. Your clothes were on the boat - it was excruciating, being at sea, alone, thinking of you - wanting to hold you, to kiss you, to make love to you. It was the first time my patience was tested. I could hardly wait to get back to you." He whispered in her ear, "I dreamt about you everyday I was away."

Maddy wanted to lash out at Adam, tell him he couldn't wipe out the hurt of his words by simply saying he loved her. She must be a weak person to be pacified by his touch, to continue to accept his body against hers when he showed up after long absences…was he manipulating her or did he really care for her…Maddy was too tired to fight. She closed her eyes, feeling lightheaded, as he kissed her neck again,

Confused by her feelings, Maddy asked Adam to continue his story.

Adam told her of his dinners with Michael Riley - Michael would bring his latest mistress and a friend for Adam. The evening either ended after dinner or not. He never saw the same woman again but realized these women were willing participants in exchange for expensive perfume or designer handbags. Michael had spoken about his friend *Blue Eyes*, in reverent terms - he said she was the best gift and the most disappointing aspect of his life. He refused to let Adam meet his *Blue Eyes*, she was the one thing in his life he was not sharing. Adam wondered how this mysterious woman would have such a hold on his colleague. Michael Riley was not easily fooled. Adam had fallen in love with *Blue Eyes* long before he met her, wanting her in his life.

"You fell in love with me?" Maddy asked sleepily.

"Yes."

"But you didn't even know who I was?"

"That's right. It wasn't until that night in the restaurant when you said his name. That's when I knew."

"Say it."

"I love you." Adam had never been more sure of anything.

"Say it again." Maddy whispered.

"I love you Madison Davis-Walker. I love you Maddy. I love you *Blue Eyes*."

"Say it in Arabic."

"*'anā 'uhibbukah.*"

Adam moved beside her, holding her, facing her. He teased her lips and when she didn't resist, he kissed her. He kissed her with a tenderness that surprised them both.

"Please come back to me." Adam touched Maddy's face, studying her eyes before meeting her lips for a kiss that made him feel like the happiest man in the world.

Maddy lost herself in the kiss, blocking out the desire to run away. It just felt right.

I'M DREAMING OF A WHITE CHRISTMAS

The blue spruce Christmas tree arrived fully decorated, complete with sparkling lights. Nate and Oliver set up the tree, presented the turkey, unloaded the brightly decorated presents and then unwrapped their red scarfs and sat down, out of breath, eagerly taking the offered eggnog.

Angela came out of the bedroom carrying a squirming little elf, speechless at the beautiful tree. She handed Adam Jr to Oliver and hugged Nate. It was a joyous scene.

Oliver caught Maddy's eye and mouthed "everything okay?" Maddy nodded and smiled, grateful for the blessings surrounding her. It was going to be a wonderful Christmas, especially since the snow began to fall outside their window.

Adam was amazed at how casual the new parents were with the infant; remembering how frightened he had been when Angela was a baby. Maddy assured him things had changed; today new parents were more relaxed and shared the duties. She had kissed his cheek, reminding him he had done it alone and if the scene before him was any indication, he had done a great job.

Christmas Day began with a pyjama party - coffee, tea, croissants and opening presents around the tree. Oliver and Nate had purchased thoughtful gifts for all - including a sandbox full of toys for Adam Jr - they were leaving on a sailing trip in the new year and wanted to be sure the baby had a years supply of playthings.

The stockings Maddy hung were distributed, creating another round of laughter and appreciation. She had added little things as she found them and it seemed this was a definite tradition to be carried on for future holiday get-togethers.

Angela was touched by the heart shaped sea glass pendant - Maddy and Adam had found it on the beach. Adam had forgotten how Maddy clasped the glass and carefully wrapped it. He had to admit it looked stunning on Angela.

Ahmed was pleased with his golfing accessories - having just taken up the sport with his colleagues.

Oliver was thrilled with his original recording of September Morn, which Sam, the Professor, had secured from his recording friends. Nate laughed at the designer socks Maddy had chosen for him, expressing delight in the thoughtful themes she had chosen.

Maddy surprised Adam with a signed copy of her recently published book - *Life of Riley*. It was unexpected - he had not known she had published. He smiled when Maddy explained a girl had to have a few secrets. She had included several smaller gifts in his stocking but they had exchanged their gifts last night, wanting to have their own celebration. Maddy had been speechless when Adam had given her the little blue Tiffany's box as they lay in bed. The beautiful *Soleste* diamond setting featured a blue diamond in the centre.

"It was the only thing I could find that matched your eyes." He had proclaimed, clearly pleased at her reaction. He reached over and wiped the tears from her cheek.

"It's…absolutely…beautiful. I'm afraid to try it on."

"Wear it - it's insured." Adam sat up in the bed, kneeling in front of her. "I was hoping you would like it enough to settle for me. I want to grow old with you. I thought you might consider marrying me."

Maddy could hear her heart beating in her ears. She looked up at Adam, not sure what to do.

"Take a chance on me, Maddy. The blue diamond signifies faith and trust."

Maddy bit her lip. She wanted to run away but Adam was watching her, his hand holding hers. She had to respond. She thought about Sebastian and how their happiness had been destroyed - how many chances did one person get in a lifetime? Adam said her loved her - he had built the cottage for her. Her mind was racing. Why marry? Things were fine as they were.

"Adam, are you sure you want to take this leap? Do you really think we can make this work?" She looked into his eyes, trying to read past his dark secrets.

"'anā 'uhibbukah." He whispered. They fell asleep in each others arms.

Adam sat back and watched everyone enjoying their coffee, sampling the mini quiche and danish Maddy had prepared. He realized Maddy had not tried on the ring. He had carried the box out to the tree. Angela saw the box and picked it up, shaking it. "Who is this for?"

"It's for Maddy. I've asked…" Adam began but was not able to continue as he was body slammed by Angela.

"I'm so happy for you both. Tell us your plans. Oh my gosh. This is wonderful." Angela leapt over to Maddy.

Adam caught his breath and sat back, wishing he had kissed Maddy first; that she had been wearing the ring. He smiled as he realized this is what life would be like - assumptions, wishful thinking, happy family gatherings sprinkled with a smidgen of insecurity.

When the hugging and best wishes were completed, Oliver and Maddy retreated to the kitchen to start preparations for a late lunch. Turkey, with sage stuffing, mashed potatoes, candied yams, carrots with maple syrup, broccoli casserole, fresh rolls, rum sauce for the pudding…it was an ambitious menu.

"I don't want to interfere but we are going to be away for most of the year. Please don't rush into anything. I'm being selfish, but I want to be there. I also want you to know there's nothing wrong with delaying for a year and being truly sure of this decision. I just want you to be happy, to be content with whatever you decide to do." Oliver embraced Maddy. He still wasn't sure Adam was the right choice for Maddy - she deserved the best.

Adam walked into the kitchen as Oliver was delivering his friendly speech. He knew he had some convincing to do in this department - Oliver must know that Adam had waited for Maddy, had pined for her, had tried to protect her, that he did indeed love her.

A moment of awkward silence passed and Maddy laughed. "We haven't had a second to talk about plans but of course you'll be included." She looked over at Adam, nodding, encouraging him to agree with her.

Nate danced into the kitchen, oblivious, "Baby is hungry. Angela is feeding. What can I do to make this wonderful day keep going?" Oliver threw him an apron and the two men poured over the menu, nudging each other and exchanging smiles.

Maddy leaned against the counter, watching them together - they were perfect for each other. How wonderful they had finally found each other.

Adam pulled Maddy towards him and wrapped his arms around her, his lips softly connecting with hers. He wanted this kiss to convey how happy he felt, how much he loved her, how much she had changed his life. He suddenly realized he wanted to slip the ring on her finger and confirm their future. Would that simple gesture really make a difference? Why did he feel so insecure?

Maddy rested her head on his shoulder. Could this Christmas get any better? She smiled at Adam as she heard her name being called from the kitchen - what was to be done with the cranberries - it was urgent.

Christmas dinner was perfect - carols in the background, the table laden with food, rosy cheeks from the pre-dinner walk, wine poured, the fire crackling - a warm feeling of sharing with loved ones filled the air.

As the plates were cleared, as the platters were returned to the kitchen, everyone agreed it was the best meal ever and declared they had eaten too much. Dessert would have to wait. The groans of contentment made for more laughter.

The constant vibration of Adam's phone was becoming annoying. Finally he answered the call, moving away from the table. Although he had moved into the next room, it was impossible not to hear his raised voice. The group at the table stared at their glasses.

"You are a fool. Don't bother me again. I warn you, do not call me again. I am not returning for you - there will be no marriage. I will not be coerced into something so vile. Do you hear me?"

Adam appeared after a few moments - his tie loosened, his top button undone - Maddy had never seen him frazzled. He sat down and asked if he had missed the pudding.

IF YOU GO AWAY

"Maddy, I have to go away for awhile. I don't know how long I'll be gone." Adam was holding Maddy in his arms. There were so many things he could have said but he wanted to tell her before they made plans.

Maddy moved away from him and turned on her back. "Please don't go. It's New Years and something doesn't feel right about this. It can't be that you need the work or the money."

"It's never been about money Maddy. I have to do this. The old uncle is dying and there are issues that need to be resolved. I have to go."

"No you don't. You have a grandson who deserves to have a grandfather, your daughter needs you to be here, I need you to be here. I don't think I can handle losing another loved one."

"I'll be back before you know it."

"Please don't go. Something doesn't feel right about this. Please, if not for me, for Adam Jr." Maddy faced him and touched his face. "I have a bad feeling about that phone call."

"We'll talk about it later. Come here, I don't believe I told you how much I enjoyed Christmas. Everyone had a wonderful day. Thank you, my amazing Maddy."

Maddy fell asleep in his arms, exhausted from his passionate thank you.

Adam smiled as he stretched under the covers, reaching out for Maddy. Before she had fallen asleep in his arms she whispered "Gold Star" which, for some reason, made him tingle with delight. He turned slowly, realizing he was alone in the bed. He sat up quickly, calling her name.

He quickly showered and dressed, hurrying next door. He walked briskly into the foyer, hoping she was at the kitchen counter with Angela and Adam Jr.

"Good morning. Have you seen Maddy?" He asked his daughter as he kissed her cheek.

"No, not this morning. It's too early to lose anyone. We are going to miss you two when you decide to be alone. I can't believe how fast the time has flown by." Angela was speaking to Adam, concentrating on bouncing Jr on her lap. "I'm pleased you were able to straighten things out. It would be awful if Maddy wasn't part of our lives."

"Where can she be? She didn't say anything yesterday. It's a holiday, isn't it?"

"You know Maddy, she's probably arranging something stupendous and we'll all be so thrilled…you look worried. What's wrong?" Angela finally looked over at her father, who was pacing the kitchen floor.

"I hope this isn't because I said I had an assignment, one last assignment…"

"You didn't. How could you be so selfish? We've just had a wonderful month together and the best you can do is tell the woman you want to marry that you have to go away…really, Father, that's just so cruel, so unfeeling, so…"

Ahmed walked into the kitchen, reached for a mug and poured a coffee. He scratched his head and looked from father to daughter, they were both glaring at each other.

"What's up?" Ahmed asked, wishing he hadn't come into the kitchen.

"Maddy isn't here and my father wonders why, after he told her he had one more assignment to do. Can you imagine how insensitive that would be?" Angela looked over to Ahmed for support.

"Maddy went to the airport to collect the nanny. She was flying into Newark. They should be back soon." He looked at his wrist, realizing his watch was still in the bedroom. He headed to the shower, confused by the concern over Maddy.

Adam leaned on the counter, relieved. "I'd forgotten, I'm sorry." He looked tenderly at Angela preparing to feed the baby. "I'll give you some privacy."

"It's no big deal. Everyone here in America feels breastfeeding is a natural thing - no need to feel uncomfortable." Angela responded, sounded very worldly.

"Well, I am old fashioned so I will go into the other room and enjoy my coffee and newspaper. Carry on." They both laughed.

Oliver and Nate arrived with fresh croissants, still warm from the oven. "Nate's specialty. Maddy will love these." Oliver insisted, noticing Adam seemed preoccupied.

Adam stared at the fire. This past month had shown him what life could be like with Maddy, family and friends. He had lived with deception, pain, regret, subterfuge, fear and loneliness for so long - he had made himself believe he was living his best life.

He looked up at the anxious faces and realized a response was necessary.

"Thank you." He stood and wondered if he had said the right thing. Obviously they had heard his telephone conversation yesterday - he wasn't sure if he should explain. He did not want to break the news but he had been called back by the old uncle - he would have to go. It was not possible to refuse. He merely told his friends he had to go.

The door opened and Maddy walked in with a young woman. She smiled tentatively at the men looking so sombre and introduced Jennifer, the daughter of her friend from Canada. Jennifer would be staying with Angela and Ahmed and now Adam Jr, as their nanny or *au pair*. Jennifer had graduated with a basic degree in Science but had no plans, as she was unsure of her career path. She was taking a year off to consider her options. Student visas were difficult to obtain but Maddy had called Dermot in Washington and here she was…ready to meet the baby and live with this family.

Angela and Ahmed were delighted to hand the bawling Adam Jr over to Jennifer, who rocked him. She whispered sweet nothings and almost immediately the baby was laughing in her arms, gumming her sweater. It was an encouraging beginning.

While Angela and Maddy showed Jennifer her room, Ahmed asked if the croissants were for eating or display. The men laughed, still not sure how to interpret Adam's news.

Adam leaned forward on the fireplace hearth, watching the flames, collecting his thoughts, trying to sort through the assignment and possible outcomes. He must tell Maddy - she had been upset with him. Not knowing where she was for only a few hours had made him anxious - he understood how his long disappearances had worried her.

Maddy hoped she could sneak out of the condo and go back to bed. She yawned as she walked towards the door. It had been a long morning. Jennifer would be a fine fit for Angela and Ahmed. As Maddy reached the door she felt strong hands on her shoulders.

Adam stood in front of her, holding her against the wall.

He leaned into her, close enough to whisper. "Don't ever do that again." His dark eyes boring into Maddy.

"Don't do what, exactly?" Maddy asked defiantly, raising her chin.

"Don't leave me alone in our bed without letting me tell you how much I love you."

Maddy looked back at him, wondering how he could be so intense and yet, so insecure. She closed her eyes and smiled, too tired to continue. "Hmmm. I'll do my best." She sighed as Adam leaned forward and covered her mouth with his.

AULD LANG SYNE

Adam was assigned the task of collecting a parcel at the courier office and showing Jennifer where the closest shopping area was located. They were to shop for dinner and brunch - Jennifer offered to prepare the meals, just to be sure her new family would approve of her cooking.

"Did you really propose to Maddy on Christmas Day?" She asked Adam.

He looked over at the young girl and smiled. "I did and the best part is, I believe she agreed."

"I'm glad. She deserves to be happy. We missed her so much when she left for England. When she came home she was still Maddy but she was different somehow, happier, I think. Dag, her partner, was so needy and all of a sudden she had a nice life in London. We did like Sebastian, mainly because he adored Maddy. He looked at her the way you read about in novels. He was always touching her, you know, in a good way, his hand on her back or touching her elbow…it was really romantic. So sad how he was shot and on their wedding day, of all days. I hope you make her happy. She's a lovely person and she's always giving….I'm sorry, I'm talking too much." Jennifer laughed. "I guess I'm a bit nervous - it's all so new to me, being here."

"I think you'll get on fine. Angela and Ahmed work hard and they need someone they can rely on. Maddy says you are very reliable and caring." Adam wanted to pat her hand but smiled at her instead. "I will do my best to take care of Maddy - you get the rest of my family." They both laughed.

The parcel contained two packages - a lovely caftan for Angela and two identical gowns for Maddy - one in a peacock blue and the other a rich burgundy velvet for New Years Eve. Sofi had worked with Sorento in Italy to design a gown they hoped would be the first in their new line *Sofisticata*. If Maddy approved and found the gown comfortable, easy to move in, it would go into production for the next season.

The velvet was soft, with intricate detailing - the front was conservative but the back was daring - low and draped. Maddy looked forward to wearing it.

Against his better judgment, Adam had agreed to attend the University party - he had hoped to spend New Years alone with Maddy. He felt they needed some time away from the rest of the group.

Oliver in his Marine uniform and Nate in his Navy uniform, made a striking couple - handsome and debonair, Angela proclaimed. They offered cocktails as the group assembled in the living room. Adam pulled his shirt cuffs down and tweaked his tie as he walked into the room. Angela looked lovely in her caftan, her long braid falling over her shoulder while Ahmed looked uncomfortable in his tailored suit. Maddy was yet to appear. She had just taken a call from her friend in Texas - she would be here in a moment, Adam advised.

Maddy charged into the room, apologizing for her tardiness, flushed from the happy conversation with her friends, oblivious to the sudden quiet in the room. Everyone in the room had stopped speaking and turned to stare at her. Maddy had no idea her entrance had rendered everyone speechless.

"You look spectacular. That dress is lovely." Angela rushed forward, breaking the spell.

Nate and Oliver whistled their approval.

Adam blinked and walked slowly towards Maddy, bowed and kissed her hand. "Selfishly, I would prefer to stay right here with you all evening but that dress deserves a ballroom and to be seen. You are a vision." He leaned close, whispering in her ear, inhaling her scent.

Angela and Ahmed were delighted to be included in the invitation to the private function at The Nassau Club. The department head had personally invited their visitors as his guests - it was quite an honour, Angela assured Adam.

The banquet was formal, with speeches and toasts, exquisite food and California wine.

Adam watched Angela and Maddy dazzle the others at the table - they were so similar in their open, unaffected joy at learning about others. Ahmed was greeted by several of the university faculty members. It seemed the young couple had made a name for themselves at Princeton.

Finally the doors were opened to the dance hall. Angela had warned Adam he must stay until after the midnight countdown. He was not looking forward to the anticipated kissing and hugging of strangers. He wanted to herald the New Year with his family alone.

Maddy moved easily around the room, dancing with Oliver, Nate, Ahmed and several professors, as well as Adam. She returned to the table with minutes to spare before the countdown. She held a bottle of champagne in her hand. She leaned over and kissed Angela on the cheek, whispering in her ear. She kissed Ahmed on the cheek and then grabbed Adam by the hand, leading him out of the room. She had found a seating room upstairs where they could watch the fireworks alone, with their champagne.

They could hear the countdown shouts from downstairs, then suddenly it was midnight and the band played Auld Lang Syne. Adam held Maddy in his arms, kissing her, tasting the champagne. It was a perfect way to start the new year.

The merrymakers made their way back to the condo and agreed to have one last drink to celebrate the new year before retiring. There were many toasts to good health and happiness. Everyone thinking about what the new year held for them.

Oliver and Nate were leaving the next day. Angela and Ahmed were settled into their jobs and new home with Adam Jr. - Jennifer was a lovely addition to their family. Maddy was heading west to ski with Dermot and his friends before heading back to London. No one asked Adam what he planned and he offered nothing.

Angela held Ahmed's hand and thanked the group for joining them and making this the best holiday season ever. She proclaimed they were the best family and she hoped they would all come back next year. It was deemed a tradition. There was much hugging as the revellers said good night, looking forward to the year ahead.

BLUE TANGO

The Washington ballroom was a blur of colour and movement - couples dancing, whirling around the polished floor. The orchestra, dressed in white tuxedos, commanded the room. Colourful ballgowns swished by, in the arms of smartly dressed politicians, lobbyists, media moguls and influential patrons. Maddy stopped to watch the beautiful scene before her, realizing she had no hand to squeeze - no arm to grasp. She suddenly felt very lonely in a room filled with laughter and music.

As she slowly made her way through the crowd she felt a hand on her elbow.

"Do you tango?" A mellow voice asked.

"As a matter of fact, I do." Maddy replied as she turned to see the inquisitor.

"Excellent." The tall, thin man with light curly hair and hooded hazel eyes reached for her hand and guided her towards the dance floor.

They danced the tango, Maddy aware of his strong arms, letting him lead her. She hadn't danced the tango since her lessons in Argentina with Sebastian - it took concentration and her partner was very adept at his direction. It felt lovely.

"Thank you. Most enjoyable." He spoke in Spanish, Maddy guessed the accent was Barcelona.

"Why did you ask me to dance?" Maddy was curious, looking around the ballroom at the many options available to this stranger.

"I thought you were someone else." He responded, smiling sadly.

"Well I hope you find *'your someone else'*. Thank you." Maddy laughed.

At that moment an officious older man moved forward, his hand extended. "Delighted to have you join us Dr Cortez. I'd like to introduce you to the Chair of our Environmental Task Force, Wellington Daniels." He turned to a bearded, rotund man. "Perhaps we could talk at the bar."

Dr Cortez cocked his head, bowed towards Maddy and turned his attention to the men. In an instant they were lost in the crowd.

Maddy felt giddy. Maybe she had only imagined the dance with a handsome stranger.

"Here you are. We thought we'd lost you." Dermot and his wife Helen appeared at her side. "I told you it was a big deal. Let's find our seats."

When they arrived at the assigned table there were several others already seated. Maddy was introduced as a friend of Dermot, someone who had been invaluable to him at the Embassy in London. She felt the cool reception from the women around the table and realized her single status made her less desirable at this event.

Dermot's wife leaned over to Maddy and whispered, "Don't worry Maddy, they see you as a threat but only because they've been the threat themselves and most are on their second or third husbands. Shallow and undernourished." She patted Maddy's hand.

Maddy smiled, agreeing the women were quite thin. They were beautiful in a fragile *China doll* sort of way. They looked like they might break if touched. She took a deep breath and turned in her chair to watch the dance floor. She found herself looking for the tall stranger, Dr Cortez. Realizing how foolish she was being, she turned back to the table and began a conversation with the lobbyist to her left. He was happy to talk so Maddy nodded and sipped her champagne, asking the occasional question and continuing to nod.

Dermot touched Maddy on the shoulder and asked her to dance, rescuing her from the long winded energy critic, saving her from falling off her chair.

As they danced, Maddy thanked Dermot for assisting with the visa for Jennifer and for inviting her skiing. She had enjoyed the two weeks of skiing and aprés-ski - Dermot was a fanatical skier - first on the chair lift - last off the mountain. They had skied hard, partied hard and slept well. She would leave tomorrow and return to London, toned and sun kissed.

"How do you know Cortez?" Dermot asked as he led her around the dance floor.

"I don't. He just asked me to dance." Maddy responded.

"You look like his wife, Isabella. She died early on during the pandemic. He was crushed. It's good to see him out. He's very involved in the climate change movement - highly regarded in Washington as a tough negotiator and lobbyist. He has a reputation with the ladies, so look out."

"You seem to have a reputation with the ladies…should I be dancing with you?" Maddy looked up at Dermot, who was scanning the room, always on the lookout for an influential politician or lobbyist.

Dermot bristled. "You are my friend and you should always dance with me - as a matter of fact, if you want to stay in Washington I can take you to the top with me. What do you say?"

"Thank you, my dear Dermot. You have lofty plans and a wonderful wife who is rather influential. I need to tend to my garden and my charitable works. I haven't been back for months. Life awaits me in London." She sighed dramatically.

"I hope you get over that Adam guy - he rattles me. I think you need to meet an accountant or someone stable - someone who adores you, just like I do."

"Right now, I need to be alone to figure out who I am. I'll be watching you - you continue to be brilliant and I'll continue to root for you. You have the perfect mate - your wife Helen is such an asset. She's one in a million and she's yours. Stay out of trouble, my friend. You are destined for great things. I'm so fortunate to know you." She reached up and kissed his cheek. "Would you mind if I left now?"

"I hate it when you leave but I understand, somehow I do understand. Keep in touch. It's been wonderful to have you with us. I'll miss watching sports with you. You know you can come back here anytime. Give Anza a big doggie hug for me, will you." Dermot squeezed her hand.

Maddy walked through the crowd, towards the entrance. The month with Angela and Ahmed seemed ages ago - she had visited friends in Texas and then returned to ski with Dermot and his entourage in Colorado. She felt apprehensive about returning to London alone, yet she felt free somehow. She had forced herself to block out thoughts of Adam and whether she would ever see him again. She missed her friends but wasn't keen on having to explain why Adam was not with her. Life was getting too complicated.

"May I walk you to your hotel?" She felt a hand on her arm and for a moment she forgot where she was - she had been daydreaming. She shuddered and turned towards the voice.

Gabriel Cortez apologized for frightening her and waited for her response.

"I'm sorry, I was miles away. Don't leave the party. I'm fine. My hotel is just down the street. Thank you."

"I want to leave the party. I would like to get some fresh air and you offer me the perfect excuse. Please, let me get your coat."

Maddy and Gabriel walked in silence until they reached the hotel. Gabriel invited Maddy for a nightcap, claiming it would be unacceptable to let your tango partner vanish without reward. He looked relieved when after a moment of contemplation, Maddy agreed.

Over several drinks they found they had much in common - they were both widowed - they had both been wildly in love - they both enjoyed dancing - they agreed on favourite foods and places to visit - they liked to entertain with friends and they were both lonely. It seemed the only thing they could not agree upon was whether Barcelona or Real Madrid could beat Bayern München in football.

Gabriel commented on her laugh, how her eyes lit up and her dimples appeared - he confessed he never wanted to sit across from her at a negotiation session.

Maddy asked about his childhood, his work and how he was coping with his loss.

They were so deep in conversation the bartender was afraid to announce last call.

"I am a gentleman, so I will go, although I would prefer to stay. May I call you when I am next in London? I would like to show you my favourite parts of the city. I particularly enjoy the Portrait Gallery."

"I would like that Gabriel. Perhaps you would enjoy my favourite parts of London as well."

Gabriel held Maddy's hand in his as he said good night. He waited for the elevator door to close before leaving. Maddy wondered if she should have invited him up to her room - he was so easy to be with. She shook her head in disbelief - what was she thinking?

In her room, Maddy leaned against the door, slipped out of her shoes and tossed her wool cape on the chair. She pulled her arms out of the sleeves of the blue gown and let it fall to the floor. As she bent over to pick it up she felt the effects of the nightcaps and groaned. She hung the dress carefully and wandered over to the bed, humming softly.

She could hardly wait to fall into that bed and close her eyes.

She stretched, realizing she had sat for some time down in the bar. She placed her hands behind her neck to unclasp her necklace when she felt hands on hers. She stopped breathing; all she could hear was her heart pounding.

"Let me help you with that." A familiar voice whispered as the gold chain with the single diamond fell away. Next he removed the comb in her hair, letting her hair cascade onto her bare shoulders.

"I missed you." The voice whispered between kisses on her neck.

Maddy could feel the goosebumps forming on her body, her breathing was uneven, she was fighting the urge to moan, biting her lip to stop the sound from escaping. His breath was hot on her neck. He hadn't touched her anywhere else and yet she felt enveloped in his presence. She was frozen in place, not daring to turn around, afraid she might lose control, over what she had no idea.

When she felt she might faint he turned her to face him, wrapping his arms around her.

"I have to leave in an hour but I couldn't pass through Washington without seeing you. Let me hold you." He was still whispering, his lips brushing her cheek.

"Are you alright? Are you hungry? Do you need something to drink?" Maddy asked, reaching for his face. She shook her head, wondering why she would ask if he needed refreshments when they only had an hour to be together.

He laughed and then he kissed her, softly and then more passionately. His arms held her tight against his body. She could feel the soft wool of his turtleneck against her skin.

"I only need to hold you. It would be wonderful to make love to you but that wouldn't be fair to you. You would hate me in the morning. Let me lie with you until you fall asleep." He was still whispering.

Maddy looked up at him, her eyes adjusting to the darkness, and asked if he was safe.

He nodded and placed a finger gently over her lips. "No more questions. I'll be back soon."

As they moved to the bed he noticed a photo box on the nightstand. "Where did this come from?"

"Angela sent it. It's a nice reminder of Christmas and the baby and…." Maddy didn't finish the thought. The photos included a lovely group shot with the baby and a separate shot of Adam and Maddy, smiling at each other, looking insanely happy.

Wrapped in his arms Maddy closed her eyes, the anxiety and worries of the last month pushed away, letting sleep in, warm and comforting.

Maddy turned and was greeted by the warmth of bright sunshine through the large windows when the alarm sounded. She stretched and felt the bed to see if she was alone. Had she dreamed that he was here last night? She reached over to the nightstand for her phone, wondering if she had time to spare. Her hand touched the photo block. She grasped the block and brought it towards her - the photo of Adam Jr in his elf suit always made her smile.

She sat up and plumped the pillows behind her. She turned the block over and over - the photos were missing.

Maddy chuckled. She had not imagined his visit. She hugged her knees. He had the photos to remind him of what he left behind, he would be home soon.

IT'S A MAD WORLD

The departure lounge at Kennedy International was filling with anxious travellers, clutching their cloth face masks, waiting for boarding instructions. It had been some time since travellers had been able to fly commercially. People were careful about crowds, not wanting to sit too close, not wanting to repeat another lockdown. The commuter flight from Washington had been easy going - New York was ramped up.

Maddy felt her phone vibrate and then text messages starting binging. She had been thinking about the gardens, seeing Grace at the coffeeshop, visiting Villa Mirage and the beach house…she would have to plan her time wisely on her return. She looked at the phone messages crossing the screen.

DO NOT COME HOME (Grace)

Stay away if you can, not good time to arrive in LGW. (Christian)

Call me ASAP. Need to talk. (Lambert)

Enjoy New York. London can wait. (Sam)

CALL ME BEFORE YOU BOARD PLANE (Grace)

Maddy smiled and then wondered why her friends would not want her to return when she had been away for months, missing them. She called Grace, confused and a little hurt by the messages.

"Oh Maddy, so good to hear your voice. I've been trying to reach you for hours. You don't want to come back just now. The media people are keen to find you. It won't be pleasant, I'm afraid. It kills me to tell you to delay but you must." Grace was hyperventilating on the phone. "Christian agrees, he's so angry."

"Grace, slow down. What's happened? What's going on? I'm at the airport waiting to board my flight."

"Oh Maddy, that witch, Barbara Hartwood, published a photo of Adam and some Saudi Princess, announcing their upcoming marriage. She's calling the marriage a double-cross and wonders how you, who were the object of his affection lately, are handling the brushoff. It's awful. The papers are eager to hear your side of the story. Did you know he was engaged? I thought he was with you in New York. Oh Maddy, it's a mess."

Maddy slumped in her seat. Adam marrying. He had told her not to believe what she saw or heard. She wasn't sure what to do. Returning to London would be painful, especially if everyone thought she had been dumped. Well, hadn't she?

"Grace, thank you for letting me know. I'm not sure what to do right now. I'll let you know once I've looked at my options. Big hugs." Maddy looked down at her phone, disappointed. She sighed, knowing she should get up and check with the airline, sooner rather than later. She had seen Adam last night…

"Is New York so hard to leave?" Someone sat beside her.

Maddy looked over, absently smiling at the question. Gabriel Cortez was staring wistfully at her.

"Hello Gabriel. My plans seemed to have changed, this very moment. I'm not sure where to go." She laughed, realizing how silly her words sounded.

"Not a problem. I insist you come with us to Barcelona. Let's get you a seat. My assistant Bruno will arrange everything. Give me your ticket and passport. Come on, you can tell me about it later." He stood and reached for her hand. "If you don't hurry, your luggage will go without you."

Bruno arranged a seat in First Class beside Gabriel, who introduced Maddy to his entourage and ordered champagne cocktails. In the lounge, the various aides, press agent and publicist rushed off to use the work stations, leaving them alone at last.

"Now, why is it you cannot fly into London?" He asked, as though it was the most natural thing for someone to change their destination while at the airport.

"It's complicated. The press would be waiting for me to comment on something I'm not even aware of, yet. Perhaps it's spineless to divert but I do appreciate your capable handling of the situation. You acted without knowing why the change was necessary. That's commendable. Thank you." She raised her glass to him.

"I'm delighted I could help. Do you know Barcelona?"

"Yes, I do. Someday I'll let you see the video we made, welcoming the world to your amazing city. I can't wait to see the Sagrada Familia and the changes since my last visit." Suddenly Maddy felt overwhelmed with sadness. The happy memories were replaced by a fleeting picture of Sebastian laughing at her, outside the masterpiece structure in Barcelona.

She looked over at Gabriel. "Why are you helping me?"

"You looked so forlorn and vulnerable. Nothing like the confident woman who agreed to tango with me. How could I leave you there, knowing you were hurting?" It sounded so matter of fact when he said the words. "Selfishly, I want to know you better."

Maddy smiled. "Thank you. I don't know what else to say right now. Thank you."

Gabriel nodded and turned back to his papers. There would be time enough to talk, later.

Gabriel was a gracious host, ensuring Maddy was settled in the pool house, suggesting an afternoon outing the next day, leaving Maddy to her own devices. He was in demand around the world so his schedule had him conducting lectures and workshops around the clock.

During an outing to see the *Miro* collection, Maddy and Gabriel stopped for a coffee at a pleasant outdoor cafe. Maddy asked if Gabriel missed his wife. She was surprised by his response.

"My wife and I got along quite nicely. She thought my work was frivolous, she thought I would do better as a lawyer or doctor. We were polite to each other and each morning she would sit with me for breakfast, ask when I would be home so she could plan her day with her lover. They spent the days playing cards, drinking coffee, reading to each other and frequenting the best restaurants in Barcelona. Silliness. Do I miss her? I have my days. It was easy to leave parties early by saying my wife was not well. Did I love her?" He shrugged. "I guess I loved that she didn't bother me or make demands."

Maddy smiled. "Have you ever had someone read to you?" She challenged him. "It's quite lovely. I'll read to you and you can judge for yourself. Deal?" She held out her hand.

"Are you offering to be my lover?" He asked, amused.

"Not exactly." Maddy smiled. "But I think it will help you better understand the allure or the intimacy involved."

Later that afternoon they chose the large round chaise at the pool for the reading experiment. Maddy patted to her lap and Gabriel reluctantly laid his head on the cushion she offered. She asked if he preferred poetry or prose. He chose prose and as Maddy began reading he closed his eyes. Her voice was soft and she ran one hand through his curls, as his mother had done when he was a boy. He felt himself drifting into a deep sleep.

Gabriel woke himself with a start, embarrassed by his inattention. Maddy laughed as he scrambled to sit up, not knowing where to put his hands.

"That was very relaxing. Shall I read to you?" He took the book from her hand and waited for her to settle into his lap. He picked up the book she had been reading from and started to read, afraid he would be distracted by her hair falling across his leg. He felt his hand reach out and stroke her hair, it felt so natural, so soothing.

"Ahem. *Disculpe doctor.* You have a delegate from the Minister's office regarding the upcoming World Congress - would you like to meet him here or in your office?" The assistant was hesitant to disturb his boss as he never sat by the pool, relaxing this way. "My apologies for the interruption." He directed this to Maddy, bowing slightly.

Gabriel sighed and climbed out of the chaise, sorry to leave. As he walked away he turned back to Maddy. "You win. I understand now. Very powerful. Oh, I would like to continue reading that book - do you know the author?"

"I do. So do you."

Maddy sought out Irena, the young designer who had worked on her Barcelona gown; the dress Sebastian had wanted to buy for her, it seemed so long ago. Irena had seen an overwhelming interest in her design business when Maddy wore the gown to the Congress dinner, but after a season she returned to designing costumes for the theatre and opera. Irena told Maddy there were real divas in the entertainment world, she didn't have the nerves to deal with society ladies who acted like divas.

Irena had created several outfits for Maddy, with fabrics left over from the high society orders. Maddy was thrilled with the colours and textures offered. They walked along La Rambla, arm in arm, exchanging stories of their journeys to this point. Irena invited Maddy to a rehearsal at the Opera, insisting she come to dinner with her family.

Barcelona had always held a special place in Maddy's heart but sitting in the cafe across from the entrance to Gaudi's Sagrada Familia, a place of wonder, she felt very lonely. She recalled her last visit with Sebastian, sitting at this very table. She brushed a tear from her cheek and looked up as a shadow fell across her table. The sun created a halo around Gabriel, his curls lit up in the profile.

"I thought I might find you here. May I join you?"

"Please. I was just reminiscing. This is my favourite place to see the Sagrada. I never get tired of the view." Maddy smiled at him.

An elderly couple sitting across from them, stood and the woman approached the table. "I'm sorry to intrude. You make such a lovely couple, you must have beautiful children. I hope you will enjoy Barcelona." She smiled at them, knowingly and joined her escort.

Gabriel reached over and held Maddy's hand in his. He looked at the amused smile on her face and wondered what it would be like to have children with her. Would he be a good father? Was he too old? He cleared his throat and stood.

"Let's go in. I'll call my cousin, he loves to see me and he will love your enthusiasm."

They spent the afternoon touring the Basilica with Hector, an engaging historian. Between sharing family gossip with Gabriel, Hector recounted interesting anecdotes making each element come alive. Hector was a treasure.

Exhausted, Maddy and Gabriel left Hector, who was still buzzing with facts and excitement about the universal work of art. They laughed as they walked away, anxious for a quiet moment of reflection. They found a cafe and ordered *Cava*, a delightful sparkling wine, popular in Barcelona.

"I've been thinking about your question." Gabriel broke the silence. "It's quite a question - who would I call if the world was ending…"

Maddy watched him, amused that he would give the question any thought.

The buzz of his mobile phone shattered the moment. He looked agitated as he listened to the caller, rubbing his earlobe, gesturing emphatically when responding.

"My apologies. I must deal with an urgent matter. May I see you back to the house?"

"I'm fine. You go ahead. Thank you for a most enjoyable and memorable afternoon. I feel guilty taking so much of your time." Maddy smiled and raised her glass to him.

"It was my pleasure. Perhaps you would join me Friday? There is a performance at the Liceu I think you would enjoy. Dinner afterwards?" Gabriel Cortez could not believe how giddy he felt when Maddy accepted his invitation to the theatre and dinner.

Maddy slowly made her back to the house. It was time to check in with Giselle at the Villa Mirage and of course Grace would want to know she was enjoying Barcelona - the bookstore and coffee shop were doing well but would soon need attention. She checked in with Lambert, who said he missed her and she should come home. Christian asked if she was keen on another week of sailing - the boat was ready.

Angela called Maddy on a video call so she could see how fast Adam Jr was growing. Jennifer was invaluable - Angela and Ahmed wanted to adopt her. There was laughter and a few tears before they said good bye.

On Friday Gabriel arrived at the pool house and found Maddy on her knees looking under the bed. He knelt beside her offering his assistance. She laughed as their heads bumped and they turned to sit on the floor, rubbing their foreheads. Maddy crawled over to the chair, delighted to find her shoes. Gabriel sat on the floor and laughed - it felt so good to laugh at something so trivial. Here he was, on the floor, watching this woman crawl across the room, with no regard for the wonderfully chic gown she was wearing.

Irena had designed the gown with repurposed textiles and fabrics - the pieces were placed cleverly to resemble a Picasso-like work. Gabriel was captivated with the way Maddy moved in the gown - it fit like a glove. He found himself staring at her; wanting to move his hands along the curves of her body - to trace the artwork - to wrap her in his embrace. He felt like a geeky teenager on a first date with a popular girl.

The play was interesting and dinner was delightful - the conversation easy. Too soon the evening was over. As they walked back to the pool house Maddy mentioned how bright the stars were - she pointed out several constellations and asked what role the stars played in the climate change movement. Gabriel responded absently, they had no role.

Maddy sighed. "How sad that something so simple and beautiful has no relevance to the future."

Gabriel said good night and walked away pondering the statement. He paced back and forth in his office, his mind racing between the stars and this woman who made him want more - more time to enjoy the simple things around him. What had he been working towards? Was his life all about science and trying to convince the world to understand the danger ahead? Why hadn't he worked harder at having a personal life? Why had he accepted his wife and her lover? Just because it was easy? His mother would say he needed to be more interested in people, not just science. Maddy had told him to smile after his presentation, to encourage questions and give his scientific persona a human face. He had a few days before the Pacific Congress - he needed a break. Gabriel drove to the country home, maybe a few days with his family would soothe the ache in his heart.

After three days of watching Gabriel struggle, his mother ordered him to return to Barcelona and deal with the demons he was fighting. He was short tempered and edgy and not very good company. As he drove he considered his options - he knew exactly what he had to do. He had to find Maddy.

He walked with purpose to the pool house, rapping impatiently on the door. He was nervous but ready. To his amazement, Franco the pool boy slipped by him, pulling on his tee shirt. He had disturbed a lovers rendezvous. On the bed he saw his latest girlfriend, Jordana, scrambling to cover herself. She was tanned and her long dark hair spread across the pillows like a fan. She was beautiful but simple-minded. She had no idea what his work meant - she just enjoyed dressing up and accompanying him. The sex was pleasant enough. They didn't speak about art or current events or philosophy or travel, as he and Maddy had done, so easily, it seemed.

"Oh Gabriel, you've become so distant and your work is always so important. A girl needs attention. It was nothing. Just a bit of fun. He's young and willing to please - shall I call him back? Come here, let me welcome you into my arms." She pulled back the sheet, exposing her nakedness.

"Get out. Go home. Take the pool boy with you." Gabriel realized he was calm, in control, without regret. As he walked away, he turned, "Why are you in the pool house?"

"Your English friend left for the airport. She was looking for you, she said she wanted to leave a package. She seemed upset - she was worried about you. I assured her you were fine. I also told her we were to be married. She seemed surprised. I think I remember we talked about it once, didn't we? She said congratulations and then she was gone. You don't really want me to leave, do you?" Jordana pouted.

Gabriel walked away, looking for something to throw. Climate change was simple compared to dealing with women.

Maddy had left a primer on identifying stars and constellations - the template at the back of the book allowed you to place the heavens in perspective. Her note was short, thanking him for his hospitality, extending an invitation to let her reciprocate when he was next in London. She also left a copy of the book she had started reading to him. He smiled when he saw her photo on the back cover - *The Life of Riley* was written by Madison Davis.

WHAT DO YOU WANT FROM ME

♥ ♥ ♥

Returning to London was exhilarating for Maddy. She went immediately to the coffee shop to see Grace and Davi and read a story with little Chance. Her first sip of chai was heavenly. Within the hour Lambert and Christian appeared - eager to hear of her travels and provide their support.

Sitting at the dinner table with her friends Maddy realized how fortunate she was. These people had become so important to her - she dared not think of life without them. Not one word about Adam, not one question about where he might be or if he was to return. Thankfully, as Maddy had no idea. At some point she wondered if it was true absence makes the heart grow fonder…she certainly missed Sebastian.

Describing her time in Barcelona with a stranger, which by any account could be considered reckless, she saw looks of understanding from those around her. Grace was first to comment.

"If anyone else told me that story I would question their sanity but hearing it from you, it sounds so reasonable. I think I'd like to meet your Gabriel Cortez."

"I've heard him speak at several functions - is he really as intense as they say?" asked Christian.

"He works continuously, all hours of the day. He has researchers and advocates around the world. It wasn't unusual to hear him speaking with Tokyo, then Switzerland, then Australia in the same day. He seems sincere - hopefully he has deputies ready to take over because no one can maintain the pace he works at for very long." Maddy responded thoughtfully. She hoped they would meet again, mainly so she could explain her sudden departure.

"When are you heading up to Henley?" Lambert asked the question but everyone wanted to hear the response.

"I guess tomorrow I'll drive up and see how it fared over the winter. Anyone want to come with me? No. No. I'm fine on my own, I know you're all worried about me. I really am fine." Maddy sighed. "Let me get settled and we'll have dinner together in a few days. Fair enough?"

Everyone agreed. They were supportive and yet they felt she needed some time to sort things out. They planned on dinner for Thursday.

Maddy sat in the car, staring at the cottage. The gardens were ready for spring, the cottage looked cared for. The drive was familiar and suddenly Maddy wanted to be inside, alone, at home.

The simple act of opening the door gave Maddy a sense of comfort. She walked from room to room, taking in the familiar feeling. The cottage felt warm and welcoming, the air was fresh and clean, the kitchen was stocked and the back door was open…had someone been living in the cottage, she wondered. Had her friends prepared for her arrival?

She turned as she heard footsteps, her heart pounding, her comfort giving way to caution.

"Welcome home. I've been waiting for you. I didn't know it was possible to miss someone so very, very much." His voice so soft, so soothing, yet so foreign.

Before she could react Adam stepped forward and wrapped her in his arms. His kisses were warm against her cheek, her eyes, her lips. His arms pressed her close, their bodies melding. Maddy couldn't breathe, her mind had gone blank, her lips betrayed her, responding to his kisses.

"Let me look at you." Adam moved back, releasing her. He gently tucked her hair behind her ear, his fingers tracing her dimples, stopping at her cleft chin, his eyes never leaving her face. "Shall we have chai or a glass of wine?"

"When did you get back?" Maddy cleared her throat and tried to collect her thoughts - her mind was reeling. Should she be angry or should she be thankful he was alright…it was difficult to know.

"Are you a Prince now? Where is your wife, the love of your life? How long are you staying? Have you been in touch with Angela? Adam Jr is growing so fast. Talk to me. Please." Maddy perched on the stool at the kitchen counter.

Adam prepared the chai and joined her. "First of all, you are the love of my life. I am not married and I have been in touch with Angela. I asked her not to warn you I was back. Second. My work is done. I will no longer be needed. I have some custom work, all easily handled from a computer anywhere in the world." He reached for her hand. "What is this about a Prince?"

"The announcement of your marriage to the Princess is the reason I didn't come home from Washington. My friends advised me to stay away until the media circus was over. Barbara Hartwood published a photo of you draped over a bejewelled woman - her headline suggested you had moved up to royalty after unceremoniously dumping me. You were, of course, not available for comment, so the wolves were at the door for a story." Maddy looked up to see surprise in Adam's eyes.

"Maddy, my love, I told you not to believe anything you heard. Before the old uncle passed on to the next life he had several old feuds to settle. His business rival and nemesis for many years had a daughter who wanted to leave her secluded life. By escorting her to a few parties, feigning interest, we were able to anger her father beyond reason - as a result we closed several outstanding deals. Her father wanted me to go away - I would only corrupt her with my western way of thinking. Once the deals were done Dahlia and I agreed we hated each other - she thought I was distant and cold; I thought she was shallow and spoiled. There was no intimacy or even respect, believe me. Dahlia will soon be married to an older, wealthier and less worldly *captain of industry* who needs another wife. She will spend his money and flourish knowing she is driving him crazy." Adam stroked his forehead, as if he had a headache.

"I am so sorry you were involved in the matter. I had no idea the news would reach London - it was so local in Dubai, hardly worth mentioning. If you have suffered from the ruse, I am truly sorry. Please understand your safety and wellbeing were, and are, always foremost in my actions."

Maddy watched him, wanting to believe him. Wondering what he would think of her escape to Barcelona, she stood, wanting nothing more than to take a bath and go to bed - alone. She hoped she wouldn't have to explain how very much she enjoyed the side trip to Barcelona and the time with Gabriel Cortez.

"I'm glad you're safe. Angela must be relieved." She smiled at him. "How was it you were in my room in Washington?"

"I had reason to be in America, just for a few days. I was basically a courier for several of the transactions. Not everything can be handled over the internet. I wanted to be sure you were safe and not associated with me in any way. Again, I'm sorry if you were frightened by my nefarious behaviour. It was impossible to be so close to you and not see you. I had hoped you would return to your room earlier."

Maddy felt guilty for a moment, knowing she had been in the lobby bar with Gabriel that night. How could she have known Adam was waiting? She smiled, more to herself than for him. "It was kinda sexy, in a weird kinda way."

Adam took her hand and pulled her close. "You must be tired. Take a bath and come to bed. As much as I want you, and I do want you, I am content to watch you sleep, knowing you are home safe."

Life always seems simpler after a hot bath. Maddy padded into the bedroom and slipped under the covers. Adam slowly put his book down and turned off the bedside lamp.

"Adam, what do you want from me?" Maddy whispered.

"I want you to love me as I love you. I want to make you wildly happy. I want to be your *happy ever after*. Do you think that's possible?"

"Hmmm. I think I need a refresher…"

HAVE I TOLD YOU LATELY

The long folding table was set with platters of food, fresh bread and wine - the music was soft, the chatter loud, the lights low. Adam poured the wine as Maddy looked around the room, adding final touches, before inviting everyone to the table.

The cottage was filled with the sound of friends, toasting the return of Maddy and Adam. The neighbours were pleased to have Maddy back in their fold, although they had seen Adam a few times during the last month. He had thwarted the developers plans for the village, defending the status quo as Maddy loved the area as it was. The villagers had no idea what backroom deals or tactics had been used.

Grace was careful not to mention the time in Barcelona but there were many questions about Dermot and the time in Washington, the ski trip and the visit to Texas.

"Maddy, is it the man or this cottage you love?" Grace asked Maddy as they prepared a tray in the kitchen.

"Hmm, that's quite a question. The cottage is wonderful and I do love it here but it's just a place. The man is complicated, but so am I. I guess that makes us a good match." Maddy looked out at the group, laughing and enjoying the garden. She smiled and touched Grace on the arm. "Give it time."

Grace nodded and returned to the food trays. She worried about Maddy. She just wanted to her to be happy.

Adam was quiet during dinner. He understood the group felt he had abandoned Maddy. He also noticed she did not announce that he had proposed. Maddy had not worn the ring or spoken about marriage since arriving at the cottage. He was reluctant to address the subject, realizing she may be having doubts. His long absences required patience and trust - he had asked her to trust him and she had, but the time lost created a gap - how would they get back to where they had been? He hoped the effort was worth it for Maddy. He had missed her so.

Maddy touched his hand, interrupting his thoughts. He looked over at her, her face flushed from the preparations and the wine. She was enjoying having her friends around her; enjoying the warmth in the room. She smiled at him, a tender, loving smile and he knew - she was the one for him. He kissed her hand and whispered he loved her. He would ask her to marry him again, tonight.

DREAM BELIEVER
♥ ♥ ♥

Christian was speaking at the Sustainable Earth Exposition in Paris. He invited Maddy to accompany him as she had met several of the other panelists and speakers with Sebastian. Christian also depended on her review of his talks or speeches - she seemed to anticipate questions she thought others might ask so he could be prepared. Adam had not been invited, although Maddy suggested he might like to join her. He decided to arrive after the Exposition.

The Paris reception room was filling, not as crowded as it had been in years past, but busy enough for those uncomfortable with large groups. Some were still wearing masks and declining any hors d'oeuvres passed on a tray.

Maddy and Christian were involved in a conversation with a group of panelists who had presented that afternoon. Maddy suggested they might have taken more time to explain the process rather than cutting short the questions. She also expressed concern about the omission of carbon taxes - why not address this issue, she asked. The conversation began in a defensive attack - Maddy passively listening, not reacting, letting them run out of steam. When they realized she was not fighting them they stopped and let her speak. She had several points to make, ticking them off on her fingers. When she was done the group applauded her understanding of the issue and asked if they could use her points for the next presentation.

Maddy nodded in agreement and Christian shook his head. The presentation would definitely be more accepted and adopted if they chose to address Maddy's points. They high-fived Maddy and laughter exploded from the gathering.

At the entrance, the conference organizer, Jeanne Doran, stood with her prized guest speaker on her arm, studied the room for an appropriate group to introduce or present her Ace. He had just arrived and was trying to escape to his room. As the laughter and high fives filled the room they both turned towards the group. Jeanne recognized the panelists and sighed - she could do better with another group of delegates.

Maddy moved her head, blushing at the compliment and did a double take. She recognized the man at the entrance. He looked miserable, as if he wanted to escape. His reaction was immediate, he removed himself from Jeanne, mumbling an apology and started towards the crowd. He would walk a mile for that smile, it started with her mouth and then lit up her face, her eyes sparkling.

Maddy was clearly pleased to see him. She noted his tired eyes and the uncontrollable curls around his collar. He was walking towards her, craning his neck around anyone who passed in front of him, obscuring his view of her.

They came together near the bar. He held out his hands and she was pleased to place hers in his. He had watched her move towards him; her head cocked, her smile unmistakeable, her dress moving slowly against her purposeful stride - he was holding his breath.

They said each others name at the same time. Laughing at their awkwardness, holding hands. Gabriel made the first move, leaning in to kiss her cheek. He whispered, "I know now. I would call you."

Christian was delighted to meet Gabriel and suggested they dine together, just the three of them. He wanted to thank Gabriel for taking care of Maddy so gallantly.

Gabriel looked over at Maddy, who seemed even more alive than he had dreamed. He admired her confidence and her way of speaking her mind without hurting or demoralizing. He wondered if Christian had been the man who abandoned her.

Once it was made clear in the introductions that Christian was a good friend, a sailor and a banker, Gabriel relaxed and enjoyed his evening.

Christian was to present after Gabriel spoke - he confessed Maddy would probably listen without bias and suggest changes to his delivery. Gabriel nodded, he had notes from Maddy as well. He asked if Christian and Maddy would like to meet before breakfast to review content on both addresses. It was a magnanimous gesture, and when Maddy touched his hand to say so, he felt undeniably proud of himself.

As they made their way to the elevator, Maddy carrying her shoes in her hand, Christian excused himself to greet an old friend. He kissed Maddy's cheek, shook hands with Gabriel and disappeared into the lobby.

"Walk with me. It's too early to say goodnight to Paris. Especially since you are here." Gabriel looked hopeful. When Maddy smiled he suggested she change her shoes. She laughed and promised to return with proper walking gear.

When Maddy appeared wearing a red cape, black leggings and flats, Gabriel was amazed he noticed - he was always being chided for not noticing human things yet he seemed to be particularly aware of what Maddy was wearing.

They walked in silence for sometime, arm in arm along the banks of the Seine. They stopped at an outdoor cafe for a tisane and continued walking.

"I wasn't sure you would come back down tonight." He confessed.

"Why wouldn't I want to spend time with you? I want to know how you are, what you've been working on, if you're happy…you know, things you'd want to know about a friend you haven't seen for awhile."

"Maddy, I went to my family home to get away, away from what, I cannot say, and I missed your departure. As soon as I returned I went straight to the pool house to find you - Jordana was there, in bed with the pool boy. She told me about a rubbish conversation she had with you. The incident would be amusing if it wasn't so sad." He shook his head as he recalled the anger he had felt.

"When I got back to London I wasn't prepared for everything to be back to normal. I wasn't sure I was ready. It was confusing, but I guess timing is everything." Maddy shrugged, realizing she had confided in Gabriel, sharing with him why her plans had changed, allowing them time in Barcelona. Yet she had not spoken to Adam about Gabriel.

"I finished your book. It wasn't the same reading it myself but someday I will read to you and change your life as you changed mine." Gabriel kissed her cheek. "Come on, we better start back, it's already tomorrow." He pulled Maddy close. "I wasn't looking forward to Paris but now I think it's my favourite city." He swung his arm, *"J'adore."*

They laughed and talked, like old friends, holding hands as they walked towards the hotel.

Adam walked into the hotel lobby, expecting to surprise Maddy with his early arrival. He saw Christian and Maddy with a group of delegates; the group was dispersing, shaking hands and waving good byes. Christian had his arm around Maddy, as they walked towards the elevator. Adam caught them as they waited for the elevator.

"Adam, what a lovely surprise. We're done for today." Maddy smiled as she greeted him, kissing his cheek.

The concierge approached, excusing himself for interrupting, and handed Maddy an envelope. "Ms Walker, this was left for you at the desk. I thought it might be important."

Christian handed the concierge several Euros as Maddy took the package. She opened the unmarked envelope and pulled out a red beret with a note pinned to it.

As if anything could top your red cape.

Maddy laughed as she donned the beret, looking over at the mirrored wall.

"Perfect souvenir of Paris. Looks great Maddy." Christian leaned forward to pull the beret down over one eye.

Adam noticed Christian did not ask who had left the beret. Maddy had not shared the note with them.

They agreed to meet for cocktails later - Christian had phone calls to return, Maddy and Adam would enjoy an afternoon in Paris.

Once in the room Adam wrapped his arms around Maddy and told her he had missed her. Maddy returned his embrace and claimed Christian's report was received with enthusiasm. He had done a wonderful job of presenting his paper.

"Are you ready to explore Paris?" Maddy asked as she changed into her casual clothes.

"Paris can wait. Let me show you how much I missed you." Adam held out his hand.

Maddy fell asleep in Adam's arms, exhausted from their passionate lovemaking. Adam moved gently, sat on the edge of the bed, reaching for the bottled water. His hand brushed the beret. He read the note attached and wondered, once more, why there was no signature.

In his mind, Adam was imagining Maddy with another man, someone she found intriguing and philanthropic - she certainly wasn't a gold digger - she wasn't extravagant - she liked simple things and was not impressed by expensive designer ware or jewellery. Dermot was not in Paris - he had checked; Christian had spent time with Maddy sailing and yet there seemed to be no physical connection; Oliver and Nate were off on their adventure. Where had Maddy gone when he last saw her in Washington? She had mentioned her ex-partner was in the Maldives - no threat.

Maddy stretched and opened her eyes. She was confused to see Adam holding the beret. She sat up and pulled the sheet around her.

"Maddy, who sent the beret?" Adam asked, knowing he'd been caught red-handed.

"Why does it matter?"

"What matters is you not wanting to tell me."

Maddy felt the anger rising in her. "Adam. Let's stop this now. You go away for months at a time - I don't know where you are, what you're doing, who you're sleeping with or being married to…I don't know anything. You ask me to trust you. So I wait, hoping you come back to me, hoping you aren't hurt, hoping you don't forget what we have…" She stood up and began dressing. "You pop back and act as though everything is fine. You don't talk about the time you've been gone while I torture myself trying to be positive for Angela when she calls, worrying about you. How you can have the nerve to be jealous of a silly beret, I just don't understand." Maddy grabbed the beret and her cape and headed for the door.

"I've always loved Paris and I wanted to share my favourite places with you but right now I am so angry I'm going for a walk. Alone. When I get back you will either be gone and out of my life or you will be here, rethinking your trust issues. If you decide to go - I'll be reasonable but I won't give up my friendship with Angela - she cannot be abandoned again." She let the door close behind her.

Adam showered, dressed and walked out of the room.

Maddy left the hotel and walked directly to the Cafe de la Paix, wishing in her heart Paul, her first lover, now long dead, would appear at the door with his usual bouquet of flowers, his welcoming smile and his soothing words of comfort. She missed him, she missed her simple life. She ordered her favourite dessert, *Ile Flottante*, vanilla custard with whipped egg whites, and for the first time ever, didn't enjoy the sweet treat.

She responded to her messages and then slowly made her way back to the hotel. On the way she did a quick business analysis of her relationship with Adam, assessing strengths and weaknesses. She wondered why she hadn't done the exercise before. It worked for problem solving and decision making…why not now?

Strengths: He was loving, when he was with her; he had built the cottage in Henley with such care and attention to detail to please her; he had made her feel welcome in his family of Angela and Ahmed. He made her feel things no one else ever had.

Weaknesses: he could be controlling and jealous; he disappeared for long periods of time. He was secretive. Was he dangerous?

Opportunities: Maybe they should start over and date, get to know each other better.

Threats: he might want the cottage and she would miss it - it was her home. What if he blew it up like the flat in London? Was she ready to be alone - on her own? Again?

Having thoroughly canvassed her thoughts, without resolution, she saw Christian in the lobby. He waved at her and stopped her at the elevator. "Maddy, have you seen this?" He held up a folded newspaper.

Confused, Maddy leaned over and saw an article circled in pen. The headline read:

London Gossip Columnist Dead

The brief article reported Barbara Hartwood, a notorious gossip columnist, had been found in her car, on a deserted road, not far from Nottingham Woods. Substance abuse was cited as the cause of death.

Maddy looked up at Christian, her eyes wide. "Oh my gosh. How awful."

"Well, no more worries about her nasty, ruinous gossip. Still, it's a sad way to go, isn't it?" Christian shook his head. "Hey, where's Adam?" He looked around the lobby.

"We had a misunderstanding…I went for a walk."

"This is about the beret isn't it?" Christian asked.

"Partly. I don't know what I'll find when I get to my room. He may have gone. I'm afraid I gave him an ultimatum. Rain cheque on cocktails?"

Christian kissed her cheek. "Of course. If you are alone, text me and I'll bring a bottle of wine, baguette and cheese, for a picnic. Maddy, don't you dare stay in your room alone." Christian stopped in his tracks. "Maddy, this isn't about the pozzolan is it?

Maddy wasn't sure what to expect as she approached her room - the death of Barbara Hartwood bothered her - she shook her head, surely Adam wouldn't have had anything to do with this. Why did Christian ask about pozzolan?

She slowly opened the door, holding her breath. A large bouquet of flowers adorned the coffee table. A large note read:

Forgive me. This is all new to me.

Adam

Maddy smiled and noticed rose petals leading to the bathroom. She followed the trail and found another note.

> *Champagne and lavender bubbles for a relaxing bath*
> *Dinner on the terrace at 9*
> *Humble pie with morels*
> *Your Adam*

She sighed and ran the bath, eager to lie back in the warm water and close her eyes. Maddy wasn't sure how long she had been in the bath but her fingers were wrinkled and suddenly that seemed very funny. She dressed and walked out to the terrace. A soft breeze made her fold her arms. She walked back into the room and sat in the velvet chair, sipping on the champagne.

The ringing of the phone startled her out of the dream she had been enjoying. She stretched and walked to the phone. The front desk was calling with a message from the hospital. There had been a shooting and the patient had asked for her before he went into surgery.

Maddy looked at the time, cried out and grabbed her cape. She hurried to the lobby and was pleased to see a cab at the door. She slid in and asked the driver to get her to the hospital as quickly as possible. She left messages for Adam as he was not answering his phone. Who would shoot him? Had he been badly injured?

Rushing through the hospital doors she stopped at the reception and gave her name. She was directed to the surgery area, where she once again gave her name and asked for the patient. This time she was directed to the room. To her surprise Gabriel Cortez was sitting up in bed, his shoulder and arm wrapped in gauze. She gave a cry, relieved Adam had not been shot.

Gabriel was touched that Maddy had such strong feelings for his predicament. He reached out and squeezed the hand she offered. Maddy leaned over and kissed his cheek, running her fingers through his hair.

"Whatever happened?" Maddy felt breathless.

"There was a demonstration outside the hotel when I left the Exposition. There was a scuffle and shots rang out. I don't believe they were intended for me. I will be flown to Barcelona tomorrow morning - I don't think the French authorities want the media to use this as a statement on their Climate Change initiative. This might end my painting career. Thank you for coming. I really wanted to see a friendly face." Gabriel was nodding, his eyes closing.

"We've given him a sedative, he needs to rest. I've already sent his staff away. I suggest you return in the morning." The nurse was pleasant but firm. She opened the room door, waiting for Maddy to exit.

In the cab enroute to the hotel Maddy called Adam several times, leaving messages, texting him, calling the hotel suite. No response.

Maddy slid out of the cab and ran into the hotel. She saw Adam at the desk with his overnight bag. As she approached he asked for a cab to the airport.

"Adam, I tried calling you. There was an emergency. I got a call that there was a shooting. I thought it was you. I can't tell you how relieved I am to see you." She stopped before falling into him. The look on his face was cold and unwelcoming. She wasn't sure he had heard her.

Adam moved forward as if she was not there. He turned, and with a voice that could freeze water, advised Maddy that it was his turn to think about this relationship. He walked out of the hotel and into the waiting cab. As he sat back he reached for his phone. It was dead. He struggled to find a cable in his bag and an outlet in the cab.

He had missed the last flight out so he stayed at the Citizen Hotel in the airport. He entered his room, loosened his tie, poured a drink and plugged his phone into the lamp receptacle. Suddenly the phone was alive with messages, texts, voicemail notices and emails. He glanced over, annoyed by the entire Paris experience.

He saw Maddy's face appear on the screen, her number flashed over and over, the beep of messages continued. He finally read the screen. Maddy had been trying to reach him. She left several messages about an emergency. She waited for him and when she got the call about the shooting she believed it was him and left. Thankfully it wasn't him - she was on her way back to the hotel. She didn't say who had been shot and that made him angrier. He realized he was angry at himself.

Adam paced the small room, wondering if he should return to the hotel and Maddy. Would she open the door to him? Would she be pleased to see the trolley with dinner in the room? Should he call? He tried calling and heard her voice advising him to leave a message. He pulled out his laptop and began searching…he would find the answers he sought, he always did.

The next morning Adam made his way to the terminal, watching the flight board, checking his search results. Maddy was booked on the noon flight out. He booked on the same flight and waited for her to arrive. According to her phone she had returned to the hospital and was now enroute to the airport.

He watched as an ambulance arrived, lights flashing, and saw Maddy step out. The back door was opened and the stretcher was removed, a wheelchair provided for the patient. A car arrived and several official looking aides clamoured around the wheelchair. Maddy leaned over and kissed the blond, curly haired patient on the cheek, held his hand and then waved good bye. She entered the terminal, looked up at the information board and began to walk towards her departure gate.

Adam watched her, the familiar walk, the way she smiled at passersby, then turned his attention to the wheelchair posse. The group slowly moved towards the lounge, speaking in Spanish. He made his way to the gate, stopping briefly for coffee and a brioche.

"Paging Mr Adam Khan, passenger travelling to London. Your flight is boarding. Please present yourself to the check in area." A heavily accented voice filled the departure area.

"I am Adam Khan." He presented his passport and showed his electronic ticket to the agent.

"Ah, the infamous Adam Khan, the man who disappears and leaves his loved ones to fend for themselves. I wondered if I might meet you someday." The curly haired man in the wheelchair called, his voice calm, with a hint of sarcasm.

"I don't believe we will be friends, Dr Cortez. I am getting on this flight, going home with Maddy. You are flying to Barcelona. There's no need for us to meet. Excuse me."

"You don't deserve Maddy. You are an arrogant bastard."

Adam turned to stare down at the man in the wheelchair. He laughed. "I've been called worse, let me tell you. Go home Dr Cortez, concentrate on saving the world."

Adam smiled at the agent and walked onto the jetway, to his seat.

Maddy was seated at the window of the Airbus, seat 1A. She closed her eyes, wondering why she had refused to return to Barcelona with Gabriel. She had no idea what awaited her in London - would she be leaving the cottage at Henley? Should she go straight to the beach house and hide out? Would it be difficult to see Adam again?

She sighed and felt a light kiss on her cheek. She opened her eyes in surprise, startled out of her reverie.

"I'm so sorry Maddy. I ruined Paris for you. Please forgive me. I love you. You know I do." Adam was whispering in her ear, his breath tickling her. She felt his lips move across her cheek, his hand moving a strand of hair behind her ears, his musky scent filling her nostrils. She wanted to scream.

She moved her head to the side. "Did you know about Barbara Hartwell?" She asked, not wanting to know the answer.

"I heard the news this morning." He sat back in his seat. "You can't think I had anything to do with her death, do you?" He looked confused.

"I'm glad you didn't. It was awful." Maddy patted his arm. "What happens now?"

"Let's go home. We need to talk. I need to work on my trust issues. I need to be a better man for you. I'm willing to try if you'll give me the chance." He took Maddy's hand in his and kissed her palm, making her shiver. "I'm sorry."

"Let's go home." She squeezed his hand. "You owe me a visit to Paris but for now, let's go home." She closed her eyes and sat back in her seat, so many questions unanswered.

Adam sat back, holding her hand in his. He closed his eyes, sighing with relief. He hoped he would never have to sleep alone again.

As they walked through the terminal towards baggage claim Adam grabbed Maddy by the hand and pulled her into the Family Washroom. Locking the door, he approached Maddy, pulled her tunic up over head, kissing her neck and running his hands along her body. She reached up and unbuttoned his shirt, feeling the urgency to have his body next to her burning skin. He somehow managed to rid them of the rest of their clothing as Maddy groaned from his touch. He lifted Maddy and she wrapped her legs around his hips. She opened her eyes as he whispered affectionately in her ear, his hands travelling up and down her naked body. His lips found hers and suddenly she was transported to another world, a world where every nerve in her body was awakened. It had been months since they made love. When Adam placed his hands against the wall Maddy somehow found the strength to unlock her legs and stand on her shaky legs. Adam held her close, one hand in her hair, one hand on the small of her back.

Maddy giggled as she looked over his shoulder and saw the flashing sign *Press for Assistance*. He followed her gaze and smiled. "We're going to be alright on our own."

They washed at the small sink and changed clothes, feeling refreshed and somewhat connected. Maddy felt you could only take a sponge bath with someone close…Adam commented he hadn't had the luxury of warm water for awhile. Maddy watched him shave and slip into a clean, crisp shirt. She saw the welts on his back and lightly traced them with her fingers. She tenderly kissed them, making him flinch. There were several colourful bruises and burn marks as well. She would ask later.

They brushed their teeth, spitting into the sink, giggling like children. They stood at the door, holding hands, took a deep breath and walked out, joining the crowds heading to collect baggage. Anyone seeing the couple would take a look at their smiling faces and say they looked as though they had just shared a sweet secret.

GETTING TO KNOW YOU

As they drove to Henley, enjoying the warmth of the sun, Adam reached for Maddy's hand. He kept looking over to watch her, hoping she would forgive him and life would continue as it had before Paris.

"Tell me about your life as a child Maddy." Adam asked as they lay in bed, neither sleeping, neither making the first move.

When she spoke it was in a soft voice. "Oh Adam, we come from different worlds. My mother denied my father what he called 'the comfort of lying beside the one you trust'. They were happy together and then my mother lost a baby, a son. After that she turned away from us. I had always travelled with my father - I sat in meeting rooms doing puzzles while he negotiated with foreign speaking men in dark suits; I was left to explore cities on my own while he conducted his business. He was relentless - learn the language, learn the culture, learn from everyone - put that learning to good use when you make decisions in life." Maddy sighed and turned towards him.

"My mother shut us out and drove my father to his other women - they were lovely to me - I think I loved them more than I ever cared for my mother. When my father died, in the arms of his lover, I couldn't mourn him - he had found comfort with someone he trusted. My mother died angry. I don't want to be angry…I want to die in the comfort of someone I trust. I want my happy ever after, just like the stories my father read to me." When Maddy blinked the tears cascaded down her cheeks. She brushed her cheek, surprised the hidden thoughts could bring her to tears.

Adam reached for her and pulled her close. Maddy snuggled into his arms. Why had she shared those thoughts? She felt vulnerable.

"Maddy, I've seen horrible things happen when men believe women are not equal. As a child I heard my mother cry herself to sleep most nights. She met my father at school in London and never imagined her life would change when they came to Dubai. She was brilliant as an engineer, her career just beginning. My father realized she was ambitious and sought after by the very firms he hoped to join. He didn't need to work, the family held land with oil reserves - it was pride, foolish pride that made him jealous of the beautiful wife he brought home." Adam paused, as he remembered his mother, her light scent lingering in the room, her long dark hair brushing his face, as she bent to kiss him goodnight and promise him the best life ever. She had always called him *Sweet Adam* although he was known as Hassan. It was an easy transition to be known as Adam.

"I walked into the room one night and saw my mother on her knees in front of my father, he was naked and he was pulling her hair, hurting her, yelling at her to obey him. He looked like a maniac and I was terrified. I remember the sad wail, my mother was begging him to leave her alone. His laughter was cruel. He pulled her closer and closer and her pleas were becoming louder." Adam wiped his forehead, he could feel beads of sweat forming.

"When my father saw me, paralyzed by fear, in the doorway, he laughed that cruel laugh and told me to come in and takeover from my mother. He threw her against the wall, a handful of her hair in his big hands. He challenged me to come and save her, to finish what she could not do. I remember walking towards him, hating him, wanting to hurt him as he had hurt my mother. All I could hear was my mother sobbing, lying on the floor. She begged me to go to my room. My father fell back on the bed, laughing. I felt the warmth of an oil lamp beside my hand and before I could reason with myself I threw the lamp at my father. The flames engulfed him and the smell of burning hair will never leave me. My mother, who a moment before had been lying in a sobbing heap, was suddenly beside me, ushering me out, telling me we would never speak of this." He stopped, closing his eyes, trying to erase the memory.

"The next morning we were sent back to London. The old uncle said it was best we left for awhile. He told my mother she was destined to ruin lives but he would call for me when the time was right. We returned to London - my mother cut her hair, began working for a large firm, marrying Conrad Kahn and living what she called, a normal life. I was sent to boarding school but we always went somewhere wonderful for school holidays. Conrad was a decent man, he accepted me and taught me to fish, to sail, to hunt…he encouraged me to make my life count. He and my mother loved each other, I believe they had loved each other at school - he waited for her to return - it seemed very Hollywood to me at the time." Adam smiled, recalling the way his mother would look at Conrad. He had yearned for someone to look at him that way.

Maddy touched his face, outlining his lips, stroking his cheek, pulling his face toward her. She kissed him with such tenderness he felt he might sob. He had not spoken of his life with anyone - he felt lighter, honest and clean, having told the truth to someone who did not judge him.

"I'm sorry you had to carry that with you - what a horrible thing for a child to endure." Maddy held him, understanding there were no words of comfort.

"I have tried to be better than my father but the old uncle, who I am not sure is actually related, had control of my life. He never mentioned the incident and we never heard what happened - we were free. However, whenever there was a negotiation with the western world, I was called. Soon it became delivering shipments, collecting debts, smuggling informers - some of the assignments were dangerous, most just required a tailored suit." Adam snickered in embarrassment.

"What happened to your mother? Did she know you were being blackmailed?"

"We never spoke of Dubai once we arrived in London. Conrad and my mother worked on several projects together - he was good to her and they seemed happy together. She contracted tuberculosis on a project in South America and died soon after. I think Conrad died of a broken heart. He hired me to find the source in the water table and we were able to close the project. I have concentrated on water related projects since then, in his honour."

"Were you taken advantage of by the old uncle?" Maddy asked, curious about the danger involved and the abuse he may have suffered.

"Ah, the old man was canny. I was well paid - there was never any reason to complain or question an order. Michael Riley was a great investment counsellor - he handled transfers and soon I had a ridiculous portfolio, which could never be traced. He called it my insurance policy. Michael understood the work, the sacrifices and the need to create a nest egg."

Maddy smiled, acknowledging Michael and his talents. "Michael was brilliant. He had street smarts, no formal training."

"Money was his lifeline - he had a horrible life but money made sense to him. I miss him and I know he would have enjoyed investing the inheritance from the old uncle. I received the bulk of the estate when the old man died. He hated to leave it to me but not as much as he hated to see his oil reserves go to his enemies."

"Are you an oil baron now? It seems incongruous with your work."

"I hate to admit this, but in the last week I succcssfully negotiated the sale of the properties. The funds should be in the Swiss account by now. Your friend Christian has been most helpful. Michael recommended him as a decent fellow, savvy banker and friend of yours. So you see, I am a fair man with many flaws and many things left to learn. I am also very wealthy. Although somehow, I believe for you that is my least attractive feature."

"We all have flaws. I like to think it's not what you have but what you do with it. Your knowledge of water systems and your worldliness should help you find ways to help others. I also feel you have more building to do - I'm amazed at your capabilities in carpentry and design." Maddy snuggled into his arms. "Thank you for sharing with me. It was important. To me."

"Maddy, there's something I've been meaning to speak with you about." Adam hesitated.

"Go ahead. We seem to be sharing." Maddy smiled at him, encouraging him to continue.

"When we visited the island to check on the water system I took samples of the soil to confirm pozzolan, which is a compound added to strengthen cement. Interesting, the buildings are crumbling on the very ground where siliceous-aluminium is found. The last time I flew over the island I noticed all the inhabitants had gone and the garbage was slowly burning. We were able to mine the pozzolan with the equipment left on site. The market is lucrative and we have made a healthy profit, paid for an ecological clean up and removed the machinery. Your island is recuperating and may someday be a paradise for the right venue or tribe. I didn't want to upset you or intimate that we were profiting from the demise of the life you wanted to provide for the islanders." Adam took a deep breath and waited.

Maddy considered what she could or might say and decided to let it ride. He left the island a better place, nothing else mattered. She could release that unfinished project from her mind.

"Now you know who I am. Can you live with that? Can you live with me?" Adam asked.

"We both have a past, reasons for who we are and how we handle life. We also have a future. It's a choice we get to make. Right now, my future includes sleep. Goodnight Adam. I'm so relieved you were not the shooting victim in Paris. Sweet dreams." Maddy reached up to kiss his cheek but he intercepted her and their lips met. Tentatively at first, then more passionate. It was the kiss that sealed a deal.

SOMETHING IN THE WAY SHE MOVES

Standing by the bar at the Dorchester Hotel in London, Christian and Adam waited for Maddy to arrive at the reception. The men had come directly from their meeting at the bank. Maddy was involved with a fund raising committee - she anticipated being late and suggested they meet at the event. Adam was uncomfortable without Maddy at his side - he knew so few people in the room - his choice - Maddy always made introductions and filled him in on who was approaching. She was his savant. He pulled his shirt cuffs down, anxious to see her.

"Adam, watch all these women arrive at the door; gripping the arms of their dates, maybe searching for a single man, some bored with the evening before it begins." Christian nodded towards the entrance.

"Observe. When Maddy appears she will make an entrance, the servers will fall over themselves to hand her a cocktail and several of the old guard will approach her with condolences. They haven't seen much of her since the shooting." Christian sipped his beer - he had long ago traded his sherry for a lager.

Christian was right. Maddy walked into the vast ballroom, head held high, a confident smile on her face - she looked as though it was her party and she was checking to see if all her guests were enjoying themselves. She was wearing black palazzo pants that seemed to float when she walked. The white silk blouse had a three button cuff and a high neck. No jewellery. Black slingback shoes with a small heel. She had one hand in the pocket of the pants and before she descended the short flight of steps she had a champagne flute in her other hand. Her walk was distinctive - she rolled her hips and never looked harried as she made her way across the floor.

Adam watched her with admiration, starting forward to meet her when he saw an older woman touch her hand, stopping her progress.

"Maddy, I'm sorry I haven't called on you, what with this silly pandemic and all. I heard you were seen with the tall foreigner over there. I suppose one cannot grieve forever. I imagine he strikes rather a dashing figure naked." Dame Clarice Fortescue chirped in her high voice.

Maddy blushed. She quickly looked over at Christian and Adam, embarrassed by the comments, hoping they weren't able to make out the words.

"I'm sure he gives you hours of beastly pleasure in the bedroom. He looks well endowed."

"Dame Clarice, I'm shocked." Maddy was uncomfortable.

"I may be old but I ain't dead yet. Enjoy it while you can, his sort never stay very long. They take what they want and move on. You'll see." Dame Clarice patted Maddy on the arm and walked away.

Maddy was outraged. She had not understood why Adam felt people judged him but the cruel words were indicative of how he must feel when in this crowd.

Adam had stepped forward to greet Maddy, cautious of the look on her face. Before he could speak, a middle aged woman with heavy make-up and an elaborate nest of hair appeared at his side.

"Maddy, really, you must introduce me to this fine specimen. Don't be selfish."

Maddy sighed. "Lady Cornelia Smythe may I introduce Adam Khan." She turned to Adam and repeated the introduction.

Lady Smythe wrapped her arm around Adam's arm and pulled him away. "You must tell me where you've come from. I don't recollect meeting you and I know everyone. We're going to be great friends." She raised her shoulder coyly, running her hand down his tie.

"Perhaps another time. We were just leaving." Adam turned to Maddy, detaching himself from the woman. "Darling, we cannot be late, the invitation clearly says we are to arrive before the guest of honour. Ready?"

Maddy smiled. "Of course. I know how important it is to you."

Lady Smythe looked confused with the rebuff. No one ever dismissed her.

Adam excused himself, bowing slightly, and placed an arm on Maddy's back, directing her towards the door. He leaned close and whispered. "Please may we leave. I will take you to dinner and then I will do unheard of things to delight you before you fall asleep in my arms."

Maddy shuddered. "Like what, *darling*?" She turned suddenly and asked with a mischievous grin. He had not anticipated she would stop, the momentum pushing him against her.

"Stop it Maddy. If you keep looking at me like that I will have to kiss you in front of all these pompous people."

"Looking like what, *darling*?" He caught his breath as she placed her hand on his chest.

Adam looked at Maddy, smiling up at him, daring him to do something unthinkable - something reckless - like showing affection for the widow of Sebastian Walker, in a crowded ballroom.

"You are trouble. You are reckless. I knew it the first time I laid eyes on you." He spoke in a hushed tone, his eyes boring into her. "I am a gentleman and therefore, I will escort you out of this room, into the foyer, where I will kiss you until you beg me to stop."

He looked around the room. "Shall we, darling?" For some strange reason the word darling was sounding natural to him.

Maddy giggled, feeling like a schoolgirl. "Promises, promises, promises… we don't want to be late, *darling*. Come along."

"Why are you mocking me? I called you darling because it felt right." Adam tried to sound light although he was hurt.

Maddy stopped and slowly turned around to face him. "I'm sorry Adam. I thought you were just acting to get away. I did like the sound of it, though. You don't use endearments often." Her smile returned. "It was nice."

Adam realized he was smiling back at her. It was strange to smile for no apparent reason. Smiling didn't come easy to him - it was exhilarating… he would make every effort to smile more. Not hard to do with Maddy.

DON'T LET THE SUN GO DOWN ON ME

"Adam, can you get Maddy to the grave site tomorrow or would you prefer we collect her?" Grace called Adam direct. "Davi is picking up the flowers from Mrs Bing. I can see how it might sound morbid but we never got to the restaurant after Maddy and Sebastian were married - we all agree it's time to celebrate his life - and acknowledge their short-lived marriage. I know Maddy would want you to be included." She stopped to take a breath.

"Of course, Grace. It's important to everyone. If you feel it's appropriate for me to be there, I will be as supportive as possible. Is there anything else I can do?" Adam was pleased to be asked to join the group. Having such a tight group of friends around all the time was not something he knew about - he had always been a loner.

"No, thank you. Just get Maddy there by 11:00 am - you know, it's going to be tough - Sebastian and Henry were such a big part of her life. Lockdowns didn't allow us to get together before this anniversary. She'll need you to understand."

Adam thanked Grace for the call and sat at the desk, unsure of how to be supportive. Maddy was always helping someone, it came natural to her. He tried to recall if he had ever grieved for another person…

When Adam drove into the cemetery he was touched by the way Maddy's friends had gathered, forming a line to the gravestones. The flowers were lovely - one bouquet of Gerbera daisies of every colour for Sebastian - another with wild flowers for Henry. The friends read poems, exchanged their favourite stories and honoured the lives of the men Maddy had changed, for the better, they all agreed.

The group slowly moved away, leaving Maddy alone on the bench in front of the graves. They waited patiently for her to rearrange the toy soldiers on the lawn between the graves. Maddy wiped her cheek with the back of her hand, assuring the souls they would never be forgotten.

She looked at the friends gathered, waiting for her. They had all been so important in her relationship with Sebastian and they had all accepted Henry and loved him. She wouldn't grieve for the loss; she would concentrate on the love she felt for each person here.

Grace had been her first friend when she landed in London, unsure of what the year would bring. Davi had been Sebastian's driver - his kindness and acceptance of Maddy led her to introduce him to Grace - they were a lovely couple.

Christian had been a colleague of Sebastian - he had given Maddy several jobs at Deutsche Bank - paying her with theatre tickets, lavish dinners and then sailing with her. He had included her in the CityScapes evolution, asking for her advice and confiding in her. She had directed several clients his way and he handled her finances. Christian had taken an interest in Henry, thankful Maddy had included him, especially since his own sons were loyal to their mother in Germany and her life.

Decades, the popular nightclub, was owned by Sam, called The Professor. Maddy remembered attending his business class with Davi, who was confused by the way The Professor taught - it was Maddy who took over the class and became a hero to the students and Sam. He depended on Maddy for hiring and training and had always been receptive to her ideas for fundraisers.

Sebastian's assistant, Lambert, felt Maddy had shown him a world of new things - she gave him the commission on the sale of a house and took him to see The Rocky Horror Picture Show - she turned the disastrous annual office party into a highly anticipated family event. Lambert had adored Sebastian but he loved Maddy - he could tell her anything.

The tall, cigar chumping Texan, known as PC, treated Maddy as a daughter. She had settled a gambling debt for him with Sorento, the Italian designer, and he would be forever grateful. Maddy always made him feel authentic - she accepted him and he loved her for it. She always welcomed him and surprised him with barbecue or something she seemed to know he enjoyed. She was special and he had invested in the Villa Mirage to ensure she was successful. She had also introduced him to Maria. Now there was a woman; prickly as hell, so Swiss in her thinking, so practical and so different from the gold digging beauties he had known after his wife passed.

Maddy and Giselle met at the hotel in France during a ski holiday with Sebastian and Philippe. PC, the Texan, had created a fuss - Giselle would always remember how Maddy calmed the Texan and saved the day. Maddy introduced Giselle to Philippe and they had married at Villa Mirage. Philippe had sold his vineyard in France to develop the winery at the Villa - Giselle had left the hotel business and invested her alimony in the Villa. Both had strong feelings for Maddy and her pluckiness.

Adam stood back, knowing in his heart Michael Riley was here, in spirit, to support Maddy. He also knew there were many others who were not here today, who loved and cared for Maddy. He looked at the faces of the group and was thankful they had included him. He was smart enough to know he had to share Maddy with everyone here.

Once seated at the restaurant, the friends proposed toasts and gave brief tributes, trying their best to laugh and keep things light. Maddy stood and thanked each one, eloquently, for being there. She was composed and genuine in her remarks. She didn't acknowledge the tears streaming down her cheeks. Adam stood and wiped her cheeks with a cotton handkerchief which brought gales of laughter. Christian finally intervened and explained how Sebastian always had a clean handkerchief for Maddy - it was such an innocent gesture - a fine way to end the Celebration of Life.

YOU'VE GOT A FRIEND

Grace was anxious to have some time alone with Maddy. Adam appeared to make Maddy happy and he did seem more comfortable around her friends since the celebration of life. She mentioned this to Maddy, who reminded her how long it took for Sebastian to feel comfortable with the group.

"It must be intimidating for him to meet you all and try to deal with the closeness and then, of course, the ghost of Sebastian. He doesn't know about our business relationship and how we got to this point…he just knows I'm fiercely loyal to you. As he gets to know you I can't help but think he will love you too, as I do." Maddy was stirring the batter for the next batch of cookies.

Chance was having his afternoon nap, lying across Davi's chest. Maddy and Grace stopped to look over, smiling at the snoring pair. When Maddy looked back at Grace she realized Grace had something on her mind.

"What's up Grace?" Maddy continued to stir, giving Grace time to respond.

"Oh Maddy, I can't keep anything from you, can I?" Grace laughed, her lovely deep belly laugh. "I think Chance will have a brother or sister soon. I don't feel as rotten as I did the first time, but I've caught you looking at me funny so I thought I better tell you."

Maddy rushed over and hugged her friend. "That's wonderful news. Davi must be delighted. He said he wanted a large family."

"True. But we want to talk to you about the building - we're doing well enough to want to expand the food offering - we've been hoping to talk to you about making the changes. The timing is always off…is this a good time?"

Maddy wiped her hands on her apron and suggested they sit for a chai. She had wondered when Grace and Davi would want to build their own brand and expand - Maddy was just the landlord/partner.

"You know we can't do this without your help. The coffee shop is booming and we need the room upstairs. We want to offer lunch and afternoon tea. The reading room is busy enough and if we added a sitter we would get the new mothers as well. Does that sound crazy?" Grace held her breath.

"It sounds wonderful. The books are a tribute to Mr Simpson and I sometimes feel the smell of the old volumes may be a deterrent for germ-conscious mothers. I'll try to move them - we have them catalogued so it should be easy to advise other booksellers. Tell me your plan and I'll work towards getting you some design ideas. Lambert will be thrilled to work with us." Maddy could see the relief in Grace's eyes.

"You and Davi need to plan for your family, don't ever be afraid to talk to me about growth. As a matter of fact, it might be time for you to think about buying me out. I just want you to be successful."

Grace hugged her friend. "How fortunate we are to have met you Maddy."

"I'm the fortunate one, believe me. Hey, my cookie dough is screaming to get into the oven."

Maddy met with Lambert and an associate from the architectural firm and they agreed on an open concept design, ideal for the building and the new direction. Sam found a buyer for the antique books and the space was cleared within a month.

Davi, Adam and Maddy worked tirelessly to scrub the hardwood floors and repair the bannisters, keeping the natural attributes of the building in tact. Adam was a great help as a carpenter, no surprise as he had built the cottage for Maddy.

Grace fed the work crew, enjoying having them around all day. Chance was delighted to carry tools and babble baby talk with Maddy between his naps. Adam and Davi developed a mutual respect as they moved and dismantled book shelves to build tables and sideboards.

Frequently they would end the day sitting on the floor, against a wall, with a drink - reviewing the work completed and setting tasks for the next day. Davi would sit crosslegged, rubbing Grace's feet as she lay on a mattress, exhausted. Chance would sit between Adam and Maddy, reading from his book - he had his own language - his expressions and emphasis on certain words were priceless. Grace believed he would be talking soon. Maddy and Adam would eventually stand and make their way home for a bath and bed.

An elegant glass elevator was installed to improve access - the curved oak staircase remained in place as the cornerstone of the design. New windows were installed to brighten the space in the upper level, with round bottle glass windows added on the main level. Adam created intricate frames for the windows, negating the need for art on the walls.

Maddy worked on the marketing plan and sent out flyers to past guests. The neighbouring businesses were motivated by the changes and began sprucing up their store fronts. The gelato shop had closed during the lockdowns so Maddy purchased the equipment and convinced her old friend to work with them to make his wonderful gelato - the addition of gelato filled the cafe tables on the outdoor patio, especially on sunny afternoons.

Ads were placed requesting donations of china cups and saucers - the boxes flooded in. Grace wondered how Maddy could ask for such treasures but soon customers were delivering their grandmothers' teapots. Afternoon tea would be a visit into the past.

Cupboards to hold the lovely teacups were soon adorning the walls - no job seemed menial or too intricate for Adam. At the end of each work day he and Maddy would walk through the building admiring the changes. Davi and Grace trailed behind them, sometimes too emotional to speak.

Gravitasse, named for Grace and Davi, opened to sell out crowds - gelato, specialty coffees and teas, tasty wraps, pita with dips, fresh bread and an assortment of baked goods were offered to neighbours, media and curious new customers. Afternoon Tea would be available Tuesday - Thursday, by reservation. When Maddy last checked the reservations on the computer *Gravitasse* was sold out for months.

Auntie and Uncle, Davi's relatives, had sold their take-out shop prior to the lockdown and were eager to assist with bread and pita making, creating interesting dips and various chai recipes. Bread orders poured in and most days they sold out mid morning. Maddy found sealable containers for the chai and when packaged with honey, it was a perfect hostess gift.

Adam suggested several dips for those with allergies or special diets - Angela and Ahmed had challenged him to find more natural ways to prepare plant proteins. His knowledge of Middle Eastern cuisine, combined with Auntie's Indian recipes, became popular with younger patrons. Adam was amazed that he should be contributing to the menu when his experience was in eating, not preparing food.

Adam and Maddy were pleased with the results and the business. They were anxious to return to Henley and care for their garden. They also looked forward to being less tired every night…they missed early morning lovemaking, reading the news sitting in bed. They missed being alone with each other.

"Thank you Adam. *Gravitasse* is beautiful and would not have happened without your willingness and building expertise. I can hardly believe the hands that create this wonderful woodwork are the same hands that touch me. I wish I had worked with you on the cottage." Maddy caressed his hands as they sat in the coffee shop, watching the activity.

Adam was pleased. "Perhaps one day we'll have a chance to build something together."

"Oh dear, the last thing I need is another address. Who knows, Angela and Ahmed may solicit our help for their home someday." She smiled. "In the meantime, we do need to visit the Villa in Italy. I promise there are no major repairs to be done."

They both laughed.

Giselle and Philippe were anxious to have Maddy visit the Villa for the financial review. Maddy suspected they too had a plan to take on ownership of Villa Mirage. They worked so hard at managing and caring for the property Maddy felt they deserved to want more. The villa had held emotional ties for her - could she give up Sebastian's birthright?

Adam travelled with Maddy to Italy, hoping to provide support for whatever decision was taken. He enjoyed the vineyards and the village and yet, he sensed it had lost much of its charm for Maddy when Father Dom passed away.

Giselle and Philippe offered to repay all investors, including PC and Maria, the Swiss conglomerate and Deutsche Bank, avoiding penalties and taking ownership. Maddy would always have her suite in the Villa and would continue to hold shares, the boutique would continue to feature Sorento designs but the product would change - Sofi had made the line popular with younger fashionistas. The Villa was transforming into a wine making/culinary college - students were already signed up for the first three courses, increasing the revenues substantially.

"Maddy, how are you doing? Are you happy?" Giselle asked as they walked arm in arm, through the vineyard, finally able to escape the group.

Maddy smiled at her friend. " Gigi, I'm good. I keep busy and I love the garden. Adam is very kind. He's away for long periods of time, I don't know how much longer he will have to be away for work, but I need my time alone and this relationship seems to suit us both. I know he seems intense but he's very lovely and caring. What more could I want?"

"Be careful Maddy. My ex-husband is in Dubai, as you know, and he is terrified that I am doing business with Adam Khan. He has a reputation. I worry for you." Giselle sighed.

"Please don't worry. Adam designed the irrigation system, remember? Maybe he's mellowed in his old age. Anyway, I'm delighted to see Philippe take an interest in the Villa. He and Sebastian were best friends, it seems only fitting you and he are ready to take it on and build your future. It's time you became the Contessa and lived your dream. Could you find a better retirement community?" Maddy laughed. "I love seeing you and Philippe work together. This is the right place and the right time for you both. It's just a memory for me but for you it's a life. Enjoy it."

"We love it here but we don't want you to feel any pressure to sell. Maddy we miss you, Anza misses you - please come back as often as you can. Keep the memories alive." Giselle wiped a tear away. "Father Dom was right. He saw that we were cool towards Adam and he wanted you to be happy. He was the one who convinced Philippe to return here. He knew Philippe would find solace here, with me, but also with the memory of Sebastian. Father Dom pointed out how happy we were and asked us why we were denying you happiness by not accepting Adam. He cared for you, a lot."

"I miss him. I miss Sebastian too. I believe there is a future with Adam. Thank you for telling me that." Maddy looked over at her friend.

"Right now, we need to taste the wine. Come on my friend, it's time to celebrate life and friendship." Giselle laughed, feeling grateful for this lovely friendship.

Maddy encouraged the investors to sell and let the couple build their own brand. Once it was clear Maddy was ready to let go, they agreed.

The investors departed, signed agreements in hand. Maddy embraced Giselle and Philippe and wished them well. She had neglected the Villa and although it would always hold a place in her heart, she had to admit, her plate was full. She would help in any way - believing in the plan presented.

Although Maddy was reluctant to leave Anza, the resident pet, she knew in her heart the dog belonged at Villa Mirage.

Father Dom, she assured Giselle and Philippe, would be proud of what they had accomplished.

"Is it wrong that I feel somewhat free, driving away?" Maddy asked Adam as they left for the airport.

IT'S THE MOST WONDERFUL TIME OF THE YEAR

Angela and Ahmed, and now Adam Jr, invited Adam and Maddy to spend the Christmas vacation with them at a chalet in Aspen. A faculty member had offered his chalet as he was on sabbatical. The four bedroom chalet was located on the mountain and would suit the family just fine. Angela was adamant they not exchange gifts as they had limited baggage allowance on their flights.

Maddy agreed and mailed the gifts to the New Jersey house - declaring they were already purchased.

After several delays due to weather, they all arrived at the chalet. Angela and Ahmed had signed up for ski lessons and encouraged Adam to join them. He reluctantly agreed to participate and found he enjoyed the freedom - he was soon joining Maddy for easier runs. His favourite part of the downhill was stopping on the slope, seeing the joy in Maddy's eyes and kissing her cold cheeks. Evenings were early as everyone, except Maddy, was stiff and sore.

Jennifer and Adam Jr spent the morning falling off the toboggan, building snowmen - always a family of snowmen. After lunch Adam Jr attended the day care and Jennifer wandered through the village. When the adults returned late afternoon, she had hot chocolate and pizza or salmon and cream cheese on bagels ready for them. Dinner was skipped several nights as the group convened in the hot tub under the stars, preferring sandwiches or wraps to a sit down meal.

Maddy and Jennifer escaped for an afternoon at the Spa. Jennifer was enjoying her time with the family - they were lovely to her. She was keen to tell Maddy about her evening job - she was allowed to work with Angela on the research. She also had learned key words in Arabic so Adam Jr would know something of his heritage. At first she thought Angela might be upset but one day when Angela and Ahmed were discussing a presentation they started speaking in Arabic and Adam Jr began to cry. Both adults stopped and realized their son was afraid, fearing his parents were arguing. Now he was able to respond to words in both English and Arabic.

"Father, you seem like a younger version of yourself. Maddy must be good for you." Angela wrapped her arms around Adam's neck as he read the news.

"Maddy is hard to keep up with and yet, we seem to get along very well." Adam nodded.

Angela rolled her eyes. "Get along? Really Father. Is that the best you can do?"

"Listen, you know I adore her and so far, she hasn't thrown me out. Life is good." He smiled. "On another subject, I am so proud of you and Ahmed. Adam Jr is a treasure and we love to visit with you. I hope you are happy. As a father I wish for nothing more than to hear you are happy, healthy and enjoying your life." He looked up at his beautiful daughter and touched her cheek.

"I know we don't say it often, and we should. We love you and Maddy and we feel blessed to have such a wonderful life." Angela leaned her head on her father's, as she had as a child. "We better go to breakfast or I'll start to cry. Come on." She held out her hand.

WHEN I SEE YOUR FACE

♥ ♥ ♥

Maddy stopped as she walked into the living room. Sprawled across the sofa she saw Adam, snoring lightly, his arm across Adam Jr, also snoring lightly. The baby was clutching onto Adam's shirt, as though he never wanted to let go. She smiled and blinked to capture the moment to her memory. It was a lovely moment. They had returned to Princeton for a few days before flying back to London.

Adam stirred, as though he felt the presence of someone in the room. He smiled at Maddy, wishing she was also here beside him on the sofa.

"We seem to be out of daytime energy. Have the others gone to the movie?" He asked sleepily.

"They should be back anytime now. You haven't forgotten our date, have you?" Maddy walked over and knelt beside the sofa, gently massaging his head.

"Oh Maddy, I did forget. I know you want to see your friends. Would I be a beast if I stayed home with the little one tonight? I'm bone weary from trying to keep up with you." He was reluctant to move from this very comfortable sofa. He looked down at Adam Jr and felt a surge of love. "May I be excused?"

"Of course. You look so peaceful and content lying there. Jr will be thrilled to have you to himself. I'll call you before I get the train home." She kissed his forehead, stood and leaned over to kiss Adam Jr as well. "Behave yourselves."

As she walked away Adam reached out for her hand. "Thank you. I'll make it up to you, I promise."

Maddy felt quite free as she boarded the train to Manhattan. She rarely had time to herself these days. She had wrapped herself in the red cape and placed the red beret on her head, feeling festive. Dermot had sent the tickets for the first lecture series at the Public Library in Manhattan. She had not been in the library for years and looked forward to visiting the familiar building.

She hurried up the steps, saluting the lions guarding the entrance, a cold wind threatening to take her beret. She showed her security pass and entered the building. She walked slowly, undoing her cape, feeling chilled but in awe of the architecture. She could see the crowd in the room to her left. She knew she should check her cape and seek out Dermot. Ephrom Gold was also attending - she could see him walking towards her.

"Maddy, how wonderful to see you. I hoped you'd come. You look marvellous in that red cape. Keep it on. Everyone will be envious of me walking in with you." Ephrom was gallant as ever and Maddy laughed as she air kissed his cheeks.

Gabriel Cortez stood in a group of academics who were attempting to put his thoughts in their own words. He was tired and needed fresh air. He looked around the room, wondering how soon he could escape. He heard laughter and suddenly he was awake and excusing himself. He pushed through the crowd, nodding and smiling at the people who touched him and wanted him to hear their thoughts.

He stopped behind her. "Excuse me. Surely you cannot have forgotten this is our dance."

Maddy turned, recognizing his voice. She smiled at his boyish pout. She was about to introduce him to Ephrom Gold when Gabriel grabbed her hand and pulled her through the crowd and out onto the stairs outside.

"I just needed to get out. Have dinner with me. Damn, it's cold. You're wearing the beret. I guess we have to go back in and get my coat." He looked over at Maddy who was laughing at him.

"Hello Maddy. How are you? Hello Gabriel. I'm fine. And you? How long are you in New York? Do you have a restaurant in mind or do you care?" Maddy teased.

Gabriel was now laughing as well. "I'm sorry. I heard you laugh and I had to find you. I've missed you. Will you have dinner with me? I guess we have to wait until after the presentations. Come on, let's go in, you're shivering."

They walked back into the building, Gabriel with his arm around Maddy. As they entered the reception room there was a deafening noise - the lights went out as the ceiling collapsed, in slow motion, spreading dust and debris over the crowd. Screams and wails could be heard over the rumble of the blast.

Gabriel wrapped Maddy in his arms and moved away from the door. The dust in the room was moving towards the door. Soon they too would be covered in dust. Maddy held her breath, her heart pounding, her legs weak. She could hear alarms ringing throughout the building.

Gabriel was whispering soothingly into her hair. "It's alright, you will be fine. Hold on *Cariño*. You are safe."

"Gabriel, what can we do? We have to help. That room was filled with people." Maddy cried. Her ears were ringing from the explosion.

"We have to wait for the fire department or the emergency service people - they will know what to do. Come, let's move away from the door." Gabriel moved towards a bench, still holding Maddy.

In Princeton, Angela and Ahmed arrived home and smiled as they saw Adam holding Adam Jr - both asleep on the sofa. Ahmed hurried to the television - his watch had signalled a breaking news bulletin. They watched in horror as the explosion at the Library, the wonderful building, was broadcast. A group of Saudi students had taken responsibility - citing their anger at the unfair treatment their Prince had received. They had left a video stating retaliation for the cancellation of the Prince's charity event after falsely being accused of murdering a journalist.

Adam sat up, forgetting he was holding the little boy. "Maddy went to the event. Has she called? Is she alright? I have to go."

Angela placed a hand on her father's shoulder. "No, you cannot go into the city tonight. It's too dangerous. Maddy will call us. We'll wait to hear from her. Please don't go."

When Angela wandered into the kitchen she was shaken, worried about Maddy and what her father might do…as she returned to the living room with a tea cup in hand she was alone. She rushed down the hallway to the guest room, hoping to find him there. Adam was gone. He would know who the students were, where to find them…Angela shut the door to the room and leaned against the wall. And then she wept.

In the library, medics walked through the rubble, removing the debris carefully, their powerful lights shining into faces, hoping to find survivors. Maddy could hear shouting as the medics called out their assessment of the bodies strewn on the floor. The fire fighters arrived and produced masks for those in the foyer. Maddy and Gabriel were questioned by the police. They were anxious to relate what they saw and begin helping rather than watching the efforts of the medical team.

Hours later, beams and debris had been lifted, bodies found and removed from the room. Maddy covered those on the stretchers with blankets, awaiting the ambulance. Many grabbed her hand, asking that she call their loved ones. She made several calls to advise families of the accident, finding it difficult to leave messages rather than speak to another human. Maddy was relieved to find Ephrom on a stretcher, speaking on his cellphone. She blew the dust from his face and wiped his forehead - no visible injuries. She made note of the private clinic he was assigned so she could visit.

Maddy and Gabriel, covered in dust, hands bleeding from the splinters and sharp objects they had removed, were seated against the wall, exhausted. Their ears were still ringing from the explosion and yet they felt fortunate to be on the other side of the disaster. Dermot had called and apologized for being late - he was told to return home.

Maddy heard a familiar voice and watched as a man dressed in black crossed the foyer with a group of technicians in bomb proof gear. The man was describing the wiring sequence as he walked by. He glanced at the row of exhausted volunteers against the wall and nodded when he saw Maddy. She was too tired to stand and greet him although it appeared he was too busy to stop and acknowledge her presence. Gabriel reached for her hand. "He'll come back when they find it and know what they are dealing with. I'm sure." His voice sounding hopeful.

"I guess it's too late for dinner but how about some breakfast? I need coffee." Gabriel stood and helped Maddy stand.

"We are a sight, aren't we?" Maddy smiled. "I'm going to the ladies to splash some water on my face. Then I'm ready for breakfast. If I'm not back in five minutes, I've fallen asleep."

Feeling somewhat refreshed, despite her filthy clothes and hair, Maddy walked out of the building for fresh air, hoping it would wake her. As she touched the exit door she felt a hand on her arm. She looked up as Adam wrapped his arms around her, kissing her eyes and then her lips. She suddenly felt too tired to stand. It was comforting in his arms.

"I came as quickly as I could. I was going crazy not knowing if you were in that room. My heart stopped when I saw you." Adam was gasping for air. "I'm so relieved you weren't hurt. Are you alright? I have work to do here and I may not be back for a few days. I have a promise to keep. I love you."

When Maddy opened her eyes he was gone.

AND I WILL TRY TO FIX YOU

After breakfast Gabriel suggested Maddy come with him to his hotel. He had a suite and they certainly needed showers and sleep. He swore he was too tired to try anything so she would be safe. He was pleased that Maddy laughed and agreed.

Sometime during the day Gabriel's aide had delivered clothing, the tags still dangling, as well as food and an assortment of magazines. It was evening before they emerged from their respective rooms, dressed and hungry. They opted for room service and enjoyed a quiet night looking out over Manhattan.

"Here's to us. We are survivors." Gabriel raised a glass.

Maddy raised her glass. "Yes, we survived. We get another chance. What do you want to change? We should think about that, shouldn't we?"

"I have been thinking about change. I am a scientist, why am I flying around the world trying to convince people the earth isn't well? Why am I the self-proclaimed fixer of the world? I want to return to my research, to my painting, to reading anything except doom and gloom. I want to spend time with someone who wants to share these things with me. Do you know anyone?"

Maddy smiled wistfully. "Your message is important for future generations but I agree, you need to re-energize yourself before you become cynical with our inability to understand what you say. Paint, read, research, fall in love - now, while you can."

"What do I do first? Fall in love? Paint? Release my staff?" He shrugged.

"How about refusing to take more speaking engagements starting tomorrow; purchasing the paint supplies to get you started; letting me read to you and after a few days we see if you can stand it…not being needed around the world. I'll stay with you until you figure it out. I don't want to see you fail at your self improvement project."

Gabriel rubbed his forehead, as if in pain. "You'll stay with me and help me through this?"

Maddy nodded.

"Deal."

"Deal."

The suite became a studio and Gabriel began painting - Maddy had to admit he was talented. The injury to his arm in Paris had healed, leaving a nasty scar. They walked each day, finding new neighbourhood restaurants and interesting sights to paint, returning late in the afternoon for cocktails and quiet time. They read to each other before choosing a dinner destination, returning to the suite ready for bed.

They travelled to Princeton to visit with Angela, Ahmed and Adam Jr. for a day. Ahmed was delighted to share his work in the lab with Gabriel. There were several research opportunities requiring expertise or leadership which Gabriel was offered.

Angela was distressed that Adam had disappeared again, mainly because she felt Maddy and Gabriel made a lovely couple and she was worried Adam might be replaced in Maddy's heart.

On the train back to the city Maddy was pleased to see Gabriel reading the research prospectus. He seemed excited by the smaller projects. She reached over and moved his curls over his collar, returned to her reading, her fingers twirling the curls on his neck.

"Stop that. Please don't do that. It's driving me crazy." Gabriel whispered into her hair, his voice husky.

Maddy shook her head, suddenly aware of what she was doing. She pulled her hand back, as if it had been burned.

Gabriel moved his mouth from her ear, across her cheek, stopping at her lips. She didn't move, she felt paralyzed. His kiss was sweet and tender. He groaned and suddenly his cheek was on her cheek, his breathing laboured. He had reached over and now held her in his arms, afraid to have her stop him. To end the moment.

The train lurched to the side and they moved apart. Neither spoke. Gabriel reached over and touched Maddy's lips, tenderly tracing them. Why did such an innocent gesture make her feel faint? She touched his hand, her body shuddering. The announcement advised them they were nearing the station.

They walked back to the hotel in silence. In the suite Gabriel stood by the door to his bedroom.

"Good night Maddy. Sleep well. Dream of me. I will be dreaming of you and what could have been."

Climbing into her bed, Maddy sighed - feeling conflicted. Gabriel was a lovely man - they could have a good life together but she had a life, in England. She wasn't sure what to expect when she got there but she was going home. She closed her eyes, feeling free. Her life had been a whirlwind of relationships - finally she was going home, single, widowed, happy with her life. She had so much to be thankful for... so many blessings. She was alive and she was going home. No regrets...well, almost no regrets.

Gabriel tossed and turned, wondering why he hadn't followed Maddy to her room. That kiss had been so full of promise. These past weeks had been the happiest of his adult life. He was such a fool, he told himself over and over.

Maddy booked her flight to London, feeling confident Gabriel had found his way. He had cancelled his speaking engagements, taken an interest in research at Princeton, completed several canvasses worthy of praise and realized which authors he wanted to read. He hoped to see Maddy on her next visit to Princeton, where he had been offered a small apartment for the year. He had no thoughts of returning to Barcelona in the short term but suggested Maddy might want to treat his home as her own. Neither had spoken about the kiss, neither wanting to damage their friendship.

They said goodbye, embracing as old friends who know they will see each other soon.

TOTAL ECLIPSE OF THE HEART

♥ ♥ ♥

If Davi was surprised to see Adam waiting for Maddy he didn't show it as he waved and welcomed her to London. Chance had come with him and on seeing Maddy he ran forward screaming "Mad, Mad, Mad" in his high voice.

Maddy was lifted off the ground by Adam, in a warm embrace. He whispered welcomes in her ear. Chance was pulling on her jacket so she picked him up for a sloppy kiss, leaning forward to kiss Davi on the cheek. Maddy felt emotional - it was such a lovely welcome.

"Maddy, I want to ask you a favour. I know you just got back but Grace is in such a state and I have to do something. Before the baby arrives I want to marry her - she doesn't want to make it a big deal but she also doesn't want to talk to me about what to do. Please can you help me? Can you help Grace? We have missed you."

Maddy turned to Davi and touched his cheek. "I know exactly what to do…is Wednesday still the day you take off work?"

Davi nodded, visibly relaxing. Maddy always knew what to do. She would handle this and Grace would be happy. Once again.

Adam watched the exchange, not sure what Maddy was committing to handle. He was sure he would be assigned a role. All would be revealed. It felt good to have her home. He had been anxious for her return, not sure why she would stay in Manhattan. He assumed it had something to do with Gabriel Cortez but he knew better than to ask. He had only returned to London two days ago himself. It had not been a pleasant task although he had managed to find the bombers and deliver them to the authorities.

Davi drove them to *Gravitasse* so Maddy was able to see the busy lunch crowd, check on reservations and visit the reading room with Chance. When the little boy fell asleep in Maddy's arms she handed him to his Auntie. Grace had prepared boxes with groceries, casseroles and croissants - she knew they would be anxious to get home to the cottage in Henley.

FOR YOU ARE MINE AT LAST

♥ ♥ ♥

The morning sun was bright, the raindrops glistening on the leaves in the garden. Maddy felt Adam's arms around her and she sighed, a contented sigh. They had arrived at the Henley cottage late last night and headed straight to bed, anxious to hold each other.

The neighbours were in the garden, checking the flower beds and commenting on the cutting back required. They had seen the lights the night before and were anxious to see Maddy.

"Darling, ring the bell. Surely they are up at this hour. Let Maddy know we have coffee."

Adam groaned as he heard the doorbell. Maddy slipped out of the warm bed and opened the window, holding Adam's shirt in front of her naked body.

"Good morning. I've been offered mind-blowing sex if I stay in bed so if you don't mind, let's have cocktails at six and I'll prepare dinner for all of us." She smiled sleepily.

The older couples pretended to look shocked. "Will you be done by six, do you think?"

"Promise. We've missed you all." She smiled, waved and closed the window.

She pounced on Adam and wrapped her arms around him.

"Mind-blowing?" He asked, raising his eyebrows.

"Oh Adam, just do the best you can." She patted his shoulder, trying not to laugh.

"You want mind-blowing, I'll give you mind-blowing…" he whispered.

And he did.

Dinner was lively, everyone talking at the same time. Adam sat back and watched the group. Maddy was enjoying the chaos - she laughed and poured wine and asked questions that required lengthy answers. She didn't offer any insight into the bombing or her delay in returning home.

When they finally said goodnight and closed the door on the neighbours, Adam turned the lights off and danced with Maddy. "I think you feel at home here."

"I do. You?" She looked up at him.

Adam hesitated, stopped moving and held Maddy's face in his hands. "I think home is wherever you are." He kissed her. "I really believe that."

"Indeed."

Maddy had little time to arrange the perfect wedding for Grace and Davi, but of course, she had help from her friends.

Sam handled the music; Lambert was enthusiastic about the decor; Christian was in charge of beverages, securing non-alcoholic bubbly drinks and mock cocktails; Auntie and Uncle supplied samosas and a selection of Indian and Caribbean casseroles; Adam was the driver - collecting the unsuspecting bride and Chance; Davi was on an errand and would arrive at the requested time. Maddy had arranged the judge and decorations. Mrs Bing arrived with flowers - insisting they were gifts. The Henley neighbours were excited to be part of the ruse - a garden party to celebrate spring.

Adam arrived at the Maida Vale home and handed Grace a package. "Maddy's village friends are dressing up in vintage clothing and Maddy chose this for you. I'll wait. Where's little man Chance? He and I can go for a walk while you get dressed." He moved back from the door, then turned, as if he just remembered an important message. "Oh, and Maddy has marked all the public toilet stops on the route, just in case you have to stop." He smiled and nodded, his tasks for the moment completed.

Grace appeared at the door, her hands clasped in front of her. She was crying.

Adam was alarmed. She looked beautiful in the silver blue gown - the dress was alive with every movement - the glass studs shimmering in the sunlight. He stepped closer and held out his arms. "What's the matter Grace? You look absolutely stunning."

"I can't believe how lovely this dress makes me feel - baby bump and all." She sobbed into Adam's shoulder.

"You look wonderful Grace. Like a fairy princess." Adam was not comfortable with women crying when they were happy.

Chance was dancing around them, clapping his hands and shouting, "Mommy, Princess."

They finally settled into the car, Chance in his child booster seat - Adam wondered who had designed it and was almost ready to give up when Chance pulled the seatbelt over and showed him how easy it was to operate.

"Adam, you know Maddy is special to all of us. Her random acts of kindness have touched us all. She is the mother, sister, best friend, mentor and confessor to me. She's suffered so much grief in the short time I've known her, yet she continues to care about all of us. I know your situation is convenient but do you love her?" Grace had never had the opportunity to be with Adam alone. She hoped he would understand her wanting to know.

Adam looked into the rearview mirror and considered the question. Of course he loved Maddy but he wanted Grace to believe his intentions.

"Grace, I never thought I would meet a woman who makes my heart melt with her smile, makes me hold my breath when she enters a room, makes me feel warm when she touches me…I just didn't believe I could be that fortunate. Nothing in my life to this point makes me deserve her, and even if she asks me to leave there will never be another man who loves her more than I do. I will do whatever it takes to protect her. It may not be enough but it's what I have to do."

Silence. Then he felt a hand on his shoulder. "Thank you." Grace whispered. "Any chance we are near one of those comfort stops?"

Adam pulled into the prearranged parking spot by the cottage and noticed there were no other cars on the lane. Maddy thought of everything. He stepped out of the car and opened the door for his passengers. Chance ran out into Maddy's arms. Grace tentatively stepped out, taking the hand Adam offered. She was going to a garden party.

"Grace, you look beautiful." Maddy embraced her friend.

"I feel beautiful. It's a lovely dress. Do I have to give it back?" Grace laughed.

"It's my gift to you. Ready to meet your future?" Maddy asked.

Grace looked confused. She reached for Maddy and squeezed her hand. "My future?"

"Come on. Trust me. I have one request…I want you to enjoy every moment, every detail." Maddy tucked Grace's arm under her elbow. "Walk with me."

When a surprised Grace walked into the garden she was given a lovely bouquet of fresh flowers. Chance and Adam walked, hand in hand, ahead of them, up the pathway to their seats. Sam was playing *Pachelbel's Canon in D* on the piano and Davi was standing nervously at the door, awaiting his bride. It took Grace a moment to understand what was happening. This was more than a garden party.

"Maddy, is that the judge…" she whispered as the judge, in his robes, motioned them forward. Grace remembered the story of this judge saving Maddy from arrest at a Starbucks - he had asked for a dance in exchange.

"Yes. He's cool. I just have to dance with him twice. It's worth it."

Grace could feel tears rolling down her cheeks, her feet were swollen but she felt she was floating. The colours of the garden, the guests, Davi, dear Davi, looking at her with such love - Maddy was right - she was enjoying every detail. She was going to marry the love of her life.

She saw Adam smiling and she wondered if Davi would love her as much as he loved Maddy. She felt the excitement in her adorable son, standing on a chair beside Adam, clapping his hands and smiling like a miniature Davi. It was a lovely image and she would save it and recall this moment over and over again. She took a deep breath and nodded, moving forward. Forward to her future. Forward to a life with Davi, dear Davi. She was going to be married and for the first time since Davi had asked her, so long ago it seemed, she was happy, truly happy. Strangely, at peace.

Clinking glasses, soft piano music, warm spring sunshine, congratulatory speeches and a few toasts so the bride and groom could kiss…the garden, budding and springing to life offered the ideal background for the wedding tableau.

Grace and Davi sat with Chance in the garden as guests walked up with plates of food, fond wishes, envelopes and advice. Grace looked over at Maddy and smiled, blowing her a kiss and touching her heart. Adam was standing beside Maddy, his arm around her waist, his face nuzzled in her hair. Grace wondered why she hadn't noticed what a handsome pair they made - blue-eyed, blonde Maddy, open and always smiling; Adam tall, dark and mysterious. They complimented one another and when they looked at each other their eyes locked - as if they were communicating without words.

Adam leaned in and kissed Maddy, slowly and tenderly. Grace realized she was holding her breath. She felt like a voyeur, peeking in the window at two lovers.

Grace shook her head, she was missing the moments Maddy told her would be important. She smiled, looked at Davi, who was clearly enjoying his role as groom, and touched his arm. He turned slowly, his eyes devouring her, making her shudder.

"Yes, my beautiful wife and mother of my children?" He smiled and she wondered at her good fortune for having met such a kind man.

"Nothing, my handsome husband. Just wanted to look at you."

"This was a most lovely day and you are a most lovely bride and I am the most happy man in the world." He kissed her, oblivious to the cheers and whistles.

The limousine driver held the door open patiently, as the bride and groom embraced the crowd. Chance had slipped into the limo and settled down for a nap. Grace had confessed she adored the bouquet and didn't want to toss it so Maddy presented a smaller version tied with ribbon. The toss was lukewarm, landing in Maddy's surprised arms. The neighbours had great fun teasing Adam.

When the thank you's and goodbyes had finally wound down, the wedding couple slid into the limo with Auntie and Uncle. They waved goodbye and drove off to their married life.

"Were the circumstances such that I was waiting for you with the judge under the trellis would you have married me?" Adam asked Maddy as she waved to the limo driving away.

"Would you have asked me?" She turned into his chest and smiled up at him mischievously.

"I ask you every day. I ask you in my sleep. I just don't know the answer. Have I heard it?" He wanted to carry her into the cottage, lock the door and make love to her, right now.

"Adam, I haven't had great luck with marriage. It doesn't seem to like me much. Besides, I'm not sure I can do a part-time marriage. When you aren't here I'm always worried about you. Not knowing if you're dead or alive is taxing - I don't feel you trust me enough to tell me what you do. I will give you all of me when I know I have all of you. I'm not saying you shouldn't have secrets but if they affect us they are harmful." Maddy looked around the garden.

"Do you have another family? Another wife? Another life? You can't imagine what goes through my mind." Maddy bit her lip and sighed.

"Maddy," he held her chin in his hand, "you are more than one man can handle…there's no other life, no other wife, no other assignments of the heart. My work has everything to do with security and secrecy. It never mattered before - now it seems too invasive." Adam looked pensive, as if he was weighing the issue in his mind. "I promise…

"Lovely party Maddy. It was a brilliant wedding. Perhaps you could do our renewal of vows?" Chelsea stumbled into them, not realizing they were in deep conversation.

Maddy smiled, looking up at Adam. "I had lots of help. So glad you enjoyed the afternoon. Let's make your special day extraordinary."

FREEZE FRAME

Blue skies and sunshine call for a garden party and Maddy was happy to oblige. The Henley neighbours filled the gardens with laughter and kind hearted banter. Adam was a hero now that the developer had been run off. All was at peace in the village.

Bernard approached Maddy with a package. "This came for you earlier. I expect you were too busy. It's fragile so be careful."

A small crowd gathered around Maddy to see what was in the package. Maddy opened the outer box slowly, not sure why everyone was so curious. She pulled out a folded frame with four panels. Maddy handed the framework to Lambert who was as anxious as a child to open the gift. As he opened the frames there was silence behind him. Friends were gazing in amazement, looking up at Maddy and then back down to the frame. Lambert slowly turned the frames toward Maddy. She froze as she saw her face in three of the frames - the first was Maddy smiling wistfully with the Sagrada Familia in Barcelona behind her; the second frame was Maddy wearing a red beret and smiling whimsically with the Eiffel Tower behind her; the third was Maddy with a tear on her cheek standing on the steps of the New York Library with a statuesque lion beside her; the fourth panel was a white canvas. Maddy gasped. The portrait paintings were so lifelike - they were too personal. She didn't offer an explanation and the crowd moved away, leaving her alone with the gift.

Adam had walked away from the group, seeking out another drink, resisting the urge to smash the frames. How much longer would Gabriel Cortez interfere with their future?

Slowly the neighbours were making their way towards the gate. The gin and tonic bar had been a great success. Adam watched Sam, Lambert and Christian put their arms around Maddy and raise a glass to friendship. He found he wasn't as envious of them as he had been in the past - he knew they would take care of Maddy if something happened to him…he knew they were probably envious that he was the one waking up with her. He took a deep breath and walked towards the gang.

I'LL BE THERE FOR YOU

Sitting in The Stag Pub with their Henley friends, Maddy pointed out to Adam this was *'their local'*. Thursday evening was trivia night at the Pub, drawing a healthy crowd of neighbours and locals. Maddy laughed at the competitiveness of her friends, enjoying every moment. Some nights Christian would join them and stay over, other nights Lambert would attend. He was always on point for entertainment responses.

Maddy sat across the table from Adam, raising her glass in salute for his correct football recall when her phone rang.

"Hey you. Good to hear from you. It's noisy here. You'll have to speak up." Maddy looked across at Adam, motioning she had to go outdoors to hear.

Adam was distracted as his teammates set down another round of drinks and pondered what year Cliff Richards was on the Hit Parade. Humming and singing started at every table, in an effort to recall the actual song, until it was impossible to hear anything.

Maddy stepped out of the Pub, hoping for better reception. She listened to the caller and then slowly made her way back to the table, struggling to concentrate on the game.

Adam looked concerned and Maddy felt she should say something.

"I just need to help a friend. Sorry to be so preoccupied. You're quite the expert on sports trivia - bravo." She smiled, wishing she could share her uneasiness.

"Let's go home. The team is doing just fine without us." Adam wrapped his arms around Maddy, wondering why she was shivering on such a mild night.

As they reached the garden wall of the cottage Maddy turned to Adam and announced she had to go into London. She would be back as quickly as possible. She refused his offer to drive her, as she seemed upset. Adam watched her drive away, his heart ripping, feeling useless and angry that she had shut him out. As he walked into the cottage he realized this feeling, this hollow void, was exactly what Maddy must feel each time he said he had to go. When she returned he would tell her he was finished, retired, no longer available for hire. He was a permanent fixture in her life, never leaving her alone again.

He fell asleep content with his decision.

The Mad Hatter Hotel, just over the Blackfriars Bridge, was a small riverfront hotel near the Tate Modern. Parking is not easily available in London so Maddy took the tube to Waterloo Station and walked to the hotel. She needed time to think.

The reception clerk was reluctant, citing privacy reasons and policies, not sure Mr Cervantes would want to be disturbed. Het eventually succumbed and showed Maddy to the room.

Maddy stood in the dark room, aware that it needed airing, waiting for her eyes to adjust. She walked towards the loud snoring noise, hoping not to trip on furniture. She sat on the padded chair, at the foot of the bed, not wanting to wake him, too weary to do anything but wait for morning.

Maddy stirred, stiff from sleeping sitting up. The blind on the window appeared to be framed with light - it must be morning. She stood and stretched, wanting more than anything to lie down and sleep. She pulled back the draperies and pulled the blinds up, flooding the room with daylight. The view of the Thames wasn't as lovely as Maddy remembered.

Stirring noises behind her, expletives uttered, movement…he was alive.

"Good morning Mr Cervantes. Really, that's the best name you could come up with? Get up and get in the shower. When you're ready we're going out for breakfast. Come on. *Darse prisa*. Hurry up." She pulled back the covers and clapped her hands.

"Why are you doing this?" He moaned. "Leave me alone."

"Gabriel, I don't know what happened but you called me and I'm here. Now get up and once you are decent, we'll have coffee, we'll have breakfast, you'll feel better and you'll explain what's going on. Get up. Shower. Now."

Maddy was standing with her hands on her hips, watching Gabriel as he opened his eyes, staring back at her and then he began laughing, hysterically laughing. Maddy tried to be stern but his laugh was contagious. Soon they were both laughing. Gabriel sat on the edge of the bed, bent over, laughing. He finally stood and made his way to the shower, still laughing.

Maddy looked around the room at his clothes thrown everywhere, his papers on the floor, his laptop open on a chair. This was not the Gabriel she knew - her Gabriel was tidy, fastidious. His work always neatly placed in folders, his laptop closed. There were no clothes in the closet so she picked up the strewn items and assembled them on the bed. She opened a window to freshen the room and wondered what had happened. She carefully gathered the papers and set them on the small desk. She made instant coffee from the portable tea station and waited.

Gabriel appeared with a towel wrapped around his waist, drying his hair with another towel. The scar on his shoulder was healing well but it was a reminder of Paris and how there were opposing views on his warnings. He offered Maddy a sheepish grin when she handed him a coffee.

"Two sugars, milk. Is that still how you take it?" Maddy asked.

"Gracias. Yes." He sipped the coffee as if he hadn't had a drink in ages. "Thank you for coming. I didn't know what to do. I told you, sometime ago, that you were the one I would call if the world was ending." He looked at her sheepishly.

"The world is not ending." Maddy assured him. "But I am here for you."

"I apologize for the mess." He rubbed his forehead and sat across from Maddy. "This is not how I wanted you to see me."

"What happened Gabriel?" Maddy looked around the room, trying to understand why he was here, in this hotel, without an overnight bag.

"Look at my laptop. There are several death threats. I am to speak at the Climate Change Conference later this week. I checked out of the Savoy and came here to finish the report. It's not good, the evidence is clear, we have to make significant changes. Not everyone agrees, as you will see. It's not safe for me to be here."

"Gabriel, I'm not qualified to speak to your report or the threats but I do know you need to report this and get police protection. Surely the organizers realize the danger you are in. Who should we call? Would you prefer to deliver your paper by video rather than in person?" Maddy was trying to understand the situation, thinking out loud. She wished she could fix this and take away the misery he was feeling.

"I thought you were cancelling your speaking engagements and concentrating on research…what happened?"

Gabriel went to the window and took several deep breaths.

"Gabriel, focus. Where is your team? Give me a number so I can call and help you. Please."

Maddy left London a few hours later, knowing Gabriel was safe. His team had been in a panic, thinking the worst, when he had gone missing. The Conference provided a security team and moved Gabriel into a safe house. He was to deliver the paper and immediately be taken to the airport. He was not to return to Barcelona or Princeton for a few days - until his labs in both countries and home could be deemed safe.

Maddy arranged for Gabriel to take a diving vacation in the Maldives. He would be safe there, with Dag, her former partner. Gabriel asked Maddy to join him there - in Paradise. In his mind it could only be Paradise if Maddy came with him. It was a tempting offer.

Turning into the lane at the Henley cottage Maddy felt tired. She didn't remember the drive home. She sat in the car for a moment, collecting her thoughts. She was startled when Adam opened the car door, looking anxious. He held out his hand and helped her out of the car.

"Welcome home my darling. Everything alright?" He kissed her and she knew, in her heart, everything was alright.

IF NOT FOR YOU

Back home, in the cottage, lying across from each other on the sofa, Adam closed his book and looked over at Maddy. She was reading and twirling her hair around her finger.

"Why won't you marry me?" He asked, rubbing her feet.

"Why do you want to marry me? I'm flighty, impulsive, impetuous, emotional, reckless, meddling - you've said so - often…" Maddy marked her page and laid her book down.

"True enough, but you are also kind, considerate, caring, exciting…you brighten up every room you enter, you see things in such a positive light and you make me very happy. Oh, and I love you. Is that reason enough?"

"Would any of that change if we got married?"

"I'm old fashioned. I will love you regardless. I would like your friends to know I have made a commitment to you. What is it about me that makes you hesitate? Is it what you know about me? Is it my name? Am I too old for you to consider a future?"

"Adam, you're amazing and why would your name matter? You are not too old. You're just right."

"That's good to hear."

"How do you not know how I feel about you? I guess I'm not very good at saying how much I care for you. I'm sorry." Maddy bit her lip, wondering why she didn't say the words.

"Maybe you don't say it but you show it in the way you touch me and look at me. I'm not as expressive as you. The words don't come easy to me so I need to speak them, to be sure you know." Adam whispered.

"I know you love me. That's all that really matters. I'm happy. If it's really important to you, I'll give the matter serious consideration. Fair enough?" Maddy sighed. "Hmm…If you keep rubbing my feet like that, I'll have no choice but to marry you."

"Fair enough."

WALKING ON SUNSHINE

Martha's Vineyard, near Oak Bluff, two months later...

By Sunday afternoon the rain had cleared, the clouds disappearing across the Atlantic. The sun seemed to have made a deal with the heavens. A soft breeze carried the scent of the floral arrangements across the terrace and into the building.

In the bright sunshine friends gathered, anxious to see two people who were so right for each other finally come together.

Adam and Oliver waited at the grapevine trellis, smiling broadly as they watched the woman they loved make her way towards them. In the front row Adam Jr, squirming in the arms of Ahmed, waved at Maddy. Angela wiped away a tear and smiled joyfully.

Flanking the officiant were six Marines in full uniform and six Navy officers. It was an imposing and powerful image of solidarity.

Adam could not take his eyes off Maddy. She looked radiant - her hair loose, her wild flower bouquet flowing down the front of her gown. She wore a simple diamond tiara that reflected the sunlight, creating a halo around her head. The tiara had belonged to the Contessa - who had passed it on to Maddy after the village party at the Italian Villa, so long ago, it seemed, when The Contessa had wished Maddy and Sebastian a long life and much happiness. Maddy reached up and touched the tiara, in a salute to her beloved Sebastian as she walked slowly forward, with a beaming and handsome Nate at her side.

The simple, yet elegant gown had been designed by Sofi, who was now a rising star at Sorento's Fashion House - the floor length creamy creation was sleeveless with a mock neckline - a loose sheath of gauze-like fabric in a light blue and pastel pink flowed as she walked. One published photo and this outfit would be in great demand. Fashion and design were international now with the internet. Sofi was already creating quite a stir in the fashion world.

Adam smiled as he realized Maddy was barefoot. A light breeze caught the fabric as she walked and he recognized fireflies in the pastels. It was beautiful. Maddy looked so sprightly and yet, so calm. Nate looked as though he would burst with happiness.

As the couple approached the trellis Adam caught his breath. Maddy's blue eyes were bright and he felt mesmerized by her smile, which lit up her face. How he wanted to reach out and caress her dimples.

Oliver looked over at Adam and they exchanged smiles as they watched Maddy and Nate approach. Oliver winked and gave Adam a mock salute.

Adam bowed slightly to Nate, bending forward to kiss Maddy's hand and then looked into her eyes, hopeful she was feeling the love he was sending her. They moved to the side as Nate stepped forward to take Oliver's hand.

Simple vows, a kiss and suddenly - Nathaniel and Oliver were married, surrounded by those who loved and accepted them.

The officers, looking dashing in their uniforms, broke rank and whistled; Adam Jr covered his ears as the crowd applauded. The newlyweds, holding hands, made a handsome couple as they made their way by the guests, towards the champagne tower.

Food, wine, dancing and laughter filled the terrace overlooking Oak Bluffs. Adam held Maddy in his arms and whispered how lovely she looked as they danced the only dance they would have together that evening. Maddy touched his face and kissed him in response. They would have ample time alone - tonight was for celebrating with friends.

Oliver and Nate approached, embracing Maddy and Adam. "Thank you for being here and making this such a special day. It was perfect."

Angela slid in between the two couples, laughing. "You know you've married all of us, don't you Nate?"

Angela asked Nate to dance while Oliver moved closer to Maddy. "This is only happening because of you, *Dream Girl*. Dance with me."

As they danced, Maddy thought she must be the most fortunate person on the planet, surrounded by such happiness and love. She wished Henry had known this happiness. She would make every effort to show Adam Jr, Chance and now, beautiful little Hope, how important friends and family were. She hoped she would be lucky enough to dance at their weddings. The Buttons were growing so fast - she was getting to know them again - life was good.

Maddy knew she should be thinking about her own wedding but that last kiss with Gabriel in London had stirred something in her. Somehow it felt comforting, soothing, safe. She shook her head, dispelling the thought.

Across the terrace Adam caught a glimpse of Maddy, knowing in his heart he was going to enjoy growing old with her. He wished they had said their own vows today - celebrating their life together. They had finally discussed getting married and where they might like to share their vows. While all the exotic places in the world were considered, they always returned to the cottage in Henley - their home.

Maddy was to be his wife. The thought filled him with such warmth and love, he shuddered. He had asked her to marry him again, as they boarded the flight to America. Maddy laughed and declared he was wearing her down. Although she was happy with their life, she was committed to him - in the end, she had agreed. They would marry at the cottage and honeymoon in Kenya on safari, in Nepal trekking and then Bali, where Adam had a water project to oversee. Maddy has started writing a second book, only her editor knew the story line.

Adam was so captivated watching Maddy and dreaming about the future, he ignored the constant vibration of the phone in his pocket. Someone was most anxious to speak with him - it would have to wait. He wasn't prepared to do anything relatively reckless, unless it was with Maddy.

Adam Jr wrapped his chubby little arms around Maddy's neck and began kissing her, chattering and making her laugh out loud. Adam watched as they both threw their heads back in laughter, the sound so pure and free. Suddenly he wanted to join them, embrace them both and be part of the love they were sharing.

As he walked towards the gazebo he felt the phone vibrate. He pulled the pin from his boutonniere and removed the SIM card from the phone. He drew back his arm and launched the phone, grimacing as he overextended his shoulder, watching the phone soar over the bluffs to the Atlantic. He skirted the crowd, wanting more than anything to be with Maddy, to hold her and tell her his heart was bursting with love for her.

Maddy gently let Adam Jr down and he ran towards his parents. She smiled as he waddled away, still laughing. She leaned against the post and looked over the crowd delighted it was such a joyous occasion. As she scanned the happy faces her eyes met Adam's. He was striding towards her, his eyes locked on hers. He was so rakishly handsome, so confident, so intense and yet, so caring.

Her heart pounding, her face flushed - she moved her hand to her heart as she was overcome with a strange, yet peaceful feeling. Was this what *happy ever after* felt like?

Everyone attending the wedding agreed it was a perfect day, in the perfect location; a perfect celebration, a perfect beginning for Oliver and Nathaniel. Perfect. Simply perfect.

Indeed it was.

No one seemed bothered by the whirring sound of a helicopter circling.

THE END

ABOUT THE AUTHOR

Anne Marshall is an adventure seeker and a romantic. She and her partner have travelled the world by small aircraft, motorcycle, by foot and most recently in a camper van. A diverse career in hospitality provided exciting opportunities, lasting friendships and signature experiences. Marshall believes the world needs more romance, even when it is reckless. Home is rural Ontario, Canada - a place where friends gather.

CPSIA information can be obtained
at www.ICGtesting.com
Printed in the USA
BVHW071615020622
638528BV00001B/1